Untethered A Story of Becoming
Table of Contents
Chapter One – Fresh Start
Chapter Two – The Color of Caution
Chapter Three – Unspoken Things
Chapter Four – The Space Between
Chapter Five – Almost Comfortable
Chapter Six – Shadows from Before
Chapter Seven – Coffee and Contradictions
Chapter Eight – The Edge of Maybe
Chapter Nine – Letters and Lies
Chapter Ten – Blurred Lines
Chapter Eleven – The Things We Don't Say
Chapter Twelve – Unraveling
Chapter Thirteen – Between Then and Now
Chapter Fourteen – The Truth That Finds You
Chapter Fifteen – Open Water
Chapter Sixteen – What Comes After
Chapter Seventeen – The Distance Between Us
Chapter Eighteen – Letting Go
Chapter Nineteen – Closer Than Expected
Chapter Twenty – What Healing Looks Like
Chapter Twenty-One – One Last Choice
Chapter Twenty-Two – The Heart Remembers
Chapter Twenty-Three – Becoming

This book is dedicated to the dreamers, the risk-takers, the ones who dare to chase their passions even when the path is uncertain. To those who have known heartbreak and the sting of loss, yet still find the courage to open their hearts again, to believe in second chances, and to embrace the messy, beautiful journey of self-discovery.

It's for the women who, like Lacy, finding themselves at a crossroads, grappling with the weight of past mistakes and the allure of a brighter future. For those who navigate the complexities of love and career, juggling ambition and vulnerability, seeking fulfillment in both the professional and personal realms. This dedication is a nod to their resilience, their strength, and their unwavering hope.

It is dedicated to the women who pick themselves up after being knocked down, who dust themselves off, and bravely step into the unknown with their heads held high. This book is a testament to their courage, a celebration of their journey, a recognition of their enduring spirit. It is a reminder that even amidst the chaos and uncertainty, even when life feels overwhelming, there is always hope, there is always a possibility of finding happiness, of creating a life rich in love, purpose, and fulfillment. For the women who embrace their flaws, their vulnerabilities, and their imperfections – this is for you. Your stories matter. Your journeys are inspiring. Your strength is extraordinary. This book is a small token of appreciation for the extraordinary women I know, for the women who inspire me every single day to believe in the power of self-love, second chances, and the boundless potential that resides within each and every one of us. May this story offer you solace, inspiration, and the knowledge that you are not alone on your path. May it remind you of your own strength, resilience, and the unwavering capacity to create the life you truly deserve. May your journey be filled with love, laughter, and the courage to pursue your dreams. And may you always remember that you are worthy of all the happiness the world has to offer.

Untethered A Story of Becoming
By A.S. Haynes

Chapter 1

The quiet rumble of the moving truck faded into the distance, leaving behind a loaded silence that clung to the sleek apartment building like mist.

Lacy stood still in the middle of the parking lot, keys in hand, heart racing under the weight of what she'd just done.

A new apartment.

A new city.

A new life.

It wasn't far from Oakland, where she grew up—barely an hour's drive—but it felt like another world entirely. The kind of world where no one knew her history. Where no one had seen her fall apart. The kind of world where she could finally start over. She looked up at the building's clean lines, the sun catching on its windows like a dare. Her palms were sweaty. Not from the heat. From the fear that she'd made another choice she wasn't ready for.

Behind her, a car door slammed.

"Okay, okay, how long you planning to stand there looking all deep before we start dragging your stuff upstairs?" Bree's voice cut through the silence, laced with sarcasm and just enough love to make it land. She came around the front of the car with a messy bun, an iced coffee, and a look that said *let's go, sis*.

Lacy cracked a smile. "Can I have one dramatic moment without you rushing me?"

Bree raised her cup. "Girl, you've had *months* of dramatic moments in my guest room. Let's go. You made it."

Lacy laughed. "Facts. And shout-out to your guest room for holding me down."

"Girl, that room barely held your suitcase," Bree said, grinning. "But look at you now—bed, couch, coffee table. Real furniture and everything."

"Don't forget my fablous patio chair," Lacy added, grabbing a bag from the trunk. "I've got seating options now."

Bree smirked. "Minimal but mighty. Clean, grown, and yours."

Lacy nodded. "It's a start. I'm rebuilding. With taste."

"Girl, with that new salary, this is *rebuilding with style*."

They both laughed, falling into rhythm like they always did—moving boxes, trading jabs, and stacking the first pieces of something brand new.

Halfway through juggling bags, Lacy's phone buzzed against her hip—the familiar, chaotic rhythm of group texts exploding all at once.
"Uh-oh," Bree said, eyeing the screen lighting up like a Christmas tree. "Let me guess. The girls?"
Lacy pulled her phone out, laughing. "Group chat's on fire. Probably arguing about brunch or inventing a reason to drink mimosas at noon."
"God forbid we miss a dress code crisis," Bree said, shaking her head but smiling.
More buzzing.
More gifs.

More all-caps mayhem.

Lacy smiled wide, slipping the phone back into her bag. "Same circus, new location."

"Wouldn't have it any other way," Bree said, bumping her shoulder.

Later that night boxes lined the hallway like cardboard reminders of everything she hadn't unpacked.

Bree had managed to find the wine glasses—well, mason jars—and now lounged dramatically on the couch, a throw blanket draped around her shoulders like a queen in exile.

"Okay, it's almost time," Bree said, sipping from her jar. "You sure you're ready for this?"

Lacy eyed the laptop, the Zoom link already open, and tugged her robe a little tighter around herself.

"I mean... it's not a court hearing," she teased, smiling despite the nerves fluttering under her skin.

Bree raised a brow. "You say that now. Wait until they start roasting your Wi-Fi setup."

Lacy laughed, the sound bubbling up naturally. "As long as no one calls me a caveman, I'll survive."

The familiar chime of someone joining the call filled the room.

One by one, the screen bloomed into tiny windows of chaos and love.

"Look who finally decided to move her cute little behind outta suburbia!" Janelle's voice rang out first, her laugh loud and bright enough to shake the walls.

Her toddler peeked into the frame with a stuffed dinosaur, waved, then vanished like a magician.

"This new background better come with a soft launch caption and a fresh eucalyptus bundle, sis," Janelle added, grinning.

Lacy cracked up, tucking her knees under her chin. "Girl, I'm just trying to find my socks, let alone my aesthetic."

"Your chaos is showing," Nina said dryly from her book-filled office, sipping tea with regal judgment. "But I respect the vibe. Minimalist breakdown chic."

"I'm calling it 'New Apartment Nervous Breakdown,'" Lacy shot back, laughing harder.

"Very exclusive," Kayla chimed in, glowing under what had to be a ring light. "Ten outta ten would repost. And if you need those shelves styled, I will fly out. Content, baby."

Chrissy popped on next, baby snuggled to her chest, typing one-handed like a legend.

"I'm just glad Lacy didn't change her number and ghost us after the move," she teased.

"I thought about it," Lacy joked, winking. "But then who would send me fifty Pinterest boards labeled 'Grown Woman Energy'?"

"I curated those boards," Ava said, raising her glass with a mock-solemn nod. "With intention."

"You made three charcuterie boards for a book club none of us finished," Lacy shot back, giggling.

"Presentation always matters," Ava replied smoothly, unbothered as ever.

"I'm just saying," Bree cut in, swirling her wine, "I deserve a medal for carrying this girl emotionally and physically all day."

"I'll ship you a batch of sea salt scrub tomorrow," Janelle said. "And some lavender oil for whatever's making Lacy look like she's been fighting ghosts."

"Thank you for your concern, you loving sharks," Lacy deadpanned, grinning.

But then Chrissy leaned in a little closer to her screen, her voice soft. "But for real, Lace—how are you? Really?"

The teasing faded into something gentler, warmer.

Lacy let the question sit for a beat, feeling it unfurl inside her chest like a slow sunrise.

"I'm... figuring it out," she said finally, smiling shyly. "This move wasn't just about work. It's about finally choosing myself. And it's scary. And lonely. And... freeing."

Nina nodded, her voice a steady hum. "The good kind of scary."

"Yeah," Lacy whispered. "It feels like I finally exhaled after holding my breath for years."

"I'm proud of you," Kayla said, flashing a bright, easy smile. "But seriously—get some curtains. That lighting is a hate crime."

Lacy burst out laughing, wiping at her eyes. "On it. Curtains first. Socks second."

"And your peace," Ava added, lifting her glass.

They stayed on the call for another hour—laughing, venting, tossing out life advice and terrible memes like confetti.

When it finally ended and the screen faded to black, Lacy looked around her apartment—the scattered boxes, the faint hum of the laptop still cooling on the coffee table—and for the first time all day, the space didn't feel so empty.

Bree caught her looking and raised an eyebrow. "Feeling better?"

Lacy nodded, a real smile tugging at her mouth.

"Yeah," she said quietly.

"I think... I'm gonna be okay."

The sun spilled through the half-open blinds like it had something to prove, landing squarely on Lacy's face. She groaned, dragging the comforter over her head. Her body protested the unfamiliar mattress, but after months of crashing in temporary spots, it still felt like luxury.

From the living room came the soft clatter of pans—or maybe plastic takeout containers—and Bree humming something off-key.

Lacy groaned louder. "You're up already?"

"Someone had to rescue this apartment from its cardboard kingdom," Bree called back. "Also, your couch is aggressively mid. I need a chiropractor and a priest."

Lacy smirked into her pillow. "It's not the couch's fault you snore like a lawn mower."

"Bold of you to say when I risked spinal injury to help you unpack."

By the time Lacy made it to the kitchen, Bree was standing at the counter in an oversized t-shirt and pineapple-print socks, scrolling on her phone and sipping coffee from a chipped mug they'd unearthed the night before.

"Please tell me that's from a working outlet and not black magic," Lacy mumbled, reaching for her own lukewarm cup.

"Little bit of both," Bree said, wrinkling her nose after a sip. "This coffee's tragic. We deserve better."

They exchanged a look—the kind only years of friendship could translate. Minutes later, they were pulling on hoodies and joggers, grabbing keys and wallets.

Bree, already tapping away on her phone, grinned.

"Good news—there's a bakery two blocks over. I may or may not have Yelp-stalked the entire neighborhood yesterday while you were setting up Wi-Fi."

Lacy laughed as they stepped into the bright morning air. "Of course you did."

"Hey, someone had to prioritize survival."

Ten minutes later, breakfast sandwiches and iced lattes in hand, they were heading back toward the apartment when Lacy's phone buzzed.

Group text. Ava.

Ava:

Event flyer into the chat.

"Global Ventures & Innovation Expo — Miami

Mark your calendars! Would be an epic girls' trip and networking gold."

The flyer was a glossy little masterpiece—sleek fonts, palm fronds, minimalist gold accents.

Bree peered over her sunglasses at the screen. "Of course Ava already has her next quarter mapped out like a campaign strategist."

Lacy raised a brow. "Doesn't she always? I barely know what I'm doing Thursday."
"I love that she thinks we're just gonna casually hop down to Miami in peak hurricane season."
"She'll probably still book a rooftop brunch and close a deal in the middle of a tropical storm," Lacy chuckled, thumbing a quick thumbs-up emoji back into the group chat. A year ago, she would've hesitated to even dream about a girls' trip. Now? She was at least willing to let herself imagine it.
"I'll see if I have PTO by then. This is, what, six, seven months away?"
"Classic Ava. Give you ample time to pretend you're going, cancel the night before, and feel no guilt," Bree said, pushing open the lobby door with her elbow. "Still... could be fun. Wine, networking, ambitious chaos."
"I'll pencil it under 'maybe, if I survive Q1.'"
Back upstairs, a breeze drifting through the open windows stirred the takeout napkins and rustled a half-unpacked moving box.
Lacy paused by the window while Bree plopped dramatically onto the couch with her sandwich and a sigh.
Outside, the city buzzed in vibrant colors—the pastel buildings, the hum of the street, the waves crashing somewhere just beyond sight.
Lacy wasn't sure yet what this version of her life would look like.
But at least the coffee was decent.
And her best friend was here.

That night the city lights blinked like lazy fireflies beyond the balcony, and the air held that soft, salt-laced breeze only an ocean city could have. Lacy leaned against the railing, wine glass tucked between her palms, while Bree stretched across the plush outdoor loveseat, a blanket draped over her legs and a half-eaten cookie abandoned beside her.
Lacy's apartment, still echoing slightly with its newness, was beginning to feel lived in.
It was a one-bedroom dream she hadn't known she needed until she'd walked through it—

Stainless steel appliances gleaming like a showroom.
Floor-to-ceiling windows that caught the sunrise like an old friend.
A balcony with a postcard view of the ocean and the bustling strip below.
The hardwood floors warmed under the late sun, and though she didn't have much furniture yet—just a couch, a coffee table, and a few essentials—everything else was on its way, one tracking number at a time.
The building itself was sleek, modern. A rooftop pool. An open-air lounge. A life that felt more like the opening credits of a show about a woman finally figuring it out.
She could walk to work now—or drive with the music up and the windows down, just because she could.
New job.
New salary.
New everything.
And for the first time in a long time, it didn't feel like she was running from something.
It felt like she was running toward something. She tilted her face toward the salt-kissed breeze, letting it thread through her hair. It felt different now—like a welcome, not a warning.
Bree took a slow sip from her wine and gave Lacy a look that meant she was about to stir the pot.
"So... Thomas."
Lacy grinned. "Girl, you love that man and still want to body slam him twice a week."
"Twice? Slow week if I don't want to throat-check him by Wednesday," Bree said, laughing. "But yeah. I do. I really love him. It's weird."
"It's not weird. He's good for you," Lacy said, settling into the seat beside her. "You're just not used to good things coming with imperfections."
Bree sighed dramatically. "You mean he's not a Hallmark movie in a fitted tee?"
"Nope. But he's real. And you don't flinch when he calls you out. Which... growth, sis."

"Ugh, gross. Personal development," Bree muttered. "But yeah. He sees me. Even when I'm being a whole problem."

They clinked glasses—the quiet kind of clink that only lifelong sister-friends share, no need for speeches.

"Speaking of problems," Bree said, grinning wickedly, "you peeped Kayla's Instagram lately?"

Lacy laughed. "She tagged herself at brunch in Paris, but there was clearly a palm tree in the background."

"She tagged Paris with a Palm Springs filter. I love her, but that girl curates her life like she's pitching a reality show."

"And Nina's been shady too. No poetry invites lately. I think she's secretly seeing someone."

"Oh, a hundred percent. Either that or she's in her brooding, artist-introvert era again."

They giggled over the group chat receipts, bad date flashbacks, and how Chrissy texted them both yesterday to ask what dry shampoo was.

"Three kids and a tech empire, but no clue what a Batiste bottle is," Bree said, shaking her head.

"Icon behavior," Lacy added.

By the time they called it a night, the city had quieted, and the wine bottle was empty.

Lacy lingered on the balcony a moment longer, letting the night air wrap around her like a promise.

The smell of fresh coffee drifted from the kitchen, mixing with the golden sunlight that poured into the apartment like it paid rent.

Lacy padded out of her bedroom, hoodie swallowing her whole, hair in full rebellion, and found Bree by the door—overnight bag slung over her shoulder, to-go cup in hand.

Bree turned, caught mid-exit. "Well, damn. Thought I'd be gone before you woke up."

Lacy blinked, still groggy. "You were just gonna ghost me?"

Bree smirked. "Please. I was gonna leave a note. I'm not a monster." She held up her coffee like a trophy. "Besides, I figured you could use the sleep. Moving is a whole-body sport, and you were snoring like it was overtime."

Lacy shuffled toward the kitchen, where a second cup waited like a peace offering. "You really went on a coffee run?"

"Crack of dawn," Bree said. "Scaled a mountain of Yelp reviews and questionable side streets to find a place open this early. Nearly died. You're welcome."

Lacy laughed, lifting her cup in salute. "Hero status confirmed."

"Oh, and while you were passed out? I fluffed your throw pillows, alphabetized your spice rack, and ate your last bag of popcorn. Basically, I'm the fairy godmother you didn't budget for."

Lacy grinned. "I owe you my firstborn."

Bree raised an eyebrow. "I'll take payment in mimosas next time."

Lacy crossed her arms, trying not to look too sentimental. "You're really leaving me already?"
Bree smiled, stepping closer to pull her into a tight hug.
"You're ready. Even if you don't feel like it yet."
Lacy exhaled against her shoulder, a small laugh escaping. "Thanks for coming. For everything."
"Always," Bree said, pulling back just enough to look her in the eye.
"You're my sister. My ride-or-die. You survived the hardest part already, Lace. Now it's time to actually live."

Lacy blinked back the sudden sting in her eyes and nodded.
"Guess I better not screw it up, huh?"
Bree smirked. "You won't. But if you do... I'll still be here. Probably with snacks."
Lacy laughed, her voice catching just a little. "Seriously. Thanks for walking with me through this."
Bree squeezed her hand. "Always. Now go be the main character of your life, okay? But like... don't get so dramatic you forget to eat."
"Deal."
Bree gave one last hug before walking out the door.
Lacy closed it slowly, her fingers lingering on the handle longer than necessary. The faint scent of Bree's citrusy body spray still hung in the air.

She stood there for a moment—missing her already, but breathing easier than she thought she would.

The morning light poured in like a promise—soft, golden, stubbornly hopeful.

Lacy stood in the middle of it all, smiling to herself.

It wasn't perfect.
It wasn't finished.
But for the first time in a long time, it felt like hers.

The first few days after Bree left were a blend of quiet bravery and little discoveries.
Lacy spent her time wandering the city like it was a living thing—equal parts intimidating and enchanting. With no set work schedule yet, she had freedom to roam, following whatever street, scent, or sudden curiosity pulled at her.
The neighborhood was a collage of contrasts: sleek cafés ducked between mom-and-pop delis, murals splashed across sun-bleached brick walls,

bougainvillea spilling from wrought-iron balconies. Every block revealed a new surprise.

She found a bakery just a few blocks away, where the croissants were so buttery they nearly melted her stress at first bite. The owner, a French woman with a salt-and-pepper pixie cut, started slipping her extra pastries "just because." Lacy had already memorized her name.

Down a narrow side street behind a flower shop, she stumbled upon a tiny independent bookstore—no bigger than her apartment—with books stacked in crooked towers. The owner and a lazy gray cat named Hemingway that was sprawled across his counter, had a knack for remembering people's favorite genres. Lacy spent an entire afternoon there, lost in used poetry collections and battered travel memoirs.

The farmer's market around the corner became another small miracle. It buzzed with color, rich smells, and the hum of weekend chatter. She bought fresh basil simply because it reminded her of her grandmother's kitchen. A vendor convinced her to try passion fruit for the first time. She wandered with a canvas tote full of produce she didn't entirely know how to cook—but she was determined to learn.

At first, the city had felt too big, too anonymous. But the more she explored, the smaller it felt—not in size, but in mystery. It began to feel like a place slowly inviting her in.

She smiled at baristas, nodded to dog walkers, traded quick conversations with shopkeepers who gave her insider tips about sunset beaches. The anonymity that once made her feel invisible started to feel like freedom.

Each evening, she tried something new—Ethiopian, Jamaican, Moroccan. Every bite felt like a rebellion against the woman she used to be. Gone were the frozen meals and lonely takeout dinners. Here, food was an act of celebration. She ordered boldly, sipped wine at candlelit tables alone, and let new flavors tell her stories she hadn't heard before.

Back at the apartment, the space was slowly taking shape.

The hardwood floors gleamed beneath her bare feet, and the sunlight poured in like a second heartbeat.

The balcony had become her favorite place—the spot where morning coffee tasted better and night felt less lonely.

She hung a few pictures: one of her and the girls laughing, one of her parents young and happy, and a framed print she bought from a local artist—a woman walking into the sea. It felt like her.

Furniture deliveries were still trickling in. There were curtain rods to install. A perfect reading chair to find. It no longer felt empty.

It felt like becoming.

And then there was Leo.

She found him on her third day, tucked under a bush near the park—skinny, dirty, full of scrappy defiance.

He hissed until she crouched down and offered him part of her tuna sandwich.

Now he slept curled up beside her on the couch like they'd always belonged to each other.

She named him Leo—for his ginger coat, but also for the quiet fierceness she recognized in him.

At night, Lacy would look around her apartment—still a little bare, still a little new—and feel something surprising:

Not fear.

Not loneliness.

Possibility.

The future wasn't defined yet. And for once, that didn't terrify her.

It felt like an open road she didn't have to sprint down.

Just walk.

Step by step.

With Leo occasionally tripping her up.

Her new life wasn't perfect. Far from it.

Some nights, shadows stretched too long across the walls. Old memories knocked at the edges of her peace.

Loneliness still crept in, soft and stubborn as fog.
But it didn't own her anymore.
It passed—quiet, temporary—and left behind something sturdier.
Hope.
She was alone, yes.
But she was also free.
Free to choose.
Free to change.
Free to exist without apology.
For the first time in years, she wasn't just surviving.
She was beginning.
And with that came something else she hadn't expected:
Power.
The quiet kind.
The kind that showed up when she cooked dinner just for herself.
When she hung art on the walls.
When she walked home alone and took the long way, just because it was beautiful.
Optimism had settled into something better:
Resilience.
Rooted and real.
The journey was just beginning.
And Lacy was ready.
The first real test arrived before she even finished unpacking the last box:
A final, in-person formality for the Senior Editor position that had drawn her to the coast in the first place.

The position was already hers on paper—the meeting was just a final formality.
Still, Lacy smoothed her blazer and took a steadying breath as she stepped into the mirrored lobby of Seaglass Press.

The building felt like something out of a film: clean lines, endless glass, sunlight pouring in from every angle.
It smelled like polished wood, expensive coffee, and ambition.
She rode the elevator to the top floor, heart thudding once in her chest.
The interview blurred by in a swirl of practiced confidence and poised answers.
She remembered the office—warm, but intimidating. A mahogany desk so polished it looked lacquered daily. Shelves lined with first editions in meticulous color order.
And behind the desk: Eleanor Vance.
Ms. Vance didn't rise when Lacy entered. She didn't smile.
She just nodded sharply toward the chair across from her.
"You've come highly recommended," she said crisply. "But recommendations only go so far. I judge talent for myself."
Lacy placed her portfolio on the desk. "As you should."
Eleanor skimmed her resume, face unreadable.
"Editor at Harbor House. Freelance acquisitions. Managing editor internship at Whitmore Publishing."
"Yes," Lacy said, steady. "I worked directly under the Editorial Director. Manuscript evaluations. Workflow. Contract support."
"Hmm."
The resume was set aside. Eleanor steepled her fingers.
Then came the question:
"How do you define a story worth publishing?"
Lacy smoothed her palms against the fabric of her skirt under the desk, grounding herself. Then she looked Eleanor squarely in the eye and answered. "A story worth publishing, is one that lingers. Something that doesn't just entertain—it unsettles, provokes, heals. It speaks truth, even through fiction. It stays with you."
A flicker passed through Eleanor's gaze—not approval, but not dismissal either.
"And if I told you truth doesn't always sell?"

"Then I'd say that's why editors exist," Lacy said calmly. "To shape the truth. To protect the heart of a story—and still find it a home."
The silence that followed wasn't uncomfortable.
It was meaningful.
Eleanor leaned back slowly, folding her hands.
"We'll see if your instincts match your ideals," she said at last, standing to offer her hand.
"Welcome to Seaglass, Ms. Blake. Don't make me regret this."

That evening Lacy stood at her kitchen counter, laptop open, wine glass half-full beside her.
There it was.
Bold.
Real:
Welcome to Seaglass Press.
Senior Editor
It hit her like a wave.
This wasn't just a new job.
It was her dream.
The kind of place she used to read about in publishing newsletters, daring herself to imagine.
It was real.
It was happening.
And next week, it would officially begin.

CHAPTER 2

Lacy's first week at Seaglass Press was a steady blend of anticipation, admiration, and moments that made her question if any of this was truly real.

Her office—yes, office—was modest but polished, with sleek glass walls, warm wood finishes, and a view that caught the afternoon light just right. A tall ficus stood in the corner as if welcoming her to a new chapter. The shelves were bare for now, but already she could see them filled with books she'd shepherded into the world. It smelled faintly of fresh paint and ambition.

Seaglass was the kind of publishing house you didn't just get hired into—you were invited. Their reputation for cultivating award-winning literary fiction made them both revered and intimidating. Which is exactly how Delia had introduced herself that first morning.

Delia Rhodes, the Managing Editor, was a woman of poised contradictions. Sharp in both intellect and wardrobe, she had the aura of someone who could kill a deal with a single glance or revive it with one word. She welcomed Lacy with a firm handshake, a knowing smile, and a stack of onboarding materials heavier than some coffee tables.

"I'll be honest," Delia said as she led Lacy through the open-concept floor, her red bottom heels echoing confidently. "We've needed fresh eyes around here. Someone with instincts. Not just polish."

Lacy blinked, flattered but caught slightly off guard. "Thank you. I'm—honored."

"I wouldn't get cozy just yet. You're here because Eleanor believes in potential. I'm here to make sure that potential performs."

Her tone wasn't cruel—just clear. Lacy appreciated that more than she expected.

On her second day, Delia circled back, poking her head into Lacy's office like a well-dressed storm.

"You'll be partnering with Andrew Mitchell," she said. "Executive Editor. Strategy, author relationships, long-term positioning—all the things we pretend we're not obsessively managing. You'll cover acquisitions, major author development, and some crossover with Book Fair planning. You two should complement each other well. Go meet him before he vanishes into another meeting."

Lacy nodded, scribbling the name, even though she already remembered it. She'd seen his name in recent press features. She knew the books he'd acquired—quiet, slow-burn novels that somehow took over entire book clubs, bestseller lists, and award circuits with graceful force.

She found him in a corner office across the hall, mid-sentence on a speaker call. Through the glass, she could already see the intensity in his posture—one hand tucked into his pocket, the other gesturing as he spoke, like the words were tools he forged as he needed them. When he spotted her at the door, he wrapped up quickly and motioned her in with an easy smile.

"Lacy Blake," he said, stepping forward and offering a firm but warm handshake. "Glad you're finally here."

He was taller than she expected, easily 6'2 or 6'3, with a quiet, steady energy that pulled attention without demanding it.

His smooth, chocolate-toned skin caught the light in a way that made him look almost sculpted, like every angle of him had been refined by patience and purpose.

His haircut was sharp and low, and the fine line of facial hair along his jaw was so perfectly kept it felt like an editorial decision—intentional, precise. A tailored charcoal-gray suit hugged his lean frame, the white dress shirt beneath it open just enough at the collar to hint at the relaxed confidence he carried.

There was a subtle, addictive scent clinging to him—sandalwood, leather, a whisper of spice—luxurious but understated.

And the shoes—designer oxfords, midnight black, polished so meticulously they caught tiny flashes of light with every step—sealed the impression.

He looked like someone who understood the weight of details—someone who edited not just words, but his very presence.

Polished, deliberate, but never performative.

He was real, and Lacy felt it immediately.

"Andrew Mitchell," she replied, her tone friendly but composed. "I hear we're about to become work-married."

He chuckled, gesturing to the chair across from his desk. "Only if you promise to be the one who answers the emails before 9 a.m."

They fell into easy rhythm. Over the next hour, they traded backgrounds, swapped stories from past publishing trenches, and reviewed the early planning documents for the Book Fair—a cornerstone event for Seaglass, and their first major joint assignment. The Fair wasn't just an industry showcase; it was where careers were made, where talent was scouted, and where the company's public face was sharpened into something marketable and brilliant.

"We've got 10 months," Andrew said, passing her a printout of the author list from last year. "This year's theme is Legacy. Mrs. Vance wants vision. That's code for: 'don't screw it up.'"

Lacy scanned the names. "Do we already know who's attending from our house?"

"Some of the big names are circling. One or two I'd love to steal from rival imprints. That's where you come in."

She glanced up. "So, seduction and strategy."

He smiled again. "Publishing's only true power couple."

By Friday, they'd had two joint meetings, shared more than one "we've got this" look across the conference table, and agreed on a framework for how they'd divide their roles. She'd already made notes for three promising manuscripts and started early outreach to an emerging author she'd admired for years.

There were still moments—when she missed a familiar face or doubted her choices—that crept in like fog around the edges. But then Andrew would knock gently on her door with coffee, or Delia would fire off a compliment wrapped in critique, and she'd remember: this was what she'd fought for. Not comfort, but growth.

And growth, she was learning, looked a lot like hard-earned confidence... and maybe a seat at the table with people who finally saw what she could do.

Saturday morning arrived wrapped in a heavy gray sky, the kind that made the whole world feel slower, quieter.

No sharp sunlight, no golden beams—just a muted, hazy light filtering through the windows, soft and still.

In the quiet, the only sound was the low murmur of the city waking up outside and Leo's paws skittering across the hardwood floors. Lacy stretched across the couch, her throw blanket tangled around her legs, a mug of coffee balanced on her stomach, and her phone cradled against her ear.

"I'm alive," she said dramatically.

On the other end, Bree snorted. "Barely. You sounded like a hostage in your text last night."

"I felt like a hostage. The first week was incredible, don't get me wrong—but there was so much. I'm still trying to figure out if Delia's secretly rooting for me or planning my demise."

"She's probably doing both," Bree said knowingly. "That's how powerful women operate."

Lacy laughed, nudging Leo off her lap with a gentle push. "And Andrew? We finally met. He's... impossible to read but impossible to ignore. Sharp, composed, devastatingly smooth. Like the kind of guy who alphabetizes his bookshelf by mood and genre."

"So he's hot."

"I didn't say that."

"You didn't have to. You said 'devastatingly smooth.' That's code."

Lacy sighed, sipping her coffee. "He's just... easy to work with. And he listens.. We're partnering on the Book Fair."

"Oh, wow. That's huge. That event's like your Met Gala."

"It is. Delia dropped it in my lap like a casual Friday task. No pressure."

"Girl, you've got this," Bree said. "And the fact that you're not crying in a bathtub with a bottle of pinot means you're doing better than half the corporate world."

Lacy smiled, the warmth in Bree's voice grounding her. "How's Thomas?"

Bree groaned. "Still in his 'maybe I'll open a brewery' phase. I'm trying to be supportive, but if he says 'IPA potential' one more time I might start hiding his hops."

They both dissolved into laughter until a ding interrupted them—first on Bree's end, then Lacy's.

Group Text:

AVA: Emergency Zoom in 1 hour. Don't ask questions. Just show up. Wear mascara.

NINA: Ava I swear to God—

KAYLA: I'm not putting on pants for this.

JANELLE: This better be juicy.

LACY: Is someone pregnant or famous?

AVA: Better. Just get on.

Bree's voice returned in a gasp. "Mascara?! Someone got promoted."

"It's Ava," Lacy said immediately. "She's the only one who uses the phrase 'emergency Zoom' like it's a gender reveal."

"Well, if it is Ava, it's gotta be big. She's been circling that exec role for months."

"I'll bring champagne to the screen," Lacy said, already heading to her bathroom with Leo tailing behind her like a shadow. "Brunch Zoom is officially back."

"Yasss," Bree replied. "Now go get mascara and mute your cat."

An hour later, Lacy settled in front of her laptop with a fresh cup of coffee, hair brushed, mascara applied, and Leo sprawled dramatically across her keyboard like he had a stake in the call. Bree's video popped up first, her curls piled on top of her head, wearing a hoodie that said Don't Talk To Me Until I've Had My Coffee.

"I did put on mascara," Bree said, squinting into the camera. "So if this isn't major, I'm driving to Ava's and hiding all her healthy snacks."

The screen quickly filled with the rest of the crew—Kayla in a silk robe with her hair in rollers, Janelle with a mimosa already in hand, Nina broadcasting from what looked like a cozy reading nook in D.C., fairy lights blinking behind her.

"Okay, everyone's here," Ava said, breathless and glowing, in a perfectly framed video window. "Are we ready?"

"No," said Kayla. "But go on."

Ava held up a piece of paper, then promptly burst into tears. "They made it official. I got the promotion. I'm going to be the Director of Strategic Partnerships at the firm!"

Screams. Literal screams. Bree jumped out of frame and came back with a tambourine. Lacy clapped so hard Leo bolted off the desk in protest.

"Ava! That's huge!" Lacy beamed. "You've been killing yourself for that role."

"I thought they were going to give it to Jeff," Nina said, eyes wide. "You beat Jeff. That's better than winning the Hunger Games."

"I did beat Jeff," Ava sniffled. "I beat Jeff with grace and PowerPoint."

"Say it again for the girls in the back!" Kayla whooped.

"This is the promotion we prayed for!" Bree added, fake-fanning herself.

"I just... I didn't think it was happening," Ava continued, laughing through tears now. "Especially not after everything. But they said I showed leadership. And vision. And... I don't know, I guess I just finally stopped dimming my light."

There was a pause—warm, proud silence.

"Don't ever dim again," Janelle said. "You're blinding us and we love it."
They all toasted—coffee, champagne, orange juice, whatever was closest.
Leo returned to Lacy's lap, now purring like he too approved.
Then Ava turned toward Lacy's little Zoom square. "Speaking of glow-ups, Lacy, we haven't even gotten the full update yet. Executive Editor? Book Fair? Working with a hot mystery coworker?"
Lacy laughed. "I knew I shouldn't have told Bree anything."
"You're not getting out of this," Bree grinned. "Tell them everything."
"Oh, I will," Lacy said, her cheeks already flushing. "But only if you promise not to say devastatingly smooth in front of the man if you ever meet him."
"No promises," the entire group said in unison.

Later that evening, Lacy was curled up on her couch, Leo purring in a loaf beside her, when her phone buzzed.

Andrew Mitchell
Sorry for the late text. Meant to send this earlier but got distracted by a very dramatic email chain about canapé options for the book fair. Who knew hummus could spark such fierce debate?
She laughed softly, brushing a hand over Leo's back as she typed back.
Lacy
I fully support hummus diplomacy. Personally, I'm rooting for sun-dried tomato over roasted garlic. But that's a hill I'm prepared to die on.
The dots blinked for a moment before Andrew replied.
Andrew Mitchell
A bold stance. I respect that. Though I think we may be on opposite sides of this hummus war.
Lacy
Then I guess we'll have to settle this the old-fashioned way: taste test in neutral territory. I'll bring the spoons.
Andrew Mitchell

Make it coffee spoons and we have a deal.
Lacy
Deal. But I expect a formal apology when sun-dried tomato wins.
There was a longer pause this time. Just long enough to make her wonder if the playful back-and-forth had pushed the boundary. Then his next message buzzed in.
Andrew Mitchell
You're sharp, Blake. The book fair team's lucky to have you. I'm glad we're working together.
Lacy felt a warmth spread through her chest that had nothing to do with the blanket wrapped around her. She hesitated, then typed back:
Lacy
Likewise, Mitchell. And hey—if the hummus wars don't break us, I think we'll make a good team.
Andrew Mitchell
Night, Lacy.
Lacy
Night, Andrew.
She locked her phone, a smile still playing at her lips. Leo lifted his head sleepily, then flopped back down against her leg.
Yeah. It was only the beginning—but this new chapter? It was already starting to feel like the right one.

Chapter 3

The weeks passed like pages turning in a well-loved book—smooth, steady, and full of quiet discovery. After the whirlwind of her first week, the city began to unfold itself to Lacy in gentler ways. The noise didn't press so tightly against her anymore; the sharp edges had softened. What once felt overwhelming now felt alive. Manageable. Almost…hers.

There was a new kind of peace to her mornings. Not perfect, not without the occasional frantic scramble or forgotten email, but peaceful all the same. She'd grown into the shape of her routine—coffee brewed before sunrise, Leo leaping to the counter in time for the first pour, his sleepy weight settling beside her as she sat with the day's first stillness.

Even Leo seemed to have found his rhythm. He no longer prowled the apartment at night like he was looking for the life they'd left behind. Instead, he curled into the window seat like a watchful little sentinel, guarding their corner of the world with one eye open and his tail twitching at the sound of pigeons.

Outside, the city murmured its morning song. She'd started walking to work—not for the exercise, but for the quiet gifts the walk offered: fog rising off the bay, the distant clang of ships in the harbor, a barista waving from a regular corner café. A violinist on the corner who played only in the early hours, his music carrying over the cobblestones like a secret just for those awake enough to hear it.

Each day at Seaglass Press added to the rhythm. Meetings, manuscript samples, emails, author calls. Her inbox stayed full, but so did her spirit. There was challenge in her work—real, invigorating challenge—but there was something else too. A spark of creative energy she hadn't realized she'd been missing. Especially when Andrew popped his head into her office, eyebrows raised, always with something clever or maddening or both.

And outside of work, the pulse of her life was slowly, sweetly building. Bree checked in nearly every day, usually with a group text full of jokes

and updates. The girls had started planning their next meetup. And her apartment, still modest, had begun to feel lived in. Like home.
It wasn't perfect. But it was hers.
And that, she was beginning to understand, made all the difference.

Halfway down a quiet side street, Lacy tapped her AirPods into place and called Bree.
"Bout time," Bree answered, playful but warm. "I was two minutes from filing a missing persons report."
Lacy grinned, shifting her tote bag higher as she walked. "You're so dramatic."
"That's why you love me. Now spill. How's life in Coastal Chic City today?"
"Good. Busy. You know. Work, manuscripts, the occasional overpriced latte. Same circus, new tent."
Bree snorted. "At least you upgraded from clowns to creatives."
"Barely," Lacy teased. "Some days, it's a toss-up."
They traded quick updates—Bree venting about her new project at work, Lacy complaining about an author who couldn't meet a deadline—until both their phones buzzed at the same time.
Lacy glanced down at her screen without breaking stride: Group Chat: Ava had dropped another flyer.
Global Ventures & Innovation Expo — Miami. Mark your calendars! Would be an epic girls' trip and networking gold.
Bree groaned. "If Ava sends that thing one more time, I'm sending her a digital restraining order."
Lacy laughed. "She's nothing if not persistent."
"She's a machine," Bree agreed. "If I had half her energy, Thomas would've been ring shopping already."
"You're still holding out hope, huh?" Lacy teased.
"Girl, manifesting is free. Let me dream."

"You're ridiculous," Lacy said, laughing as she dodged a guy on a skateboard.

"But low-key? I hope it happens. Y'all are good together."

Bree softened a little. "Yeah. Me too."

They lingered on the call a little longer, trading more jokes and life updates, until Lacy turned a corner and spotted a cozy little café tucked between a bookstore and a plant shop. A chalkboard sign out front read: Be Kind. It's Cool.

Soft jazz floated from the doorway.

"You'd love this café I just found," she said, smiling as she pushed the door open.

"Ugh, rude. Why do you get to discover all the cute spots first?"

"Manifesting," Lacy teased, tossing Bree's favorite word back at her.

Bree laughed. "Alright, fine. Enjoy. And take mental notes. I need a full vibe report later."

"Will do," Lacy promised, slipping inside as the soft hum of jazz and espresso wrapped around her.

They said their goodbyes, and Lacy tucked her phone away, letting the cozy atmosphere pull her in like an old friend.

The air smelled like fresh pastries and cardamom, and the space glowed with amber lighting and the charm of well-worn wood. She ordered her favorite: a large oat milk vanilla latte with an extra shot and light foam, then headed to the back of the café, snagging a sunny window seat tucked beneath a cascade of hanging plants. The kind of spot that made her want to open a blank notebook and just... breathe for a second before the day officially began. She let the quiet settle around her like a favorite sweater.

"Thought I spotted a free seat back here," said a voice—smooth, friendly, a little amused.

She snapped out of her moment and looked up.

He had the kind of face you notice twice. Tousled curls that refused to stay in place, a dusting of freckles that made him look younger, and a denim

jacket that had clearly seen a lot of paint and even more afternoons like this. Slung over his shoulder was a canvas bag stuffed with sketchpads and brushes, the corner of a watercolor poking out like a secret.
"Mind if I join you?" he asked, nodding toward the open chair. "The rest of this place feels like a coworking space with caffeine."
Lacy smiled. "Go for it."
"Thanks." He dropped into the seat like he'd just been handed a good twist in a story. "Didn't want to risk sitting next to someone plotting their novel's next murder."
"You joke, but I passed a guy muttering about plot twists like he was rewriting a crime scene."
He chuckled. "You're sharp. I like that."
He opened his sketchbook but didn't start drawing—just glanced around like he was letting the place breathe onto the page. "Lucas, by the way."
"Lacy."
"Nice to meet you, Lacy." His grin turned lopsided.
"You've got that 'hatching an evil plan' face."
Lacy raised her cup with mock seriousness. "World peace. After caffeine."
Lucas chuckled, leaning back in his chair. "Dangerous. I like it."
She just smirked over the rim of her cup, letting the warmth of the coffee —and the easy, sparking energy between them—settle in her chest.
Their conversation unfolded with surprising ease. Lucas talked about his art—the layers of city life, rooftop views people overlooked, how he chased light and texture more than perfection.
"I like finding the stories that hide in plain sight," he said. "Not the glossy kind. The ones with cracks and fingerprints."
Lacy leaned in a little. "That's really beautiful."
He shrugged. "Just how I see things."
They kept talking—weather, favorite cafés, how cinnamon should be its own love language. Lucas was funny without trying, thoughtful without pressing, and present in a way that made her forget the time.

Eventually, he tapped her cup. "You don't seem like a 'same drink every day' kind of person."

"You're not wrong."

"You've got curated chaos vibes."

She laughed. "Still deciding if that's an insult."

"It's a compliment," he said, completely sincere. "Like someone who plans everything but still ends up dancing in the rain."

She raised a brow. "Now that one I'll take."

Lucas stood, slinging his bag over his shoulder. "Thanks for the seat. You made my third coffee the best one yet."

"Glad I could help."

He smiled once more. "Maybe I'll run into you here again?"

"Maybe."

She watched as he walked out, sketchbook swinging by his side, the sunlight catching on the corner like a flicker of something not quite ordinary.

The café was still calm, still hers—but something about the day had shifted.

She didn't know it yet, but Lucas wouldn't stay a stranger.

Not for long.

The following week swirled into a rhythm of tight deadlines, editorial meetings, and early mornings. Lacy found herself thriving in the demanding pace of Seaglass Press, her confidence growing stronger with each passing day. Andrew remained her north star—steady, sharp-witted, and reliably good at bringing her back down to earth with a well-timed joke or an unexpected insight.

Late one afternoon, as they reviewed a stack of submissions in the break room, Andrew leaned back in his chair and gave her a sidelong glance. "You doing anything this weekend?" he asked casually, tapping the edge of a manuscript.

Lacy looked up from her notes. "Other than catching up on sleep and maybe doing laundry for the first time in forever? No, not really."

"Good," he said, sliding her a glossy invitation. "Charity event. Dress up, show up, pretend to enjoy mini crab cakes while pretending to network. It'll be fun."

She eyed him warily. "Is this one of those things where I end up in a room full of tweed blazers and awkward elbow touches?"

Andrew smirked. "There might be tweed. But there will also be free wine and good music. And… someone's been asking about you."

Lacy raised a brow. "Who?"

He shrugged, maddeningly cryptic. "A guy I ran into at a publishing mixer a few weekends ago. Said he saw you there, knew we worked together, and wanted to know who you were."

She blinked. "Seriously?"

Andrew's grin widened. "Seriously. He invited me to this thing—and gave me an extra invite just in case I wanted to bring you."

Lacy narrowed her eyes. "That sounds suspiciously like matchmaking."

"Or maybe fate," he said with a wink. "Either way, wear something nice. You might want to make a good impression."

As she walked back to her desk, invitation in hand, Lacy caught herself smiling.

Not nerves.

Not pressure.

Just... possibility.

She tucked the invitation next to her planner in her Channel tote and glanced out the window, the city sprawling wide and open beneath a silver-threaded sky.

Anything could happen.

And she was ready for it.

Chapter 4

The rooftop buzzed with low conversation and clinking glasses, a canopy of twinkling lights stretched above as the city sparkled below. The crisp evening air carried the scent of aged wine and expensive perfume, the kind of atmosphere that whispered old money and ambition.
Lacy stepped into the event like a secret finally revealed.
The hush of the room didn't shift—at least, not loudly—but energy curved toward her like a slow inhale. Her navy silk dress clung in all the right places and flowed in all the others, pooling gently at her ankles with the kind of elegance that didn't need a second glance to command attention—but got one anyway. The fabric shimmered subtly as she moved, catching the light in waves, like liquid night washing over her 5'11" frame.
Her skin—caramel with a golden undertone so rich it looked lit from within—seemed to drink in the warm ambient lighting, reflecting it back in a soft, burnished glow. Her almond-shaped eyes, ever-shifting hazel with hints of green and gold, sparkled with intent—curious, composed, and vaguely amused, as though she were walking into a play where she already knew the ending.
Thick lashes fanned above her cheeks, and a sweep of bronze shadow caught the light with every blink. Her hair—luxurious, voluminous, a glossy tumble of deep waves—cascaded past her shoulders like it had stories of its own. Everything about her was effortless and deliberate at once.
She wore diamond studs—small, sharp points of light—nestled just above the elegant line of her jaw. A soft rose flush colored her full lips, like a secret held gently between them. When she smiled—just enough to be dangerous—it was the kind that made people lose track of conversations mid-sentence. A minimal gold cuff clung to her wrist like it belonged there. Her clutch, the faint shimmer of champagne silk, looked like something whispered into existence just for this night.

And then there was the way she moved—
Not rushed. Not rehearsed.
She glided.
The click of her Jimmy Choo's echoed faintly against polished marble, her stride slow and self-assured, hips swaying with rhythmic confidence that wasn't meant to be watched... but always was.
Lacy didn't command the room. She invited it—without saying a word—to orbit her.
The effect was instant. A ripple of admiration swept across the room as if the music itself took a beat to adjust to her presence.

Andrew, mid-laugh in a circle of editors, caught sight of her—and froze. His glass dipped slightly as his jaw slackened. "Holy—" he muttered, mostly to himself. Recovering, he straightened with a grin that was equal parts pride and disbelief. He made his way toward her, navigating through the crowd like a man on a mission.
"You're kidding me," he said when he reached her, his eyes wide. "You trying to give the entire publishing industry a heart attack tonight?"
Lacy laughed, lifting her wine glass in mock innocence. "Is it too much?"
Andrew shook his head, clearly stunned. "It's criminal. Absolutely criminal. I should've warned security."
"I clean up well, huh" she teased, twirling a bit of hair behind her ear.
"You obliterated the dress code, that's what you did."
She smiled, cheeks flushed from the attention. "Well, you did say this would be fancy."
He held his hands up. "And I am thanking myself right now for saying it."
They shared a laugh, the moment light and full of ease.
"You remember that guy I mentioned?" Andrew said, leaning in just slightly as he handed her a glass of champagne. His tone was casual, but his eyes gave away the gleam of mischief.
Lacy tilted her head, intrigued. "The one who asked about me?"
"That's the one." he said

She narrowed her eyes. "And you're still not telling me who he is?"

"I gave you enough. Tall, sharp suit, apparently a fan of your work… the rest is part of the charm," Andrew said, smirking.

She rolled her eyes, sipping her drink. "You are infuriating."

"And yet," he said, backing away with a crooked smile, "you love it."

Lacy shook her head as he melted back into the crowd, leaving her beneath a canopy of soft string lights and a haze of curiosity. The band's smooth jazz mingled with low laughter and clinking glasses, giving the room an air of something cinematic—something unfolding.

She turned toward the bar, her heels whispering across the floor, her clutch tucked close to her side. The cool stem of her glass grounded her, but her thoughts floated just above the surface—half in the moment, half chasing the possibility Andrew had dangled in front of her all week.

Then—

"Lacy, isn't it?"

She turned around.

And saw a gorgeous tall man.

He stood before her, his eyes—intense and thoughtful, with a glint of something playful—met hers like they already knew her.

She blinked, slightly caught off guard. "Yes… I'm sorry, have we met?"

"Not officially," the man said, his voice smooth, deep—velvet wrapped around steel. His smile curved with practiced ease, confident but not rushed. "But I've heard a lot about you."

Her eyes narrowed slightly, intrigued. "From…?"

"Andrew." He let the name hang there just long enough to confirm he wasn't some random admirer. "He's mentioned you a few times. I figured it was time I introduced myself properly."

Lacy straightened, taking him in fully now.

He was tall—easily 6'4"—with the kind of presence that made everything else around him dim slightly. His skin was a rich, even shade of chocolate, luminous under the ambient lighting. He wore a sleek tailored suit in a deep charcoal gray, paired—boldly and somehow perfectly—with a crisp white tee and a pair of pristine, vintage Jordan 1s that looked like they belonged in a museum. The blend of luxury and edge was so precise, it almost felt like a signature.

His fade was sharp, his beard sculpted close and clean, framing a strong jawline. There was something quietly dangerous in the way he carried himself—controlled, smooth, and unbothered. The type of man who didn't just walk into a room, but commanded it without needing to announce himself.

"I'm Patrick Ellis," he said, offering a hand that felt warm and strong in hers. "Managing partner at Havenstone Capital. We've backed a few media startups—book tech, hybrid presses, a few international plays. I've been orbiting your world for a while now."

Lacy raised an eyebrow, intrigued but playing it cool. "So you're the mystery man Andrew wouldn't tell me about."

Patrick chuckled, low and easy. "Guilty. I figured it was better to introduce myself properly."

Her smile curved slowly. "And you've been asking about me?"

He tilted his head, that confident glint never leaving his eyes.

"I saw you once," he said, shifting slightly closer. "At a conference mixer. You were mid-conversation with someone, and I didn't want to interrupt. But you stuck with me."

She tilted her head, amused. "So this is what? Fate part two?"

"I don't do fate," he said, eyes steady on hers. "I do strategy. And when I see something I want, I make sure I get close enough to understand it."

Her heart skipped—a barely perceptible shift—but she didn't let it show. "And what exactly are you trying to understand?"

"You," he said simply. "But I'll settle for a drink first."

She nodded, choosing to meet that bold energy with her own. "White wine."

"Coming right up," he said, turning toward the bar with a kind of swagger that made heads follow him without even knowing why.

They talked for what felt like hours, even though the clock told a different story. Patrick was a master conversationalist—eloquent without being showy, intelligent without the need to dominate. He spoke of global ventures and emerging markets with the same ease he used to describe a graffiti artist he'd commissioned in Lisbon. His love for curation extended beyond just business—it lived in the way he observed the world, always assessing, always collecting.

And yet, he never made her feel small.

He listened, really listened. When Lacy spoke about her authors, about the manuscripts that cracked her open or made her late for work because she couldn't put them down, Patrick leaned in—not just physically, but emotionally. Like every word she spoke was currency.

"Publishing isn't for the faint of heart," he said. "It's chess. Vision, patience, timing. Sounds like you thrive in it."

"I do," she said, surprised at how easy it was to open up under his gaze. "It's... home, in a way."

Patrick smiled, slow and calculated. "And you look damn good doing it."

She laughed, shaking her head. "Do you always flirt like this?"

"Only when I mean it."

As the crowd began to thin, Patrick offered to walk her to the elevators. He didn't rush. Every step beside her felt deliberate, like he was memorizing the rhythm of her presence.

"It was a pleasure meeting you, Lacy," he said once they reached the elevator bank. His voice dipped, soft and intimate. "I'd like to see you again. Soon."

"I'd like that too," she admitted, the words tasting like both risk and promise.

He brushed his fingers lightly against hers—not a full touch, just enough to leave a trace.

As the elevator doors closed, Lacy caught a glimpse of herself in the mirrored panel. Still composed. Still radiant. But inside, something thrummed.

Patrick was more than charming. He was magnetic, intense, and deeply attuned. But beneath all that polish was a current of something tightly wound—like every move he made was part of a long game.
Still, she couldn't deny it: she was curious.
And curiosity had always been her weakness.

The next morning, her phone buzzed beside her toothbrush.
Patrick:
Still thinking about that smile. Last night was… something else. Let's not make that a one-time thing.
Lacy smirked at her reflection, her cheeks warming as she rinsed her mouth out, still half-tangled in the memory of the night before—the way Patrick's voice dipped low when he said goodbye, the way he looked at her like she wasn't just another woman in the room, but the only one.
She wiped her hands on a towel and quickly typed back:
Lacy:
Flattery before 8 a.m.? You're bold.
The reply came almost immediately:
Patrick:
Only when the stakes are high. And I have a feeling they are.
She grinned wider, feeling that unmistakable flutter again.
Lacy:
You always this smooth, or is this just for me?
Patrick:
I plead the Fifth.
But I do plan on proving it wasn't just the wine talking.
Can I call you later?
Lacy bit her lip, heart tapping a quick, giddy rhythm in her chest.
Before she could overthink it, she dropped her phone onto the bathroom counter, grabbed it again, and hit Call—this time dialing Bree.
Bree answered after one ring, her voice already half-laughing. "Took you long enough. I was about to call out a wellness check."

Lacy flopped down onto her bed, staring at the ceiling, the biggest smile pulling at her mouth. "Bree. Girl. You're not ready."

"I'm sitting down," Bree said dramatically. "Give me the tea. Full pot. I want details."

Lacy launched right in, her words tumbling out in a rush. "Okay, first of all, he's even finer in person. Like… God took his time. Tall, chocolate skin, fitted suit, kicks that looked custom—and the man smells like wealth and good decisions."

Bree howled. "Wealth and good decisions! Go on, I'm dying."

"And he listens," Lacy said, sitting up now, animated. "He asked about my work, about what kind of stories keep me up at night. Not just the usual 'what do you do?'—he cared."

"So he's fine and emotionally intelligent?" Bree sounded skeptical, but intrigued. "Sis. Are you sure he's not a simulation?"

"I'm not sure of anything right now," Lacy laughed. "But I do know I haven't stopped smiling since last night."

"Okay, so... you like him," Bree teased, voice lilting.

"I don't know him yet," Lacy hedged. "But there's something there. Energy. Chemistry. Potential."

"And he texted you already?" Bree gasped. "Girl, he is pressed!"

"In a good way," Lacy said, cheeks aching from smiling. "He wants to call me later."

"Let him!" Bree said immediately. "Let him pursue you like the prize you are."

Lacy laughed, feeling lighter than she had in weeks. "You're too much."

"I'm just enough. Now, before you get off the phone—what's the vibe? Like, what's your gut saying?"

Lacy paused, serious now. "Honestly? My gut says be curious... but stay sharp. There's a lot of charm there. And you know me—I don't want to get swept up in the surface."

Bree's voice softened. "Good. Stay centered. Enjoy the attention, enjoy you, and let him show you who he really is."

"Exactly," Lacy said. "I'm not in a rush."
"Well, call me the minute he does something swoon-worthy... or suspicious," Bree added. "Either way, I'm ready."
"I love you," Lacy said, meaning it.
"Love you more, glow worm. Talk soon."
Lacy ended the call, setting her phone down with a little sigh.
New beginnings were tricky. They came wrapped in excitement, sure—but also in uncertainty.
Still, as she glanced at the new message thread with Patrick flashing back to life on her screen, she couldn't help but feel a little thrill run through her veins.

The soft steam still clung to the bathroom mirror as Lacy wrapped a towel around her hair, humming absently while she moved through her apartment. Her skin was still warm from the shower, the faint scent of lavender and vanilla lingering in the air, calming her nerves after a long day.
Just as she reached for her moisturizer, her phone buzzed from the nightstand, screen lighting up with a name that made her smile without thinking.
Patrick Ellis.
Heart skipping, she crossed the room, tugging her robe tighter around her waist as she picked up the phone. For a second, she just stood there, staring at the screen, feeling the familiar tangle of nerves and excitement build in her chest.
With a deep breath, she answered. "Hello?"
"Hey, beautiful," Patrick's voice rumbled through the line—smooth, low, and entirely too effective. "Hope I'm not interrupting anything important... like a Netflix binge or plotting your next career move."
Lacy laughed softly, settling onto the edge of her bed. "Just getting out of the shower, actually. You're right on time."

"Timing is everything," he said, the smile in his voice unmistakable. "I was thinking about last night... and about how we definitely didn't get enough time."

"You mean you didn't get enough time to interrogate me properly?" she teased, her tone light.

"I prefer the word discover," Patrick replied, chuckling. "And trust me, I'm just getting started."

She pulled her knees up onto the bed, tucking them beneath her. "Alright, Mr. Investigator. What's the next step in your grand strategy?"

"Simple," he said. "I want to see you again. Somewhere without a crowd. Somewhere we can actually finish a conversation without someone trying to sell us a foundation grant or an overpriced painting."

Lacy smiled, feeling the soft tug of anticipation. "That sounds dangerously close to a date."

"It is dangerously close," Patrick said smoothly. "And entirely intentional. Are you free tomorrow night?"

"Depends," she teased. "What's the plan?"

"Something easy," he said, his voice dropping into that intimate register again. "Good food, a little music, somewhere we can hear ourselves think. Nothing heavy. Just... us."

Her heart fluttered in that careful, thrilling way—like standing at the edge of something she hadn't fully named yet.

"I think I can make that work," she said, pretending to deliberate.

"I'll text you the details," Patrick promised. "And Lacy?"

"Yeah?"

"I'm really looking forward to this."

The sincerity in his voice wrapped around her, warm and real, and for a moment, she didn't feel the need to guard herself so tightly.

"Me too," she said, barely above a whisper.

They said their goodnights, lingering just a little longer than necessary before hanging up.

Lacy set the phone down gently, the smile refusing to leave her face. Outside her window, the city twinkled in the distance, alive and humming. She wasn't sure exactly where this was going.
But she was excited to find out.

Lacy stood in front of her full-length mirror, her phone propped against a stack of books, Bree's face lighting up the screen with wide, delighted eyes.
"Girl, spin again. Slowly this time," Bree demanded, leaning closer to the screen like she could somehow reach through and adjust a curl if needed. "This man is not ready."
Laughing, Lacy twirled obediently. The hem of her soft yellow dress flared around her toned legs, the lightweight fabric skimming her skin like a second whisper. The fit was effortless—classy, sultry, unforgettable. The neckline dipped just enough to tease without giving away too much, while a daring slit ran up one thigh, offering a glimpse of her long, sculpted legs—thank you, endless Pilates sessions.
Leo, perched on the windowsill, blinked slowly in what she swore was approval before turning his attention back to the street below, his tail flicking lazily.
Lacy's caramel skin practically glowed beneath the warm lights of her apartment. Her almond-shaped hazel eyes, rimmed with a soft shimmer of bronze, sparkled with excitement. Her lips—full, heart-shaped, and glossed in the perfect nude—curved into a grin she couldn't seem to suppress. Her hair, freshly styled into soft, glossy waves, tumbled past her shoulders, framing her face with an effortless glamour that made her feel like she belonged on the cover of a magazine.
"Oh my God," Bree said, fanning herself with exaggerated flair. "You look like a whole plot twist he's not ready for."
Lacy laughed, slipping on a pair of gold strappy heels that showcased her freshly manicured nude toes. She looped a dainty clutch over her wrist and fastened her gold hoop earrings, pairing them with a delicate layered

necklace and a slim gold watch. The subtle, warm notes of vanilla and sandalwood from her favorite perfume kissed the air around her, wrapping her in a signature scent that made her feel untouchable.

"I feel good," Lacy said, smoothing her hands down her hips. "Nervous butterflies... but the good kind."

"As you should, boo. You look like a dream," Bree said, raising a glass of wine in salute. "Now remember: enjoy yourself. Laugh too loud, dance if he asks, and call me the second it's over. I'm invested."

Lacy winked, blowing a kiss at the screen before ending the call.

Leo hopped down from his perch as if to escort her to the door, his soft paws padding along the hardwood floors.

"Hold the fort down, little man," Lacy murmured, grabbing her keys and giving Leo a quick scratch behind the ears before heading out into the evening.

The night air was balmy, brushing against her skin like a whispered promise.

Patrick had texted her earlier with the address—an intimate, tucked-away restaurant known for its cozy lighting, incredible food, live music, and late-night dancing. The kind of place you didn't just stumble into—you had to know it existed. And somehow, it already felt like the perfect backdrop for whatever was about to unfold between them.

Tonight wasn't about making promises.

It was about possibilities.

And Lacy, was ready to say yes to all of it.

When she pulled up to the restaurant, the city seemed to hush around it, as if the evening had conspired to create this perfect little pocket of magic. Twinkling lights draped from the wrought-iron awning, soft jazz spilling from somewhere inside, blending with the murmur of quiet conversation.

As Lacy stepped out of her car, she spotted Patrick immediately.

He was standing casually near the entrance, one hand tucked into the pocket of tailored navy trousers, the other cradling a phone he slipped away the second he saw her. His crisp white shirt stretched perfectly across broad shoulders, the deep navy blazer hugging his frame like it had been made just for him.

And on his feet—because of course—an immaculate pair of vintage Nike Air Force 1s, midnight blue with a silver swoosh, so clean they almost looked brand-new. Somehow, the sneakers didn't clash with the rest of his polished outfit—they elevated it, gave him that effortless edge that made Patrick Ellis unforgettable.

His signature cologne—rich, smooth, slightly spiced—hit her just as he stepped forward, a slow, appreciative smile spreading across his face.

"Wow," he said slowly, his eyes trailing over her with open admiration. "I should've brought sunglasses."

She smirked, stepping forward, the slit of her dress catching the faint breeze.

"If you look at me like that all night," she said, her voice a velvet tease, "you're gonna start something you can't finish."

Patrick's slow smile was all heat and intent, his voice dropping to a low, dangerous rumble.

"Who says I don't finish what I start?"

His eyes dragged over her body with the kind of appreciation that made her skin flush.

"You walked out here and changed the whole damn forecast."

Heat bloomed up her neck, but she masked it with a smirk, tossing him a look that was all cool confidence—even as her heart pounded harder against her ribs.

Patrick's hand found the small of her back, his touch light but sure, sending a slow ripple of awareness down her spine.

It wasn't possessive—just intentional—the kind of touch that made her hyper-aware of every breath, every inch of space shrinking between them as he guided her toward the entrance.

Inside, the restaurant was pure ambiance—warm lighting, soft shadows, tables intimate but not cramped. A live trio played in the corner, the sounds of a slow, velvety saxophone weaving through the air. Candles flickered on each table, their flames dancing like they knew something she didn't.

Their server, Dante, introduced himself with a charming grin and a flair that immediately put them both at ease.

As they settled into a corner table—half hidden by heavy velvet drapes but still close enough to the music—conversation slipped between them like silk. They laughed over the menu, teasing about who was more adventurous with food, and ended up sharing a selection of small plates: buttery seared scallops, roasted vegetables dusted with sea salt, lamb skewers drizzled with some sauce Lacy couldn't pronounce but would dream about for days.

Patrick's playful side came out more with every course, but there was an undercurrent of something else too—something deeper, more focused, like all that charm had been sharpened just for her.

"Okay, what is this flavor?" he said after one particularly bold bite. "This tastes like regret and high tax brackets."

Lacy snorted into her wineglass. "Right? Like it's been through generational trauma."

They dissolved into laughter, their shoulders brushing, knees knocking under the table with a little more purpose each time. Gravity, not accident. When the trio shifted into a slow, sultry rhythm, Patrick pushed his plate away and stood, extending his hand without hesitation.

"Dance with me," he said—not really a question, more a certainty that she would.

She hesitated, savoring it, just long enough to make him grin wider.

"I thought you'd never ask," she teased, sliding her hand into his.

He led her onto the small, open space near the band. There weren't many couples dancing yet—but the second Patrick pulled her close, the rest of the room ceased to exist.

His hand found her lower back, firm and deliberate, holding her just tight enough to say you're not going anywhere, without needing to say a word. His other hand clasped hers lightly, their fingers fitting together too easily. The music slowed further, the lights dipped low, and Patrick leaned in, his lips brushing the shell of her ear.
"You're trouble," he murmured, voice a low, claiming rumble, "in the best way."
Lacy tilted her head to meet his gaze, her smile wicked. "Takes one to know one."
He chuckled, and the sound vibrated against her skin, leaving goosebumps in its wake.
The pull between them simmered hotter, deeper—a tension spun from barely-there touches, lingering glances, promises not yet spoken aloud.
They stayed wrapped around each other song after song, until it wasn't dancing anymore—it was just them, moving to a rhythm only they seemed to hear.
By the time he walked her back to the valet, the moon was high, casting a silver glow over the quiet street.
They lingered beside her car, the space between them charged and crackling.
"I had an amazing time," she said softly, the truth of it settling somewhere deep in her bones.
"So did I," he murmured, stepping closer, his hand brushing hers again—this time a little more possessive, like he couldn't help needing the contact. "Can I kiss you?"
Instead of answering, Lacy rose onto her toes and closed the distance herself.
Their kiss was slow at first—an exploration, a dare—and then deepened, his hand sliding to her waist in a way that felt like a silent vow: Mine.
When they finally pulled apart, Lacy smiled, wicked and breathless.
"That's all you're getting... for now."

Patrick chuckled, a low, heated sound. "You say that like you're not gonna be on my mind all night."
He opened her car door, lingering for just a second longer, brushing his knuckles lightly down her arm in a touch that promised he wasn't nearly done with her.
"I'm not good at waiting, Lace," he said, voice pitched so only she could hear. "But for you? I will."
She slipped into the driver's seat, heart hammering, body still humming. In her rearview mirror, she caught him standing there—hands in his pockets, those immaculate vintage sneakers catching the glow of the streetlights—watching her leave like he already knew she'd be back.

As she drove off, the city lights blurred softly through her windshield, matching the glow that hadn't left her face since the kiss. Her phone rang through her car's Bluetooth, and she didn't even have to check the screen to know who it was.
"Okay," Bree's voice burst through the speakers, no hello, no pleasantries. "Spill. I know you're driving, so just start talking. I want everything."
Lacy laughed, still reeling. "Bree… it was perfect. Like, movie montage perfect."
She dove into every detail—the way Patrick opened her car door, how charming and funny he was, the incredible food they shared, the music that turned into slow dancing under the soft glow of candlelight. And of course, the kiss.
"A real kiss?" Bree asked, half-gasping, half-giggling.
"The realest," Lacy sighed, dreamily. "Not too much tongue. Just enough. He smelled like expensive wood and good decisions."
Bree cackled. "Girl, you better stop before I propose to him."
Then she quieted suddenly.
"Wait, what?" Lacy asked.
"My night was cute too…" Bree said, and Lacy could hear the smile in her voice. "Thomas asked me to marry him."

Lacy gasped. "What?"

"He did it! Finally! And it was so sweet. I'll send you a pic, but you can't look until you park, I swear I'll haunt you if you crash."

"Oh my God, Bree!"

By the time Lacy pulled into her spot, her cheeks hurt from smiling. She cut the engine and finally opened the photo Bree had sent.

The diamond sparkled from her screen, and so did Bree's radiant face.

Lacy screamed. And Bree screamed right back over the speaker.

More squeals. More laughter. It was joy layered on joy, hearts full, and the kind of moment they'd both remember forever.

Still smiling, Lacy headed up to her apartment, her phone still warm from the call, her heart even warmer.

Later, just as she was slipping into her pajamas, her phone buzzed.

Patrick: Made it home safely. Just wanted to say goodnight again. Tonight was unforgettable. Can't wait to see you again.

Lacy smiled, heart full, cheeks aching from how hard she was grinning.

Lacy: Home safe. You weren't so bad yourself... Sleep tight, Mr. Trouble.

She set the phone down, turned out the lights, and sank into bed, her body still buzzing from the night.

For the first time in a long time, sleep came easily.

And it was sweet.

The kind of sweet that lingered.

Chapter 5

The weeks that followed felt like a dream stitched together with wine-sweet nights and laughter that lingered. Patrick and Lacy were finding a rhythm—slow and steady, yet undeniably electric. Their dates were a mix of charming restaurants, private art galleries, and walks through the city under streetlights that flickered like stars.

At work, Lacy was thriving. Her schedule was packed, her calendar color-coded, but the highlight of her day often came in a crystal vase—Patrick had sent flowers again. This time, a bouquet of creamy peonies and pale pink roses sat proudly on her desk. A note tucked inside read: "For the woman who's completely taken over my thoughts."

Andrew poked his head around the corner, dramatically squinting at the arrangement.

"Another one? If this man sends one more bouquet, I'm calling HR. For harassment. I'm emotionally overwhelmed," Andrew said, leaning against the edge of her desk with an exaggerated groan.

Lacy laughed, setting her coffee down. "You're just jealous you don't have a secret admirer."

"Secret?" Andrew snorted. "Girl, these aren't secret. He's basically sending billboard-level love notes. Does he get frequent flyer miles with the florist or what?"

She grinned. "You know he's a Managing Partner at Havenstone Capital, right? Man probably has an expense account just for grand gestures."

Andrew made a face. "Same thing. Professional flower buyer. You're being wooed by the Amazon Prime of affection."

Lacy laughed again, but beneath the teasing, she noticed it—the slight flicker in his eyes, the way he lingered at her desk a little longer than necessary. Their after-work drinks had started feeling... different too. Still lighthearted, still full of banter, but lately there was something softer threading through his jokes. Something almost tender.

Still, Lacy treasured what they had. Andrew was steady, solid. A safe place to land in a city that was still learning her rhythm. Their friendship was easy, familiar, and quietly important.

It felt like—for the first time in a long time—things were falling into place.

Easy. Good. Settled.

Until Mrs. Vance knocked on her door.

"Lacy, you have a new client," Mrs. Vance said, stepping into her office with her usual clipped efficiency. "High-profile. I want you to handle him personally."

Lacy stood, smoothing her skirt automatically. "Of course. Who is it?"

Before Mrs. Vance could answer, the door swung open.

And in walked Lucas.

Tall. Effortlessly cool. That same amused glint in his eye. The casual artist energy that somehow felt even stronger here, inside the polished halls of Seaglass Press.

Lacy's mouth dropped open. "You've got to be kidding me."

Lucas grinned wide, one hand casually shoved into the pocket of his worn jeans, the other holding a leather portfolio.

Mrs. Vance's eyebrows rose, her gaze flicking between them. "You two know each other?"

"We've met," Lacy said quickly, straightening. "Coffee shop. Brief encounter. Nothing... major."

Lucas flashed a look that said otherwise, but he kept his smile polite.

"Well, he's officially yours now," Mrs. Vance said, handing her a slim client file. "Lucas writes under the pen name C.J. Hart."

Lacy blinked.

Froze.

Felt her heart stumble right into her ribs.

"Wait," she managed. "You're C.J. Hart?"

Lucas's laugh was low and warm. "Guilty."

Lacy nearly dropped the file. "I love your books," she blurted out. "The Paris Letters? The Glass House? I binged them both in a weekend."

His grin widened, something both proud and a little bashful hiding behind it. "I'm flattered. Guess I picked the right editor."

Mrs. Vance gave them one last assessing glance—amusement tucked beneath her usual professionalism—before slipping out, leaving them alone.

The moment the door clicked shut, the air thickened with something heavier than surprise. Something... charged.

Lacy gestured toward the sitting area of her office, doing her best to compose herself. "Come on, let's sit. We should talk about the project."

Lucas settled across from her, casually sprawling into the chair like he owned it, like he belonged there. His presence filled the room without even trying.

"So," she said, easing into her seat. "You're not just an artist. You're... that artist."

Lucas chuckled, elbows resting loosely on his knees. "I knew you worked in publishing when we met. I just didn't expect you'd be the one I'd end up working with."

She smiled, a little dazed. "It's a small city, apparently."

"Smaller than I thought," he said, tilting his head. "But seeing you again? Yeah. Definitely a good surprise."

She raised an eyebrow but couldn't help the tug of a grin. "Well, Mr. Hart. I'm honored you chose Seaglass."

"You're the reason I did," he said easily, his voice soft but sure. "When Mrs. Vance mentioned your name on the shortlist, it just... clicked."

Lacy's heart kicked harder against her ribs, but she kept her tone even. "You're lucky I'm a fan. I binged The Paris Letters in two days. Your characters are so real. Messy. Beautiful. Broken in all the right ways."

Lucas leaned forward slightly, that playful glint back in his eye. "So you've already psychoanalyzed me?"

"Something like that," she teased. "But now I get to help shape your next masterpiece. That's exciting."

"I'm glad you think so." His voice lowered just a notch, warm and intimate. "Because I was hoping for more time with you—both as an editor... and maybe..."

He let it linger, just enough.

"...outside the office too. Would you want to grab dinner sometime? Just us. Not work."

For a breath, the air between them snapped tight. Lacy felt it—all of it—the invitation, the ease, the soft attraction simmering just beneath their words.

She hesitated, giving him a careful, genuine look. "Lucas…"

"Too soon?" he said quickly, chuckling, lifting his hands as if to pull the words back.

"It's not that." She smiled, a little sadly. "I'm... seeing someone."

Something flickered across Lucas's face—not disappointment exactly. More like curiosity.

"Ah. Got it," he said, sitting back without missing a beat. "Serious?"

"It's new," she admitted. "But it feels like something I need to see through."

Lucas nodded slowly, thoughtful. "Okay. I respect that. No pressure. No weirdness."

She smiled wider, grateful for how easily he took it. "You sure about that?"

"Positive," he said. "I still want to be around. Friends who maybe grab a drink. Talk about weird city art. Pretend we're literary snobs for an hour."

Lacy laughed. "Friends, huh?"

"Friends who happen to have a great vibe," he said, tossing her a wink. "No secret agendas. Just... good company."

She mock-sighed dramatically. "Alright. But professional boundaries stay intact. Clear?"

Lucas lifted his hand solemnly. "Scout's honor."

And just like that, a new current passed between them—different now. Still charged, still layered. But respectful. Open.
Whatever this was, it wasn't going away.
And Lacy, for better or worse, was curious enough to see where it might lead.

Later that night, Lacy lounged on the couch, hair still damp from her shower, her favorite oversized hoodie hanging off one shoulder. Leo curled at her feet, purring softly as she flipped absentmindedly through TV channels.
Her phone vibrates.
Patrick.
A smile bloomed without her even thinking. She answered on the second ring, her voice warm.
"Hey, handsome."
His answering laugh rumbled through the line, low and familiar. "Hey, beautiful. I was hoping you weren't too wiped from work today."
"Barely hanging on," she teased. "But surviving."
"Well, good. Because I was thinking…" he paused, his voice dipping into that softer, coaxing tone he used when he wanted something. "How do you feel about an overnight getaway?"
Her interest piqued immediately. "Where to?"
"There's this boutique winery upstate. Great food. Private spa. Sunset views you won't believe…" He let the words hang for a beat, then added, "I just want you all to myself for a little while. No phones, no distractions. Just us."
Lacy bit her lip, heart already racing in that delicious, reckless way Patrick always seemed to spark.
"That sounds... incredible," she said, her voice a little breathier than she intended.
"So you're in?"
She laughed softly. "I'm in."

They spent the next few minutes hammering out details—bantering about wine tolerances, packing lists, whether she'd need to bring three outfits "just in case" like he teased her about.

When they finally said goodnight, their voices had dropped to a quiet, lingering murmur, heavy with promise.

The call ended, but Lacy sat there a while longer, phone still in hand, smiling into the silence.

She wasn't just excited about the trip.

She was excited about him.

But Lacy wasn't done talking. She hit Bree's facetime.

"I knew you'd call!" Bree said, answering from her bedroom, robe on, hair wrapped, face mask in full effect.

"You won't believe my day."

"Spill it."

Lacy dove in. The client reveal. Lucas. The weekend getaway.

Bree gasped at all the right places. "Wait, wait. Lucas is C.J. Hart? Girl, no wonder you were floating after that coffee."

"I know. It's crazy."

"And Patrick's taking you on a weekend trip? Look at you, jet-setting and juggling men."

"And also—how's bachelorette party planning going?" Bree asked "I know you got a lot on your plate with juggling men and all."

"Locked and loaded," Lacy said proudly. "You, me, the rest of the crew and a house in Palm Springs, and a few very questionable games."

They laughed and talked until Lacy yawned into the phone.

"I should go," she said, finally pulling her blanket around her.

"Don't forget to pack something sexy for that trip."

Lacy smirked. "You know I already did."

She hung up, cheeks flushed, heart full.

And just as she was about to drift off, her phone buzzed one more time.

Patrick: Just wanted to say goodnight again.

 Sleep tight, Lacy. I'm really looking forward to this weekend.

Lacy smiled in the dark, her screen glowing soft in her hands.
The week stretched longer than it had any right to.
Emails, meetings, deadlines—each day seemed to crawl by slower than the last, piling weight on Lacy's shoulders. She powered through anyway, fueled by coffee, good playlists, and the small, secret thrill that carried her through even the busiest moments:
This weekend.
Patrick.
Escape.
Their last conversation had been late Thursday night, her phone lighting up just as she was slipping into bed.
Patrick: Can't wait to have you all to myself. No work. No distractions. Just us.
Lacy: I'm counting down the minutes.
Patrick: And I'm picking you up. No arguments. I want to start this weekend right—with you already next to me.
Lacy: Bossy.
Patrick: Only when it matters.
She tugged the covers tighter around her, that delicious warmth unfurling low in her stomach.

Now, Friday evening, the excitement was a steady hum beneath her skin. She stood outside her apartment building just as Patrick's sleek black Genesis GV80 pulled up to the curb.
He stepped out of the driver's side, looking devastating—tailored charcoal slacks, a crisp white shirt unbuttoned just enough to hint at smooth, warm skin, and a fitted navy blazer that clung perfectly to his broad shoulders. His cologne—deep sandalwood, something smoky and expensive—hit her like a soft punch in the chest.
And the shoes, of course—deep burgundy vintage Jordans with subtle gold accents, perfectly balancing effortless and elite.

Patrick's face lit up when he saw her, and for a moment, he just stood there, like he was soaking her in.
"Come here, beautiful," he said, his voice a low drawl.
He opened the passenger door for her like it was second nature, hand extended with a teasing bow.
Lacy smiled as she slid in, her powder-blue silk dress whispering against the leather seat.
Her long frame was a vision—every curve kissed by the soft fabric, a delicate gold anklet flashing at her ankle as she crossed her legs, nude strappy heels catching the last of the sunlight. Her hair, freshly curled, framed her face in soft waves, and her skin—smooth caramel aglow in the evening light—seemed lit from within.
As Patrick pulled away from the curb, he reached for her hand, threading their fingers together as naturally as breathing.
"Finally," he said, glancing at her with a grin that sent a shiver up her spine. "All mine for the weekend."
The city faded behind them, the concrete jungle giving way to open roads lined with golden fields and distant hills. Their conversation was easy, playful—talking about everything and nothing, stealing glances, laughing at old inside jokes that were starting to feel like theirs.
Every few miles, he'd lift her hand to his lips and kiss her knuckles, each small touch building a slow, simmering tension that neither of them dared to rush.
When they finally turned down a winding road flanked by endless rows of grapevines, Lacy felt the rest of the world slip away.

Chapter 6

The vineyard estate looked like something pulled from a storybook—elegant and secluded, framed by lush hills that shimmered under the soft glow of early evening. Rows of grapevines unfurled like ribbons across the landscape, and a gentle breeze carried the scent of lavender and earth. Patrick circled around to open her door again, his hand extended like a gentleman from another time.

"Welcome to our weekend," he said, voice rich and warm, his dark eyes sweeping over her like she was the only thing that existed in the frame.

She stepped out slowly, letting the moment settle around her—golden sunlight kissing her skin, the slight brush of evening air lifting the hem of her dress.

The scent of lavender thickened in the air, mingling with the faint sweetness of ripening grapes.

He offered his arm. She took it.

Hand-in-hand, they made their way toward a private tasting area set beneath a pergola wrapped in ivy.

Their sommelier, Simone—quick-witted and full of sass—guided them through a curated flight of wines. Her humor made them laugh, but her knowledge had them genuinely impressed.

"You two are trouble," Simone teased after Patrick made another off-the-cuff joke that had Lacy laughing so hard she had to set her glass down.

"I like her," Lacy whispered, leaning closer to him. "But I like you more."

He grinned, that crooked smile she was learning to crave. "Good. I plan on making that permanent."

Each wine had a story, and each story turned into a new inside joke between them. As the sun dipped lower in the sky, Patrick suggested they move to the patio for dinner—open-air seating with a perfect view of the sunset's watercolor sky.

Candles flickered as they ate, the conversation slowing into something more intimate. He talked about his childhood, his dreams. She shared

pieces of herself that she hadn't offered to anyone in a long time. Their hands found each other across the table, palms brushing together before their fingers slid into a familiar knot, as if they'd been doing this forever. "You're beautiful," he said softly, not for the first time that evening, but this time it carried weight. His eyes lingered on hers, unguarded.
Lacy's breath caught. "You make me feel beautiful."
As dusk settled fully, a small live band began playing under a nearby pergola. Jazz standards mixed with modern covers, all with the same dreamy lilt. Patrick stood and extended his hand.
"Lets dance gorgeous"
She didn't hesitate.
They swayed under the stars, their bodies moving in an easy, unspoken rhythm. Patrick's hand rested firmly at the small of her back, guiding her with a touch that was both confident and tender. Every subtle spin, every slow turn felt like a secret shared only between them—like the world had narrowed to just the two of them and the music threading through the night.
Some songs made Lacy smile against his shoulder, especially when Patrick would pull her closer with a playful smirk, his movements smoother than she ever would have guessed. She could feel his low chuckle vibrate through his chest every time she teased him under her breath.
Other songs slowed them down completely, and she found herself melting into him, her cheek pressed against the warm plane of his chest. His heartbeat thudded steadily beneath her ear, grounding her, wrapping her in a sense of safety she hadn't realized she craved until right then. The night air was cool, but wrapped in his arms, she felt nothing but warmth.
In those moments, it didn't matter where they were or what tomorrow would bring. It was just him. Just her. Just the quiet, perfect rhythm of something real taking shape between them.
When the last song faded into a low, lazy instrumental, Patrick leaned down, his mouth brushing the shell of her ear.

"Let's get out of here," he murmured, his voice thick and low.

Lacy didn't hesitate.

She nodded, heart hammering beneath her skin.

He laced his fingers through hers—warm, firm, possessive—and led her back across the terrace, past the scattered tables and lingering couples, toward the dim glow of the path that wound back toward their suite.

The vineyard at night was breathtaking.

Rows of vines stretched like velvet ribbons in the moonlight, the sweet scent of grape and damp earth hanging thick in the air.

The only sounds were the soft crunch of gravel beneath their shoes and the rhythmic chirp of distant crickets.

Patrick didn't rush.

He walked slowly, pulling her closer every few steps, pressing light kisses against her temple, her hair, the top of her shoulder when the path dipped them briefly into shadow.

By the time they reached their door, the tension between them was strung tight, vibrating through every stolen glance, every lingering touch.

Patrick unlocked the suite and pushed the door open, stepping aside to let her walk in first.

Lacy brushed past him, hyper aware of his gaze tracking every movement.

The room was dim, lit only by the faint spill of moonlight through the balcony doors. Their untouched bottle of wine still sat on the coffee table, two glasses gleaming beside it.

Behind her, Patrick closed the door with a soft click.

The final sound before the whole world seemed to hush.

Lacy turned slowly, meeting his eyes.

Everything they hadn't said, everything they'd been holding back all weekend, hummed between them now—louder than any music, sweeter than any wine.

Patrick crossed the room in three strides.

And when he kissed her, it wasn't gentle this time.

Patrick kissed her like a man starved, pulling her flush against him, his hands mapping her body through the silky material of her dress.
Lacy melted into him, her fingers curling into the back of his jacket, drinking him in.
But just when she thought he might lose control, he slowed—tugging back slightly, his breathing ragged.
His forehead rested against hers.
"Come with me," he murmured, voice thick and low.
He led her gently toward the bathroom, one hand sliding down her arm until their fingers laced together.
The bathroom lights were low, casting the room in a golden glow.
Patrick turned on the shower, steam filling the air almost immediately.
Then, wordlessly, he turned back to her—his hands reaching for the thin straps of her dress.
Slowly, reverently, he slid the fabric down, his knuckles grazing her skin as the dress pooled soundlessly at her feet.
She stood before him in nothing but her delicate lace underwear, her breath catching in her throat.
Patrick's dark gaze roved over her, full of heat, but when he stepped closer, it was almost worshipful.
His fingers brushed her sides, then down to her hips, hooking into the band of her panties.
With one slow, deliberate motion, he tugged them down and away.
Still holding her eyes, he pulled off his own clothes—shirt, slacks, everything—until they were bare before each other, the rising steam cloaking them like a secret.
When they stepped under the hot cascade of water, their bodies pressed together immediately—skin to skin, heartbeat to heartbeat.
Hands roamed.
Mouths found damp, sensitive skin.
Fingers explored every inch, teasing, testing, claiming without fully taking.

Patrick cupped the back of her neck, tipping her face up to kiss her—deep, slow, endless.

His hand slid between her thighs, teasing her expertly until she was gasping into his mouth, clutching his shoulders for support.

But just as her body arched against him, ready, needing him to take it further—Patrick pulled back.

Slow.

Firm.

He pressed one last kiss to her forehead, then shut off the water.

Without a word, he grabbed a thick towel, wrapped it around her trembling body, and swept her into his arms.

Lacy stared up at him, dazed, her whole body humming with need.

She was ready—aching for him.

But Patrick only smiled, soft and wicked at the same time, as he carried her back to the bed.

He laid her down carefully, then slid in beside her, pulling the covers up over them both.

He kissed her again—slow, lingering—but kept his hands at her waist.

She buried her face in his chest, overwhelmed with desire and gratitude all at once.

He could've taken her right there.

She was ready to give him everything.

But instead, he just held her, his breathing gradually slowing, his body heat wrapping around her like armor.

It was maddening.

It was intoxicating.

It made her fall for him even harder.

He wasn't just after her body.

He wanted her.

The night drifted into silence, their bodies tangled together under the covers, and sleep found them both easily.

The first thing Lacy felt was warmth.
A slow, molten heat that started at her hip and worked its way down.
Soft, teasing kisses skimmed across her skin—along her stomach, the sensitive inside of her thigh.
She stirred, a sleepy moan escaping before she could stop it.
Patrick's voice rumbled against her skin, full of wicked amusement.
"Good morning, beautiful."
Before she could form a coherent reply, his mouth found her—lower, deeper—and Lacy gasped, arching into him instinctively.
His hands gripped her thighs firmly, anchoring her as his tongue drew lazy, devastating circles against her sweet spot.
He worked her with a patience that felt like a slow torture, pulling her higher and higher until she shattered with a cry muffled against the pillow.
When she finally collapsed back, panting and limp, Patrick pressed a kiss to the inside of her thigh and chuckled low in his throat.
"Time to get dressed," he teased, standing up and tossing her a wicked smirk over his shoulder.
"We've got a full day ahead. Lunch in the vineyard. Horses to ride. Wine to drink."
Lacy could only blink up at him, stunned and still trembling, a ridiculous grin spreading across her face.
"Oh," Patrick added as he slipped on his jeans, "Don't worry..."
He tossed her a wink so sinful it made her toes curl.
"We're not done yet."

They dressed casually, but the air between them crackled like a live wire.
Lacy slipped into a breezy white sundress that skimmed her thighs with every step, the light fabric brushing against her still-sensitive skin in the most maddening way.
She paired it with simple gold jewelry and tan leather sandals that wrapped delicately up her calves, but there was no denying it—she practically glowed.

The loose tendrils of hair framing her flushed face, the faint shimmer of her vanilla-sandalwood perfume clinging to her damp skin—she looked like a walking daydream.

Patrick, leaning against the doorframe, watched her like he wanted to devour her all over again.

He wore fitted dark wash jeans and a crisp white T-shirt that stretched just enough across his chest and arms to hint at the strength underneath.

Over it, he threw on a deep olive jacket, the rich color making his skin look even darker and smoother.

And of course—today's sneakers: a vintage high-top Jordan pair in muted earth tones that somehow made the entire look even more sinfully casual. Effortless. Dangerous.

"Another pair?" Lacy teased, eyeing his shoes, her voice still a little husky from the morning's wake-up call.

Patrick grinned slowly, tucking his wallet into his back pocket. "You say that like you're not dying to see the rest of the collection."

She gave him a long, lingering once-over, her mouth curving into something far too wicked for this early in the day.

"Oh, I'm impressed," she murmured.

"But at this point? I'm convinced you have a sneaker shrine hidden in a secret vault somewhere."

Patrick chuckled, that low, magnetic sound that always seemed to find the spot right beneath her ribs and set it vibrating.

"Maybe," he said, stepping closer until she had to tilt her chin up to meet his gaze.

"Or maybe... I'm just collecting treasures. Gotta have something priceless to show for when I get old."

His hand skimmed her waist, slow and possessive, and his voice dropped to a near-growl.

"Pretty sure I already found the best one."

The heat in his words seared straight through her.

Lacy swallowed, breath catching—because it wasn't just flirting anymore.

It was a promise.
A warning.
She rolled her eyes lightly to save herself, but the flush on her skin had nothing to do with the sun.
When Patrick caught her hand and laced their fingers together, his thumb tracing lazy circles along her pulse point, Lacy knew this wasn't just a stroll through a vineyard.
They weren't playing it cool anymore.
They headed out into the golden morning, side by side, hand in hand— still smiling, still teasing—
but every step felt like they were walking toward something inevitable.
And neither of them planned to stop it.

The vineyard had curated a full experience for them.
First up: horseback riding.
Patrick had arranged a private ride through the rolling hills, the guide giving them space to trail behind and fall into their own world. Lacy, surprisingly good with horses thanks to a few summer camp adventures, teased Patrick mercilessly about his stiff posture and over-serious focus.
"Loosen up!" she laughed, trotting ahead, her hair streaming behind her in the breeze.
"I'm not trying to end up on YouTube," he called after her, pretending to wobble dramatically in the saddle.
She threw her head back and laughed, the sound ringing across the open fields, and Patrick knew in that moment he would do just about anything to hear that sound again.
By the time they slid from their saddles, laughter clinging to them like the afternoon heat, Lacy's cheeks ached from smiling.

Lunch was a private picnic tucked deep in the vineyard, hidden between the rows of sun-drenched vines.

A white linen blanket was stretched out beneath a thick oak tree, shielding them from the afternoon sun.

The spread was simple but perfect—chilled wine, crusty bread still warm from the oven, soft cheeses, ripe figs, and chocolate-dipped strawberries glistening in the light.

Patrick lounged back against a plush pillow, one arm stretched lazily behind Lacy as she nestled close, her bare legs draped over his lap like it was the most natural thing in the world.

Every now and then, he'd trail his fingertips up the inside of her thigh, featherlight, pretending to reach for a piece of bread or pour more wine—but each innocent touch made her shiver just a little.

Their conversation stayed low, intimate.

Lacy fed him a piece of strawberry, laughing when he caught her fingers between his teeth for just a second, making her heart race.

The teasing scrape of his teeth sent a shiver straight through her.

He brushed crumbs from the corner of her mouth with the pad of his thumb, then leaned in to kiss her slowly—deep enough to taste the sweetness lingering on her lips.

They spoke in soft murmurs, about nothing and everything. Favorite songs. Places they wanted to see. The kind of dreams you only confess when you're full of sun and wine and the feeling that the person next to you might actually be part of your future.

Patrick toyed with a lock of her hair, twirling it around his finger as he watched her with that heavy-lidded gaze that made her whole body heat from the inside out.

"You have no idea how beautiful you look right now," he murmured, voice thick.

Lacy smiled against the rim of her wine glass, her pulse fluttering wild beneath her skin.

"Careful," she teased softly. "I might start believing you."

"Good," Patrick said, leaning in, his hand slipping behind her neck. "Because every damn word is true."

They kissed again—slower this time, deeper—the kind of kiss that made the vineyard, the world, everything else fall away.

By the time they finally stretched out side-by-side on the blanket, the bottle of wine half-forgotten between them, Lacy realized she hadn't stopped smiling for an hour straight.

Or maybe it was just him.

Maybe it was this feeling she hadn't dared to hope for—easy, effortless, electric.

And she was nowhere near ready for it to end.

Chapter 7

As the sun dipped low behind the hills, streaking the sky in molten gold and rose, Patrick and Lacy returned to the estate for a quick change before dinner.

Lacy chose a soft silk maxi dress in deep emerald, the fabric whispering against her skin with every step. The color turned her caramel skin into molten gold, catching the last bits of light like she was spun from the sunset itself.

Patrick waited for her, looking devastatingly good in dark tailored pants and a crisp white button-down, the sleeves casually rolled to his elbows, hinting at forearms that made her mouth go dry. His signature cologne—warm sandalwood and something darker, more dangerous—wrapped around her like a spell.

Dinner was held outdoors on a sprawling stone terrace, tucked behind the main estate. Tables were scattered under a canopy of fairy lights, and a small band played, soft and easy, letting the night settle like velvet.

They dined slow, savoring each course, stealing glances and secretive smiles across the table. Every brush of his hand against hers, every lingering look, built the tension higher, tighter, until even the warm summer air felt charged.

After the last course—a decadent dark chocolate tart they fed each other between bites—Patrick leaned in, his voice low and intimate.

"Come with me."

No asking. No hesitation. Just certainty.

He stood, offering his hand. She didn't need to think. She slid her hand into his, letting him lead her away from the glow of the terrace lights, down a winding stone path lit only by the stars.

They climbed a narrow stairway tucked behind the gardens and emerged onto a small, secluded rooftop terrace.

It was quiet, just them and the open sky, the faint music from dinner drifting up on the breeze. Fairy lights draped the railings, and beyond them, the vineyards stretched into infinity, bathed in silver moonlight. Patrick pulled her gently into his arms, no words needed.
They moved together, slow and easy, swaying to a rhythm only they could hear.
His hands slipped around her waist, hers curled against his chest.
Their bodies brushed, pressed, melted into each other.
His forehead tipped against hers, the world falling away until there was only the heat of his breath, the steady beat of his heart against her palm.
He kissed her temple.
Her jaw.
The corner of her mouth.
Each touch was a promise.
Each kiss a slow unraveling.
By the time they made the walk back to the suite, it felt less like walking and more like being pulled by something inevitable.
Their hands stayed locked the whole way—thumbs brushing, fingertips tangling, a silent conversation in every small, desperate touch.
At one point, Patrick tugged her against him beneath an archway, stealing a kiss that had her knees buckling and her heart slamming against her ribs.
When they finally reached their door, the tension wrapped around them thick and hungry.
Patrick unlocked it without breaking eye contact, stepping aside to let her slip inside first like she was something precious he had to protect.
Lacy turned to him, her lips parted, her breath shallow.
"Give me a minute," she whispered, voice trembling with anticipation.
She disappeared into the bathroom, the soft click of the door leaving him alone in the dim light of the suite.
Patrick wandered toward the window, cradling a half-finished glass of wine.
Outside, the vineyard rolled out in endless, moon-drenched rows.

Inside, the air vibrated with everything unsaid, everything about to be unleashed.

He gripped the wineglass tighter, willing himself to be patient even as the seconds stretched taut.

He heard the bathroom door click open.

Turning, slowly, drawn like gravity, he caught sight of her—

Lacy stood in the doorway, barefoot, wrapped in a towel that clung precariously to her curves.

Her skin was still dewy from the shower, glowing in the soft golden light spilling from the room.

Their eyes locked.

The air between them pulled tight, crackling with something sharp and electric.

She didn't speak. She didn't have to.

The look in her eyes said everything.

This was choice. This was want. This was her.

And then—slowly, deliberately—Lacy let the towel slip from her fingers and fall to the floor.

He drew in a sharp breath, his pulse racing wild and erratic as the towel hit the floor.

Then he moved—across the room, across the invisible line they had both been dancing around for months.

Patrick's hands cradled her face first, the softest reverence, like she was something sacred.

Then he kissed her—deep, slow, claiming.

A low sound rumbled from his chest, all hunger and awe, vibrating through her bones.

He didn't rush. He didn't ask.

She'd made the first move. She was his now.

And he planned to ruin her for anyone else.

He kissed her until she was breathless, until she was clinging to him, nails digging lightly into the back of his neck.

Then he scooped her up effortlessly, carrying her to the bed like she weighed nothing.

He set her down with a tenderness that almost broke her.

Patrick knelt before her, his dark eyes blazing.

He kissed the inside of her ankles first.

Then her calves.

Her thighs—slow, teasing kisses inching higher and higher, until she was trembling beneath him.

Without a word, he dragged his mouth up her center, flicking his tongue just once over her sweet spot—

and she gasped, her hips jerking off the bed.

He chuckled low and wicked, like he'd just discovered his new favorite toy.

And then he buried his face between her thighs and devoured her.

Lacy writhed, hands tangled in the sheets, as he worshiped her with long, slow strokes of his tongue, savoring every trembling reaction.

When she was teetering on the edge, he pulled back—

only to flip her onto her stomach, dragging her hips up into the air.

"Stay just like that," he rasped.

Before she could catch her breath, he leaned in again—licking, teasing, tasting her backside with slow, filthy strokes that had her moaning into the pillow, her body shaking with pleasure and disbelief.

No one had ever touched her there before.

No one had ever claimed her like this.

It was obscene.

It was perfect.

When he finally rolled her back over, Lacy was wrecked—eyes dazed, lips parted, every nerve ending on fire.

Patrick kissed his way up her body again—her thighs, her stomach, the underside of her breasts, taking them in his mouth—taking his time, building her back up until she was pleading without words.

When he finally slid inside her, it was excruciatingly slow, a deliberate claiming that made her gasp. Lacy cried out, nails raking down his back, and Patrick groaned so deep it rattled in his chest.
He braced himself above her, his forehead dropping to hers.
"Mine," he whispered against her lips. "All fucking mine."
The pace was slow at first—deep, dragging strokes that made her eyes roll, her breath catch.
But soon it built, fast and hard and relentless, like a storm that had been building for months.
Their bodies crashed together again and again, slick with sweat, desperate for more.
Patrick's hands were everywhere—tugging her hair, gripping her hips, pinning her wrists above her head as he took her deeper, harder.
When she shattered again—crying out his name, her whole body convulsing—he followed, growling against her throat as he emptied himself inside her with a shudder that shook them both.
They collapsed together, trembling, clinging.
Patrick didn't pull away.
He kissed her—soft, messy kisses all over her face, her shoulders, her collarbone—as if he couldn't get enough.
His hands roamed lazily over her spent body, like he was memorizing every inch.
"I warned you," he murmured into her hair.
"You started it," she whispered back, breathless and giddy.
He chuckled against her skin, pure male satisfaction.
Eventually, he rolled them onto their sides, spooning her close, one arm thrown possessively around her hips.
Their bodies stayed tangled, heartbeats slowing together, syncing like two halves of a whole finally made real.
Nothing would ever be the same again.
And Lacy, even in the thick, sweet haze of pleasure, knew it:
She was falling.

Hard and fast.
And she might never want to come back up.

The next morning, golden light spilled across the white linen sheets, wrapping the room in a soft, heavy glow.
The kind of glow that felt slow and decadent—the kind that only came after a night that rewrote the way she understood pleasure.
Lacy lay tangled against Patrick, her body deliciously sore, her skin humming with the lingering echoes of him.
Somewhere between midnight and morning, Patrick had pulled her under again—
slow and deep this time, coaxing multiple orgasms out of her with maddening, unhurried precision.
She was wrecked.
And floating.
And if she never moved again, it would be too soon.
Her fingers traced slow, lazy circles across his chest, sketching secrets into his skin without even thinking.
Patrick's arm was slung possessively over her waist, his hand splayed wide, like he was still staking his claim even in sleep.
Neither of them spoke.
There was no need.
The silence between them was heavy but peaceful, full of a new, unspoken understanding.
Patrick shifted slightly, brushing a kiss against the crown of her head, his voice still gravelly with sleep and something deeper.
"I want this," he murmured into her hair, his breath hot against her scalp.
His fingers skimmed down her spine in a lazy caress, raising goosebumps in their wake.
Lacy tilted her face up, her hazel eyes heavy-lidded, heart thudding slow and steady against his side.

"Are you saying what I think you're saying?" she whispered, voice still wrecked from the night before.
Patrick smiled—slow, sure, devastating.
"You," he said simply. "Me. Just us. I want to wake up to you—every day. Not just sometimes. Not just weekends. Always."
Her chest squeezed tight, and she pressed her palm against his heart, feeling the solid, steady beat beneath her hand.
"You have me," she whispered. "You already do."
Patrick didn't rush to respond.
Instead, he kissed her—slow and reverent, a kiss that sealed the promise he hadn't needed to make out loud.
Then he rolled her onto her back, covering her with his body again, moving with a tenderness that melted her bones.
This time, when he entered her, it was slow and unhurried, just the sheer need to be connected.
No urgency.
No barriers.
Just them.
Raw and real and wide open.
They made love again—sweetly, sleepily, with lazy strokes and whispered laughter.
They kissed so much it blurred the line between kisses and breaths.
It wasn't just sex.
It was a tether binding them tighter than either of them fully understood yet.
Later, they moved reluctantly around the room—packing bags between stolen kisses, between lingering touches.
They couldn't seem to help themselves.
A brush of fingertips.
A tug of a sleeve.
A soft smack to her ass that made her squeal and him chuckle low.
Every small touch said the same thing:

This isn't over.
This is just the beginning.
At checkout, they stood side by side on the sun-drenched porch, the vineyard stretching out before them in lazy, golden rows.
Patrick curled his hand around hers, their fingers locking naturally, instinctively.
Lacy glanced back at their suite one last time, a pang of something bittersweet tightening in her chest.
Not sadness.
Hope.
Certainty.
She wasn't just leaving behind a perfect weekend.
She was stepping into something bigger.
Something terrifying.
Something real.
Something that, felt like home.
The ride back to her apartment was a gentle blur—soft music humming in the car, Patrick's hand resting casually on her thigh.
He kept stealing glances at her at stoplights, his smile slow and possessive, like he couldn't believe she was real.
Lacy spent most of the drive biting her lip, still aching in the best way, still dazed by the way he made her feel.
They didn't talk much.
They didn't need to.
The silence between them said it all.

The city buzzed beneath her office window as Lacy set her oversized purse on her desk and hung up her coat. She had barely taken a sip of her vanilla oat milk latte when the receptionist peeked in with wide eyes and a teasing smirk.
"Um, Lacy... something just arrived for you. Again."

A massive bouquet—roses, peonies, and lilies in rich pinks and creamy whites—sat regally on the receptionist's desk like it owned the place.
Lacy's mouth fell open.
"Oh my god," she whispered, approaching it with wide eyes and a stunned smile. Tucked inside was a note in Patrick's familiar handwriting:
Lacy pressed the card to her chest, cheeks heating as a giddy smile broke free.
Every time she thought Patrick had peaked with the grand gestures, he topped himself.
And every time, it felt harder to pretend she wasn't falling faster than she should.
She let herself savor it for one more heartbeat—then the sharp buzz of her phone dragged her back to reality faster than she wanted.
She was still lost in the high of it when she picked it up without thinking.
Lucas:
Hey. Hope you've been well.
Would you be up for grabbing coffee before our meeting later this week? Just want to catch up a little. My treat. :)
She stared at it for a moment, her heart giving a confused, guilty flutter.
It was just coffee.
They were friends.
He was a client now too, technically.
Still, things with Patrick were... different. Real.
And suddenly the idea of another man taking up space in her day—no matter how harmless it was supposed to be—felt complicated.
Before she could overthink it further, Andrew's familiar knock rapped once against her open door.
"Knock knock," he said casually, stepping inside with his usual effortless swagger.
His eyes flicked immediately to the massive bouquet dominating her workspace.
He let out a low whistle. "Patrick trying to win a medal or something?"

She laughed, rolling her eyes. "You're just mad no one's sent you flowers."

"Wrong," Andrew said, grinning. "I'm mad they didn't send me those flowers."

He leaned a hip against the edge of her desk, giving her that sideways, assessing look he reserved for moments when he was trying—and mostly failing—to be subtle.

But his grin faded a little as he caught the slight crease between her brows. "You good?" he asked, voice dropping into something quieter.

"Yeah," she said too quickly.

Then her phone buzzed again and Andrew's gaze flicked to it instinctively. He raised an eyebrow. "Let me guess. Lucas?"

She stared at him, caught. "How the hell do you always know?"

Andrew smirked. "You get this look. Like you're trying to convince yourself something is harmless when you already know it's not."

Lacy groaned, dropping her forehead to the desk for dramatic effect. "It's literally just coffee. Before a work meeting."

"Mmm," Andrew said, unconvinced.

He crossed his arms, the fabric of his fitted button-up pulling just slightly across his chest. "You really think it's just about coffee?"

She lifted her head to glare at him, though it lacked any real heat. "We're friends, Andrew. He knows I'm seeing someone. He respects that."

"You sure about that?"

Andrew's voice wasn't teasing anymore—it was careful. Guarded. Like he didn't want to say too much but couldn't quite help himself.

"I'm sure," Lacy said firmly, brushing it off with a wave of her hand she hoped looked breezier than it felt.

She didn't want to have this conversation. Not when the air still smelled like roses and fresh promises.

Andrew hesitated, then pushed off the desk with a shrug that didn't quite mask the tightness in his shoulders.

"Alright," he said easily. "I'm just saying... if he starts sketching sad poems about your eyes, don't say I didn't warn you."

She laughed, the tension easing just enough, but something about the way Andrew glanced back at her as he left—that half-second too long—hovered long after the door clicked shut.

Later that night, Lacy tossed herself onto the couch, propping her phone against a throw pillow as Bree's face filled the screen.

"I just got a text from Lucas about grabbing coffee," Lacy said, blowing out a breath. "Is it weird that I feel... weird about it?"

Bree sipped from a glass of wine, giving her a look. "You already told him you're with Patrick. If he's reaching out, he knows the deal."

"I know," Lacy said, running a hand through her hair. "It's just... different now. Patrick and I are official. It feels more serious. I don't want any blurred lines, even accidentally."

Bree shrugged. "Then you're good. You're not leading anybody on. Lucas knows where you stand."

Lacy nodded slowly, gnawing on her bottom lip. "I guess I just don't want to disrespect what I have with Patrick."

"You're not," Bree said firmly. "You're allowed to have friends. Just keep it friendly. Keep it clean. If Lucas tries anything stupid, then you can karate-chop his feelings."

Lacy laughed, the tension easing from her shoulders. "Deal. No karate necessary unless provoked."

"And anyway," Bree said, switching gears. "Forget Lucas—what's up with my bachelorette party? My bride vibes are tingling, and I know you're cooking something up."

"Oh, I'm planning the event of the year," Lacy grinned. "It's a couple months out, but I've already got a vision. Think coastal glam, sexy itinerary, matching robes, a private chef—"

Bree squealed. "YES. I love you. Just make sure it's classy but wild enough that I can deny anything that might go viral."

"Say less."
They chatted late into the night, Lacy glowing with the sweetness of her romance and the excitement of planning her sister's big weekend.
But deep down, she knew she was falling for Patrick, hard.
When she finally set her phone down, the truth hummed in her chest: she was already in too deep—and she wouldn't have it any other way.

Chapter 8

The coffee shop buzzed with the gentle vibe of espresso machines and quiet conversation, the kind of spot that made people slow down. Lacy stepped inside and immediately spotted Lucas at a table by the window—same confident slouch, same devil-may-care grin, but this time, there was a glint of something more intentional in his eyes.
He stood as she approached, arms opening wide for a friendly hug. "Look at you, right on time. That's intimidating."
She laughed as she hugged him back. "Please. I'm always on time when there's caffeine involved."
He gestured to the seat across from him. "You want the usual? I remembered it—vanilla oat latte, right?"
Her brows lifted, impressed. "Look at you doing homework."
"Please. This is the easy stuff."
She settled in as he flagged down a barista, placing her order along with his usual black coffee. The conversation began casually—weather, books, shared New York frustrations—but she quickly realized this wasn't about business. Not really.
"So," she said, giving him a knowing smile, "shouldn't we be talking character arcs and deadlines?"
Lucas leaned back, sipping his drink. "Technically, yes. But I figured we'd start with you. You know—get to know the person behind the red pen."
Lacy smirked. "You mean the woman who's about to tear your manuscript to pieces?"
"Exactly," he said with a wink. "If I'm gonna get dragged, at least let it be by someone I like."
She laughed, eyes twinkling. "You are something else."
"Thank you. I work hard at it."
The vibe between them was easy, comfortable, laced with curiosity. Lucas asked about her background, her favorite authors, what she did when she

wasn't working. His questions weren't intrusive—they were thoughtful, genuine. She caught herself relaxing more than she expected to.
But she also knew she had to be clear.
After a beat, she leaned in slightly, stirring her drink with a casual flick of her wrist. "You still good with the whole 'just friends' thing?" she teased lightly.
Lucas grinned, easy and unbothered. "I'm good. Promise.
Besides, sounds like you're exactly where you're supposed to be."
Lacy smiled, letting his words settle warmly between them. "I think so too."
He raised his glass in a mock toast. "To good choices—and even better company."
She clinked her glass against his, the clink light and full of understanding.
Lucas sipped his coffee, then set the cup down and tilted his head. "But for the record…" He gave her a playful smirk. "If he fumbles, I'm fully prepared to slide in and save the day. Rain, trench coat, the whole dramatic entrance."
Lacy rolled her eyes, laughing. "You are such a writer."
"I take that as a compliment."
They talked a little longer—books, travel, bad edits, weird fans—until the moment felt right to wrap it up.
"Well," she said, rising from her seat, "we should probably get back and actually talk about your manuscript."
Lucas stood too, holding the door open for her. "Whatever you say, boss."
As they stepped out into the chill of the afternoon, Lacy felt a flicker of something she couldn't quite name—something warm, but wrapped in caution.
He didn't push. But he wasn't hiding either.
And that made things... not complicated, exactly. Just hard to ignore..

Lacy walked back into the office with a mix of nerves and caffeine still humming in her bloodstream. The coffee with Lucas had been light, flirtatious, and unexpectedly personal. He didn't cross any lines—technically—but the way he looked at her still played in the back of her mind.

Focus, girl.

She slipped into work mode, gathering her notes for their afternoon meeting. Just before diving in, she glanced at her phone and saw a group text notification from Ava—another reminder about that conference in Miami she'd invited everyone to a couple of months ago. Lacy had meant to RSVP, but things with Patrick had just started to shift, and she hadn't had the energy to commit to anything that didn't involve sorting through her feelings.

She tapped her phone screen, clearing the notification away with a small sigh.

She'd figure it out later—right now, she needed to stay focused.

When Lucas arrived, right on time, he wore his usual easy grin—but there was a sharper edge now, a purposeful glint in his eye that hadn't been there over coffee.

Once they sat down, the shift was undeniable: casual familiarity gave way to real, focused collaboration.

He asked sharp questions, listened with a kind of attentive patience that made Lacy lean in without even realizing it.

The banter was still there—floating just under the surface—but it never got in the way.

For the first time that day, she found herself relaxing.

They could do this.

They could be something steady without crossing any lines.

"Okay," he said, standing up as their meeting wrapped. "I was a little nervous about this whole editing thing, but now I feel like my book's in good hands."

"You should be nervous," she said, arching a brow with a smirk. "I'm ruthless."
He chuckled. "Yeah, but you're cute when you're ruthless."
She shook her head, smiling despite herself. "Get out of here."
"Until next time, editor-in-chief."

Later that evening, Lacy sat cross-legged on her couch, laptop open, notepad in hand, and Bree's voice in her ear as they ran through the growing list for the bachelorette party.
"I'm just saying," Bree teases through the phone, "if there's not at least one half-naked man in a bowtie, I'm demanding emotional compensation."
Lacy laughs, sinking back into the couch. "You do realize I'm the one planning this, right?"
"Exactly," Bree says, her voice warm. "Which is why I know it's gonna be epic—because no one gets me like you do."
They were mid-discussion over venues and signature cocktails when Lacy's phone buzzed.
She glanced down, and her mouth immediately curved into a smile.
"Hold up," she said, lifting the phone. "Patrick just texted."
Bree gasped dramatically. "Read it out loud. I need to live through you."
Lacy laughed, clearing her throat like she was about to deliver Shakespeare.
"'You home, beautiful? Been thinking about you. Mind if I come by?'"
Bree squealed so loud Lacy had to pull the phone away from her ear.
"Girl, if you don't open that door so fast you sprain an ankle—!"
Lacy giggled, thumbs already flying across the screen.
Lacy: I'm home. Come over.
"I said yes," she told Bree, smoothing her hand over her satin shorts. "Obviously."

"Obviously," Bree said, still grinning. "Now go light a candle, fluff the couch, and put on that lip gloss that makes grown men forget their last names."

"It's already on," Lacy said smugly, adjusting one of her curls in the mirror. "I stay ready."

"That's why you're my hero," Bree said. "I expect updates. Real ones. Not that 'it was nice' nonsense."

They joked and bantered a few more minutes—Bree throwing out wild guesses that Patrick was about to show up with an overnight bag, a ring, or a spare toothbrush.

When they finally hung up, Lacy tossed the phone onto the coffee table, heart fluttering—not from nerves, but from the sheer anticipation of seeing him again.

The knock was firm, deliberate—like him.

Lacy opened the door without hesitation.

Patrick stood there, broad shoulders filling the frame, a look on his face that made her knees weaken.

Hungry. Intense. Inevitable.

Before she could say a word, he stepped in, kicked the door shut behind him, and cupped her face in his hands.

"You look like something God handcrafted just for me," he said, voice low, roughened by something he wasn't bothering to hide anymore.

She barely had time to gasp before his mouth was on hers—hot, sure, claiming.

The kiss wasn't sweet. It was devouring.

He kissed her like a man who'd spent the entire day trying not to think about her—and failed.

Patrick's hands were everywhere—tangling in her hair, skimming down her body, lifting her against him like she weighed nothing.

Somewhere between the kiss and the urgent pull of his hands, he scooped her up and carried her down the hallway without a word, only breaking the kiss long enough to murmur against her mouth, "Need you, Lace. Need all of you."

In the bedroom, he set her down, peeled the satin from her body with agonizing slowness—stripping her not just of clothes, but of every single defense.

When she was bare, trembling, wanting, he took a step back and just looked at her.

His control was a living thing—visible in every tight breath, every clenched fist at his sides.

But tonight, he wouldn't be patient.

Tonight, he was done being nice.

Patrick undressed with quick, rough movements, his body every bit as intoxicating as she remembered—and somehow more.

She reached for him, but he caught her wrists gently, pushing her back onto the bed with a look that told her, I'm in charge tonight.

And she wanted that.

Desperately.

He knelt between her legs, tracing slow, reverent paths up her thighs with his hands.

His mouth followed, worshipping her, tasting her like she was the only thing that could satisfy a hunger he'd been starving under for months.

He didn't stop when she cried out.

He didn't stop when she twisted the sheets.

He didn't stop when she shattered once—twice—beneath his mouth, making sounds she would have been embarrassed by if he hadn't looked up at her with such raw passion it made her forget her own name.

Only when she was wrecked and trembling did he finally slide up her body, pausing just long enough to kiss her trembling lips.

"You're mine," he whispered against her mouth. "And I'm yours."

And then he entered her in one deep, soul-stealing thrust that made her entire body arch off the bed.

No hesitation. No barriers. Just them.

Patrick moved like a man on a mission—slow at first, savoring the way she tightened around him, then deeper, harder, each stroke a deliberate claiming.

"I love you," he breathed against her skin, against her heart, against the desperate moans spilling from her mouth.

"I fucking love you, Lacy."

She couldn't speak.

Could barely think.

Her body answered him, clinging to him, meeting every thrust with helpless abandon.

When he shifted her hips just right, when he found that perfect rhythm, she shattered again—loud, uncontrollable, his name a broken prayer on her lips.

He followed her over the edge seconds later, burying himself deep, grinding out her name in a raw, reverent groan that sounded like promise, need and forever.

When the storm finally broke, he didn't move.

He stayed locked to her, their bodies slick, trembling, entwined.

Lacy buried her face against his shoulder, gasping for air, feeling the tremor still rolling through her.

Patrick lifted his head, brushing kisses over her temple, her jaw, her mouth.

Soft now. Sweet now.

But his next words hit harder than anything else.

"I want to wake up to you every day."

He kissed her again, deeper this time, before pulling back just enough to see her eyes.

"Move in with me, Lace."

Her breath caught.

He kept moving inside her, slow, deep, hypnotic, coaxing her through the overload.

"I know it's fast," he whispered, hips rolling into hers like a second heartbeat. "But I want it. I want you. Not just weekends. Home. You and me."
Lacy's body responded even when her mind trembled.
Her moans answered where words couldn't.
"Think about it," he rasped. "I'm serious."
And then he kissed her again, and she let herself drown.
Because tonight, she loved him too.
And that was enough.

The next morning, the soft light pressed against her closed eyelids, warm and insistent.
Lacy stirred, stretching lazily beneath the sheets.
For a second, waking up felt easy. Light.
Then she remembered.
Patrick's words. His kiss. The weight of everything he'd laid at her feet.
The question sat in her chest like a heavy, humming thing, alive even in the morning light.
She stayed still for a moment longer, letting the sunlight crawl over her skin, until finally she swung her legs over the side of the bed and planted her feet on the cool hardwood.
Move in with me.
Leo appeared like a shadow summoned by stress, padding silently into the bedroom.
He hopped up onto the bed without hesitation, settling next to her with a heavy, dramatic sigh.
"Well, look who decided to rejoin the land of the living," she said, eyeing him.
"What's it like being emotionally unavailable and still somehow judging me?"
Leo stared at her, unbothered, his tail flicking once, twice.

"You disappear for days, then pop up when I'm mid-existential crisis. Classic."

She sighed, rubbing his head.

"But thanks for showing up. I needed a therapist with fur."

Leo purred, the tiniest hint of approval.

Lacy closed her eyes and exhaled through her nose.

"Patrick wants me to move in," she whispered to the ceiling.

Leo paused mid-paw-lick, giving her a suspicious side-eye.

"Exactly," she muttered, pointing at him. "That's exactly how I feel too."

She didn't not want it.

She loved him — she was terrified to admit just how much.

But she also loved the life she was building. Her space. Her independence.

And that scared her even more.

Still sitting there, heart tangled in about sixteen different knots, she reached for her phone on the nightstand.

Instead of calling Bree directly, she opened the group chat: Bree, Kayla, Nina, Chrissy, Janelle, Ava.

Lacy:
Emergency Zoom call. 1 hour. Bring wine. And opinions.
Almost immediately, the read receipts lit up.
Bree:
On it. Putting Leo on the attendance list too.
Nina:
Wine already chilling. Say less.
Kayla:
Ooooh it's juicy if you're giving us one hour notice.
Chrissy:
I'm cancelling plans. You better not disappoint.
Janelle:
If this ain't about a man, I'm fighting you.
Ava:

I'll even bring cheese. Virtual cheese. But still.
Lacy laughed quietly to herself, some of the panic easing.
Her girls. Her safe space. Exactly what she needed.
She flopped back against the bed, Leo curling up at her side, and stared at the ceiling again.
Tonight she'd tell them everything.
About Patrick. About moving in. About being in love — and scared out of her damn mind.
But for now, she had one hour to get herself together.
And maybe... finish another bottle of wine.
Or two.
Later that night, Lacy curled up on the couch with Leo sprawled across her feet, laptop balanced on her knees, hair twisted into a messy bun, and a glass of wine within reach.
The familiar ding of Zoom logging in sounded, and within seconds, all her girls' faces started popping onto the screen in a glorious mosaic of laughter, side-eyes, and barely-contained chaos.
"Finally!" Bree crowed, leaning in so close to her camera it was just forehead and wild curls. "Our queen has arrived."
Kayla sipped from an oversized wine glass. "Okay, Lace, emergency meeting called. You better deliver. I put down my contour brush for this."
"I cancelled Pilates," Chrissy said, raising her eyebrows dramatically. "Do you know how hard it is to get a spot with Elena?"
"Girl, if this is about you buying a new couch or some random plant, I'm ending this call," Janelle warned, pointing at the screen.
Nina tilted her head, calm but lethal. "I'm holding the block button right here."
Only Ava sat back, sipping something sparkling from a flute, her gold hoop earrings flashing. "I'm just here for the drama. Also, quick sidebar — y'all still ghosting my Miami RSVP, so we'll circle back."
Lacy laughed, holding up both hands in surrender. "Okay, okay! Chill. This is real."

Bree smirked, settling back into her chair. "Real like HC-real?"
Lacy's cheeks warmed. She tucked her legs under her, feeling Leo flick his tail at the disturbance.
"Yes," she admitted. "HC real."
A chorus of ooohs and clapping broke out across the call.
"Tell us everything!" Kayla demanded, practically bouncing in her seat.
Lacy took a deep breath, setting her wine down. "Okay. So... after our weekend away— which was amazing— he came over and... he told me he's falling in love with me."
Absolute silence.
Even Leo paused his tail flicking.
"Wait." Bree sat up straighter, the grin already forming. "He said the L-word?"
"He said the L-word," Lacy confirmed, voice soft but glowing.
Nina pressed a hand dramatically over her heart. "A man. Using full sentences. Without being threatened. Love that."
Janelle fanned herself with her notes. "And here I was thinking good men were just Instagram myths."
Chrissy raised a brow. "So... then what's the emergency? That sounds perfect."
Lacy hesitated, twirling the stem of her wine glass. "He also asked me to move in with him."
Dead. Silence.
Then all hell broke loose.
Bree immediately leaned into the screen like she could physically shake her. "Lacy, you have been dating five minutes!"
Kayla screeched. "That's not moving in, that's a hostage situation!"
Janelle cackled, nearly knocking over her wine. "Girl, blink twice if you need a rescue!"
Nina, ever the calm center, lifted one brow. "Okay, let's not panic. Let's assess."

Ava, somehow both amused and intrigued, leaned forward. "Define 'move in.' Like, toothbrush and drawer? Or full-on lease-signing, life-merging, Netflix-password-sharing move in?"
"Full move in," Lacy said weakly. "He wants me to live with him."
Everyone groaned at once.
"You barely finished decorating your apartment!" Chrissy said. "You still owe us a proper housewarming!"
"I love my apartment," Lacy blurted out. "I love my space. I like missing him sometimes."
Bree nodded solemnly. "And that, my dear, is called healthy boundaries. Don't let HC steamroll you with big gestures."
Kayla sipped her wine with a smirk. "Big... other things too, huh?"
"Kayla!" Lacy choked, laughing as the whole group erupted again.
Ava finally held up her hands. "Okay, okay, now that we've gotten the gossip out— y'all still haven't RSVP'd for Miami. And flights are going up."
A chorus of groans followed.
"I might go," Janelle said. "But don't expect me on any party yachts."
"I'm a maybe," Nina added. "Depends on court dates."
Chrissy shrugged. "If I can get childcare, I'm in."
Kayla grinned wickedly. "If HC's moving in, Lacy might need a distraction."
Bree shook her head. "Focus. Miami second. HC drama first."
They ended up talking for another hour—debating moving timelines, sharing updates, talking about Nina's new case, Chrissy's daughter's latest science project, Bree's slow-burn with Thomas. Ava (in true Ava fashion) offered to send everyone personalized travel itineraries for Miami "if" they ever committed.
By the time they signed off, Lacy felt lighter.
Still unsure.
Still tangled up in nerves and love and fear.
But lighter.

Because whatever happened next—move in or not—she wasn't doing it alone.
She had them.
And somehow... she knew she was going to be okay.

Chapter 9

The buzz of office chatter was a welcome distraction from the chaos inside her head. At her desk at Seaglass Press, the soft click of keys and distant buzz of conversation grounded her—if only slightly.

Her own screen, however, was no help. The blinking cursor mocked her, perched at the top of a blank document. The manuscript she was supposed to be editing blurred before her eyes, the words slipping off the page like water through her fingers.

She rubbed her temple, trying to will herself back into focus. But no matter how many times she blinked or shifted in her chair, her mind circled back to the same, burning sentence.

I want you to move in with me.

The memory hit her like it always did—part warmth, part weight.

She hadn't answered. Not really. Not yet.

And now, weeks later, Patrick was starting to assume the silence spoke for itself.

Just then, there was a knock against her office door frame.

Andrew leaned in, holding a coffee in one hand, his smile easy and familiar. "You've been staring at that screen for fifteen minutes. If you're trying to win a staring contest, I think it's cheating."

Lacy looked up, her lips twitching. "Guess I lost track of time."

He stepped inside, setting the coffee on her desk like a peace offering. "Rough morning?"

Lacy looked up, forcing a smile. "Something like that."

He tilted his head, watching her carefully. "You've been in your head a lot lately. Want to talk about it?"

Lacy offered a tight smile and shook her head. "Not right now."

Andrew nodded, backing off with a quiet understanding only a good friend could pull off. "Fair enough. But if you change your mind... I'll be around. With better coffee than whatever's in the break room."

She gave a soft laugh. "Noted."

He reached into his blazer pocket and offered her a piece of dark chocolate. "Stress remedy. Works better than therapy—cheaper, too."

That got a small laugh from her, the first real one of the day. "Thanks, Andrew."

By noon, the blinking cursor still hadn't moved.

Lacy had reread the same paragraph three times when Andrew popped his head into her office again, this time holding up two takeout menus like peace flags.

"Come on," he said, wiggling them. "Let's get out of here for a bit. Fresh air, questionable tacos, maybe a little sunshine therapy?"

She raised an eyebrow. "You bribing me with tacos?"

"Absolutely. And a guilt-free hour away from that screen. I'm doing this for your mental health."

Lacy chuckled, grabbing her coat. "Okay, okay. But if the tacos are bad, I'm blaming you."

"Fair."

They found a quiet spot on a patio two blocks from the office—rustic picnic tables, hanging lights, and a soft breeze that tugged at her hair like it knew she needed the calm. Lacy poked at her taco, her appetite somewhere back at her desk with the blinking cursor.

Andrew, thankfully, didn't rush her.

"So," he said finally, after a stretch of silence. "Want to tell me what's really going on?"

Lacy sighed, setting her taco down. "Patrick asked me to move in."

Andrew blinked. "Whoa. That's... big. And only after 6 months?"

"Yeah." She looked up at him, her eyes tired but clear. "And I haven't answered him. It's been weeks. I've just been... avoiding it."

Andrew leaned back in his chair, giving her a long, knowing look. "So... that 'special project' you're supposedly buried under?"

Lacy winced, setting her coffee down with a sigh.

"Completely made up. No secret manuscript. No urgent deadline. Just me... needing a little breathing room."

He smiled, but it was gentler than usual. "I figured. You're good, but you're not that good at lying."

She laughed, a little sheepishly. "I just needed some space without having to explain every feeling I was sorting through. It's... a lot."

Andrew nodded, not pushing. Just there — steady as ever.

He gave her a soft smile. "Lacy, you don't owe me an explanation. But if you want to talk it through, I'm here."

She paused, then leaned back in her chair, arms crossed. "It's not that I don't love him. I do. A lot. And when he said it—'I want to wake up to you every day'—God, part of me wanted to say yes right then."

"But?" Andrew asked gently.

"But I froze. Because I've been there before. The last guy I moved in with... it ended with me on Bree's couch, trying to figure out how to rebuild my life."

Andrew's expression sobered. "That's not something you forget."

"No," she murmured. "And even though Patrick isn't him, even though he's shown me nothing but love... it still lives in me, that fear. That loss of control. That voice saying, what if it happens again?"

Andrew was quiet for a beat, then said, "You don't have to be ready just because someone else is."

Lacy glanced at him, the wind brushing against her cheek like a hand. "I don't want to say no just because I'm scared," she whispered. "But I also don't want to say yes just because I'm scared I'll lose him if I don't."

"That," he said, "is exactly the kind of thing you take your time figuring out. Anyone who really loves you will understand that."

She gave him a small, grateful smile. "Bree said something similar. Right before joking that she would've been moved in by week two."

Andrew laughed. "Your sister is funny."

Lacy chuckled, looking out over the street. "Dinner's coming. I told Patrick we'd talk once the 'project' was done. He probably thinks my silence means no."
"Do you know what your answer is yet?"
She thought for a moment, then shook her head. "Not yet. But I think I'm getting closer."

A few days later, Patrick pulled into the valet lane of her high-rise in a sleek black Genesis GV80, a bouquet in hand—her favorite blush-colored peonies, wrapped in crisp white paper.
Lacy met him in the lobby, but before she could say a word, he leaned in to kiss her and handed over the flowers like they were a promise.
He wore a tailored navy blazer that hugged his broad shoulders perfectly, a crisp white tee underneath, and a fresh pair of vintage Jordan 1s—this time in a rare navy-and-cream colorway that somehow made the whole look feel even sharper.
The clean, magnetic scent of sandalwood—and something darker, something unmistakably Patrick—trailed in with him as he kissed her, then pulled her into a hug that lingered just a beat too long.
"Hey, beautiful," he murmured, voice low enough to make her knees consider giving out.
She clutched the bouquet loosely at her side as he finally pulled back, grinning at her like she was the best part of his day.
"You look incredible," he murmured, his eyes lingering.
Lacy had dressed with care—soft curls grazing her collarbone, her makeup glowing just enough to catch the light, and a pale blue dress that cinched at the waist before floating gently around her thighs. She looked stunning. And felt it. But the weight in her chest reminded her why this night wasn't just dinner.
She tucked a curl behind her ear, still smiling.
"Every time I see you, you make it harder to believe you're real."

He smiled, wide and warm. But there was something behind it. Expectation. Maybe even hope.

The restaurant was moody and elegant, tucked away on a quiet downtown street. Low lighting. Dark wood. Candlelit corners. The kind of place that whispered: Big conversations happen here.
They ordered wine, and the small talk flowed easily—updates on work, funny client stories, Lacy sharing a disaster involving her intern and a missing chapter draft.
But under it all, the weight of the real conversation pressed between them, waiting.
When their entrées arrived, Lacy barely touched hers. Patrick, usually a man who finished every meal with smooth precision, only toyed with his food, cutting small pieces but leaving them untouched.
He set his fork down with deliberate calm, then reached across the table, linking their fingers.
"So," he said, voice low and velvet-rich, "I've been thinking."
Lacy braced herself, heart thudding.
"I want to get you out of the city for a weekend," Patrick continued, his thumb stroking hers. "Somewhere warmer. Somewhere we can just... breathe. No work. No stress."
She blinked. "That sounds amazing."
A slow smile curved his mouth, predatory and sweet all at once. "There's a getaway coming up in Miami. Gorgeous hotel. Sunset views. Rooftop bars. Maybe even a conference we could pop into if we're feeling ambitious."
Lacy laughed softly. "Workaholic."
He squeezed her hand. "Only if you are too."
The idea was tempting. A break. A few days wrapped up in Patrick, away from the noise of real life.
But before she could answer, his gaze sharpened slightly.

"And while we're away," he said, casual like he was ordering another glass of wine, "maybe we could talk about us."

Her stomach tightened.

"Patrick..." she started.

He held up a hand, smile never slipping. "No pressure tonight. I just want to know we're heading in the same direction."

Lacy took a sip of her wine, gathering courage. "I love you," she said, steady and sure.

Hope flickered across his face—bright, immediate.

"But I'm not ready to move in," she finished, gentler now, feeling the sting of disappointment even before it flickered in his dark eyes.

He leaned back slightly, the candlelight throwing hard shadows across his face.

"Why not?" he asked, deceptively soft.

She twisted their linked hands slightly, needing something to hold onto. "It's not you. It's me needing... space. A little longer to be my own before I'm someone's again."

He sat there, unreadable for a moment.

Then he smiled.

Tight.

Polished.

Dangerous.

"I get it," he said smoothly. "You're not ready."

But everything about the way he said it made Lacy's skin prickle.

They finished dinner politely, almost warmly.

But the softness between them had changed—thinned into something fragile. Brittle.

When Patrick walked her to the car, his hand still found the small of her back. His mouth still brushed her temple in a lingering kiss.

But the energy was different.

A thread pulled too taut.

As she slid into the passenger seat, she caught the way his hands…gripped the wheel like he was holding something back, jaw tight, shoulders rigid. And somewhere deep down, she felt it:
The shift in their dynamic.

Over the next few months, things with Patrick slowly, painfully shifted.
He was traveling more.
Calling less.
Still affectionate when they were together—but there was a distance now, one Lacy could feel even when he held her close.
The intimacy between them, once all-consuming, had cooled to something quieter.
Excuses piled up.
"I've got an early meeting," he'd say.
"Another trip this weekend."
"I'll make it up to you soon, baby."
And every time, Lacy wanted to believe him.
She clung to hope the way you hold a delicate thread in a storm—desperately, stubbornly.
But her intuition whispered louder with each passing week: He was slipping away.
The only constant was Andrew.
Their long hours at the office—late nights prepping for the upcoming book fair—turned into long conversations.
Shared dinners when takeout was the only option.
Laughter over ridiculous deadlines.
The quiet comfort of someone who didn't expect anything from her except to simply be.
Andrew became her anchor without either of them really noticing.
And somewhere between manuscripts and midnight coffee runs, without realizing it...
Andrew started falling for her.

One Friday evening, with Patrick away on yet another business trip, Andrew invited her out for drinks at a cozy little jazz lounge tucked between the heartbeat of downtown streets.

It was the kind of place that didn't need to scream for attention—dim lighting, velvet saxophone melodies, tables tucked into intimate corners.

The perfect place to breathe for a while.

To forget everything heavy.

They slid into a corner booth, close enough their knees brushed under the table without meaning to.

Their cocktails came—an old fashioned for him, a lavender gin fizz for her—and slowly, the tension of the week unwound between them.

"So," Andrew said, lifting a brow over the rim of his glass, "how's everything going with Mr. Move-In?"

Lacy huffed a tired laugh. "Still... complicated."

He set his drink down, watching her carefully. "Complicated like he's waiting you out, or complicated like... he's already started to drift?"

She traced the rim of her glass, her nails clicking softly against the condensation.

"I told him weeks ago I wasn't ready. He said he understood."

Her voice dropped lower.

"But lately... he feels farther away. Busier. Like maybe... maybe it mattered more to him than he let on."

Andrew leaned in slightly, the golden light catching in the dark depths of his eyes.

"You're not crazy, Lace. You know when something shifts. Trust that."

She gave him a small, grateful smile. "I've been leaning on you a lot more than I meant to."

He didn't even blink.

"I like being there for you."

Their eyes caught and held—longer this time.

Something unspoken flickered in the charged air between them.

Something neither of them was ready to name.
Not yet.
Lacy looked away first, clearing her throat. "Bree's wedding's next weekend."
Andrew nodded. "You ready for all the chaos?"
She laughed softly. "I think so. Bachelorette party first, then the wedding... Patrick was supposed to come, but now he's saying he might not be able to get away from work."
Andrew's mouth tightened—not a frown, not exactly.
Just a flicker of something restrained.
"Doesn't sound like the guy who said he couldn't breathe without you."
"It doesn't," she whispered. "And the thing is... I think telling him no about moving in... it shifted something. Like he doesn't know how to want me if I'm not giving him everything exactly when he wants it."
Andrew's voice was low, steady.
"You don't owe anybody your life on their timeline."
Her chest ached at the truth of it.
At how easy it was to be honest with Andrew.
At how safe she felt sitting there, across a tiny table from him, sipping gin and talking about the things that mattered.
"I just want," she said, voice breaking a little, "someone who wants all of me. As I am. Not on their schedule. Not on their terms."
Andrew raised his glass, voice rougher now, almost too quiet to hear over the music:
"Then you need someone who's willing to throw the whole damn plan away... just to build something better with you."
Their glasses clinked softly.
And Lacy, for the first time in weeks, let herself exhale.

Lacy needed a reset.
So, like clockwork, she wandered into her favorite coffee shop—the little escape that had become her sanctuary when the rest of life felt too loud.

The scent of fresh espresso, the low murmur of conversation, the soft clink of mugs against marble countertops—
Here, everything slowed down.
Here, she could breathe.
And lately...
She found herself running into Lucas more often than pure coincidence would explain.
He was sitting alone at his usual table near the back, a cup of espresso half-finished beside his large leather-bound notebook. He was mid-sketch, pencil dancing across the page, brows furrowed in concentration until he looked up and saw her.
"Well hello there," he said with a grin that started in his eyes. "Must be fate."
"I think you're stalking me," she teased, sliding her sunglasses up onto her head.
He laughed, leaning back in his chair. "Only in a friendly, caffeinated way. You want to sit?"
She took the seat across from him, letting the warm aroma of roasted beans and baked pastries wrap around them. The conversation picked up easily, a blend of professional curiosity and casual charm. They talked about his latest manuscript, where the plot was dragging and where it sang, and how he didn't know what he'd do without her feedback. She offered insight without overstepping, careful to maintain their working relationship—but she liked these moments, when the line between them blurred just enough to let her see who he was beyond the pages.
Lucas talked about his freelance design gigs—album covers, branding for indie startups—and how he balanced the visuals of his work with the storytelling of his writing. He mentioned his new rescue dog, Pablo, a grumpy old French bulldog who snored like a freight train, and his deep love for trivia nights at a local pub.
"Next time you need a partner, I'm your girl," she said, smiling over the rim of her cappuccino.

"Deal," he replied, his eyes sparkling as he closed his notebook. "But only if you promise not to show me up."

"No promises." she winked.

They shared a warm laugh, that kind of laugh that lingered just a second too long. And then he looked at her, head tilted thoughtfully.

"You doing anything after this?" he asked casually. "There's a park a couple blocks over. Feels like a good day for a walk."

For half a second, she almost said no. But something easy in his smile loosened the knot in her chest. "Sure," she said, rising from her seat with a soft smile.

The park was quiet that afternoon, tucked like a secret between city blocks. The sun filtered through the trees in lazy rays, dappling the cobblestone paths and casting a soft glow over the budding flowers lining the walkways. It was the kind of day that asked nothing of you but to enjoy it—and Lacy found herself doing just that.

Lucas walked beside her, hands in his pockets, his shoulder brushing hers every now and then. It wasn't on purpose. Or maybe it was. Either way, she didn't mind.

They talked about everything and nothing. He told her about the first story he ever wrote—something about a boy and a magic bicycle that could fly—and how his teacher gave him an A and said she'd keep it forever.

"I think that's when I knew," he said, glancing over at her.

"Knew what?"

"That I wanted to make people feel something with my words. That I wanted to tell stories for the rest of my life."

She smiled at him, the kind of smile that reached her chest. "Well, you're doing it."

"You're part of that now, you know. You don't just edit my work, Lacy. You shape it."

The sincerity in his voice caught her off guard. She looked away, toward a pair of kids chasing each other near the carousel. It was too much, and not enough, all at once.

They walked a bit farther, falling into a comfortable silence. The kind that didn't need filling.

"I like this," she said, pausing by the fountain, her fingers tracing the cool stone.

"What's this?" he asked, his voice curious but easy.

"Just… spending time with someone without all the pressure," she added, her gaze drifting to the water's surface.

Lucas chuckled, a lightness to his tone. "I'm not really one for pressure. Unless we're talking about who wins at trivia night. Then it's all bets off."

She laughed softly, the unease in her chest easing just a little. "Good to know."

Later that evening, just as Lacy was slipping off her heels and tossing her purse onto the entryway table, her phone buzzed.

Patrick.

She stared at the screen for a second, exhaling slowly before answering.

"Hey, love," she said, keeping her voice easy, steady.

"Hey." His tone was warm enough on the surface—but clipped underneath, like he was rushing through a conversation he didn't really want to have.

"I just wanted to catch you before it got too late. About this weekend…"

Lacy's stomach tightened.

Here we go.

"I'm not going to be able to make it to the wedding," he said, words almost too quick.

She leaned back against the wall, pressing her palm flat against the cool paint.

"Oh. Everything okay?"

"Yeah, yeah. Just work stuff," he said casually, too casually. "Last-minute client thing. Presentation I can't move."

She let the silence stretch.

Long enough for it to sting.

"We've had this date on the calendar for months, Patrick."

"I know," he said, and for a second, she almost believed he meant it. "I'm sorry, Lace. I wanted to be there."

"But you're not."

Her voice was even. No accusation. No pleading. Just the truth hanging between them.

He went quiet for a moment, and then—

"Lacy… is there something else going on here?"

She smiled, but it was the tired kind—the kind you give when you're too worn out to fake it.

"Maybe. I don't know. You tell me."

He let out a breath through his nose, a sound too close to frustration.

"I've been busy. You know how my schedule is."

"Yeah," she said softly. "I know."

Another long pause.

"I'll make it up to you," Patrick said. It sounded like a promise he wasn't even sure he could keep.

Lacy closed her eyes for a beat, swallowing down everything she wanted to say.

"Okay," she said simply. "Take care of what you need to."

"I'll call you later this week."

"Sure," she replied, already knowing he probably wouldn't.

When she hung up, she stood there for a long moment, the quiet of her apartment wrapping around her like a too-thin blanket, the weight of the silence pressing in.

She turned toward the couch—only to stumble slightly as Leo shot out from under the coffee table with a sharp, dramatic meow, weaving between her legs like he'd been waiting for his moment to be seen.

"Jesus, Leo," she muttered, scooping him up as he swatted playfully at her necklace. "You could warn a girl."

He purred loudly, completely unbothered, and she plopped down on the couch with him still in her arms.

A second later, her phone buzzed again. FaceTime this time. Bree.

"Hey sis hey!" Bree beamed the second her face popped up on the screen. "Mental Health check, how we feeling"

Lacy sighed, her whole body sagging into the cushions. "You've got timing. Patrick just called. He's not coming to the wedding."

Bree blinked, her smile fading. "Wait—what? Seriously?"

"Yeah. Last-minute work thing." Lacy made air quotes, the words tasting bitter in her mouth.

Bree's face tightened with instant suspicion. "Mmm. How convenient."

"I know," Lacy said, scratching distractedly behind Leo's ears. "Ever since I told him I wasn't ready to move in, it's like... he's been different. Distant. And I keep telling myself I'm imagining it, but..."

"You're not imagining it," Bree cut in, voice firm. "You're feeling it. Trust yourself."

Lacy stared at the ceiling for a moment. "I just thought we'd find a middle ground, you know? That we could ease into something real, without it having to be all or nothing."

"And instead, Mr. Hot Chocolate is acting like patience wasn't part of the package," Bree said, crossing her arms. "Meanwhile... aren't you spending a lot of time with a certain artist and a certain editor lately?"

Lacy gave a tired laugh. "Lucas is just a friend. Andrew too. It's not like that."

"Uh-huh. Tell that to Andrew's face next time he looks at you like you hung the moon."

"Bree."

"I'm just saying," Bree sing-songed. "Options, sis. You got 'em."

Lacy shook her head, smiling despite herself. "Andrew's just... easy to talk to. Especially with Patrick being so... I don't know. Slippery."

"You know what you need?" Bree said, voice brightening. "You need a distraction. Preferably one involving cocktails, sequins, and embarrassing party favors."
Lacy laughed. "The bachelorette party."
"Exactly. And you better have a fire outfit lined up, because your sister's last wild night is about to be one for the history books."
"I'm afraid," Lacy said, but she was smiling now.
"As you should be. And don't think you're getting out of dancing just because your love life is messy."
They talked for another hour—about dresses, decorations, and whether Leo should get his own bowtie for the wedding. Bree's teasing was relentless but full of love, and Lacy let herself lean into it.
Because when the call ended and the apartment fell silent again, she wasn't left with just her doubts. She was left with hope too.
One weekend, two events, and maybe—just maybe—a chance to figure out where she was really supposed to be.

The week blurred past in a haze of deadlines and half-finished thoughts. Lacy moved through each day like she was underwater—functioning, floating, but slightly detached. Patrick was now even harder to reach. Every call went to voicemail or was met with a clipped "I'm in a meeting" or "I'll call you later," which he rarely did.
She didn't want to be the needy girlfriend. She didn't want to pressure him. But still, the silence was loud.
She spotted Lucas again at the coffee shop, two orders ahead of her in line. He turned, caught her eye, and smiled like they were old friends.
"This place is starting to feel like our accidental hangout spot," he said as she stepped beside him.
"Right?" she laughed. "At this point, we should just set a standing coffee date."
They chatted for a few minutes before parting ways—casual, warm, familiar.

Later that afternoon, she popped her head into Andrew's office. "Hey, you still good to be my plus one this weekend?" she asked, leaning on the doorframe.

Andrew looked up, grinning—and for just a heartbeat, Lacy noticed how good he looked, casual but sharp, the sleeves of his button-down rolled to his elbows like he always belonged exactly where he was.

"Patrick's out?"

"He said he has to work. Again." She rolled her eyes. "But yes, if you're still free, I'd love the company."

Andrew's smile softened, something sparking quietly in his eyes. "I'm in. And don't worry—I clean up pretty well."

"I never doubted it," she said, and walked off, her cheeks warm.

That night, as she sat on her couch, Leo curled on her lap, purring softly, she stared at her phone. Still no message from Patrick.

The wedding weekend was coming. Her mind should've been full of champagne flutes, Bree's bachelorette party, and choosing the right heels for dancing. Instead, her heart felt like it was tiptoeing across something fragile.

But she had her sister, Leo and now, Andrew by her side.

She was ready for the weekend—whatever it decided to bring.

Chapter 10

Lacy chuckled from the chair beside her, feeling equally boneless from the full-body massage they'd just finished. Her white spa robe, embroidered with delicate gold script, felt like a soft cocoon. She lifted her glass of cucumber-mint water, savoring the coolness against her fingers.
"Only the best for the bride," Lacy said, winking.
"You really outdid yourself," Bree sighed. "I thought you were gonna drag me to some wild brunch with shirtless waiters and bad decisions."
"Oh, don't worry," Lacy grinned. "The day's still young. I just figured you deserved some peace before the chaos. You've been running on fumes planning this wedding."
Around them, the rest of the girls—Janelle, Chrissy, Kayla, Nina, and Ava—lounged in a cloud of white robes and cucumber water bliss, occasional laughter drifting through the warm, fragrant air.

"This is a whole vibe," Janelle murmured, her voice dreamy. "Hot towels, champagne, no kids screaming in the background… I could cry."
"Seriously," Kayla said, eyes closed behind cucumber slices. "Lacy, you did that."
"I told y'all," Bree said, lifting her glass. "My sister-slash-maid-of-honor does not play."
"To Lacy!" Chrissy called out, lifting her flute.
"To Lacy!" the others echoed, clinking glasses.
Lacy shook her head, laughing as her cheeks warmed. "Y'all better stop. I didn't do anything Bree didn't deserve. She's been everything to me since we were kids. Of course I'm going all out."
Bree reached over, squeezing her hand. "I love you. But don't get it twisted—I'm still expecting tequila shots and twerking later."
"Oh, there's a plan," Lacy smirked. "Chef's already on the way to the Airbnb. Pajamas are hanging up in garment bags—silk, matching, bougie. And the playlist? Laced with bad decisions."

Kayla raised a brow. "Is this chef single, though? I brought lashes just in case."

Nina chimed in with a laugh, "Girl, we're getting fed in more ways than one."

Everyone burst into laughter, the kind that came easy between old friends and new bonds, their voices bouncing warmly around the tranquil room.

Later that afternoon, after everyone had floated out of their spa bliss with glowing skin and a collective sense of serenity, the vibe took a playful turn. Robes were swapped for sundresses and oversized sunglasses, the speaker playlist changed from soft jazz to R&B, and mimosas were topped off with a heavier hand.

Lacy checked her phone and smirked to herself. "Alright, ladies," she said, raising her voice slightly. "Hope y'all didn't think the spa was it."

Bree narrowed her eyes suspiciously. "Lacy… what did you do?"

"Don't worry," Lacy grinned. "Just a little arts and culture. Grab a drink and meet me on the back patio. You're gonna love this."

They followed her outside, greeted by a long table set up with easels, canvases, paints, and wine glasses at every seat. A woman in all black—cool, collected, and clearly the instructor—stood at the front with a clipboard and a knowing smirk.

"Welcome, ladies," the instructor said. "Today, we'll be doing a figure study. Loosen up your wrists and your expectations."

"What kind of figure?" Kayla asked, already suspicious.

Before anyone could answer, out walked him—tall, sculpted, absolutely beautiful, wearing nothing but a towel slung dangerously low around his hips.

"Oh my God," Ava gasped, choking on her wine.

The towel dropped.

There was a beat of stunned silence.

Then chaos.

"LACY!" Bree shrieked, both horrified and delighted. "You got us a naked man?!"

"He's a model," Lacy said innocently, holding back laughter. "It's for art."

Janelle was already painting, eyes locked on the man like she was studying for an exam. "No one disturb me. I'm in the zone."

The model struck a pose—confident, completely unbothered, arms above his head like a living Michelangelo sculpture. The instructor kept a straight face as she handed out instructions, but the rest of the group? Absolutely unhinged.

Bree kept wheezing laughter behind her glass. "I swear, this is the horniest version of Bob Ross I've ever experienced."

"I'm not even painting," Kayla admitted. "I'm just pretending to so I can keep staring."

"I'm suddenly great at art," Ava muttered, fanning herself.

Even Lacy couldn't keep it together, laughing so hard her brush slipped and painted a bright red streak across her canvas. "I was not prepared for... all of that."

The model glanced her way with a wink. Bree caught it instantly. "He winked at you."

"He winked at everyone," Lacy protested, flushed and giggling.

"No, sis," Bree said, raising her brows. "That was extra. You better tip him or something."

By the end of the session, the patio was filled with half-finished paintings, empty wine bottles, and women doubled over with laughter. The model gave a courteous bow, wrapped himself in a robe, and made his exit to applause and catcalls.

The instructor, clearly unfazed, clapped her hands. "Great job, ladies. You're naturals. And you've officially ruined ocean scenes for me forever."

As the group started migrating back inside, still laughing and teasing each other, Bree wrapped an arm around Lacy's shoulders. "Best. Maid of Honor. Ever."

Lacy grinned. "You haven't even seen the pajamas yet."

As the night settled into a cozy haze of laughter and glowing candlelight, the private chef finished plating the last round of tapas and retreated with a respectful nod. The music played low, and half-empty glasses of wine were scattered across the coffee table. The girls were curled up in their matching pajamas, each embroidered with their names—like a soft, slumber-party version of armor after a long day of pampering, painting, and prosecco.

Bree flopped onto a floor cushion, raising her glass with a mischievous glint in her eye. "Sooo... when's Andrew showing up to save you from this single life?"

Lacy laughed, rolling her eyes. "First of all, I'm not single. Second, Andrew is just my backup wedding date because somebody bailed."

The room buzzed with curiosity. A few heads turned.

"What happened to Hot Chocolate?" Kayla asked, setting her glass down.

Lacy shrugged, swirling her sangria. "Work trip. Emergency meetings. Haven't seen much of him lately."

There were murmurs of sympathy, but Ava leaned forward, practically glowing.

"Well," Ava said, her voice sing-song sweet, "somebody's got some news."

"Ohhh?" Bree said, smirking, already sensing the chaos brewing.

"I met someone," Ava announced proudly. "At the Miami conference I told y'all about."

Excited chatter broke out instantly.

Ava beamed. "He's amazing. Grown. Fine. Managing partner at a huge firm. Venture capital. Super polished, charming... seriously, he's the total package."

Lacy's heart gave a weird little kick. Bree's head snapped up.

Bree's head snapped up.

"What's his name?" Bree asked casually, her eyes locking onto Lacy's without the others noticing.

"Patrick Ellis," Ava said brightly. "Girl, I didn't stand a chance. He's like... perfect."

Silence hit the room like a slap.

Lacy's chest tightened so hard it felt like her ribs might snap. Her sangria nearly slipped from her fingers. Her stomach dropped to her toes.

Bree sat up straighter, eyes narrowing. "Patrick Ellis?" she echoed carefully.

Ava nodded. "Yeah! He's a managing partner at Havenstone Capital. We met at the mixer after one of the panels. You guys would love him."

Lacy's world tilted slightly.

Tall. Chocolate skin. Gray eyes. Designer vintage sneakers with every outfit.

Bree's hand clamped around her wine glass so tight her knuckles turned white.

"Uh... Ava," Bree said slowly, shooting Lacy a quick, sharp glance, "what's he look like? Besides fine?"

Ava laughed, not catching the tension yet. "Tall, dark, and edible. Always fresh. Dresses down his suits with these bomb sneakers—seriously, he's like if GQ and Complex had a baby."

"Oh... my God," Lacy whispered.

"What?" Ava said, confused.

Lacy licked her lips, her voice breaking a little. "Ava... HC is Patrick."

The room froze.

Kayla blinked. "Wait, what?"

"Hot Chocolate—HC—Patrick Ellis," Bree confirmed grimly, staring dead at Ava. "Same guy."

Ava's smile crumbled into horror. "No. No, no, no—he said he was single."

Janelle leaned forward, jaw dropped. "Wait, hold UP. You're telling me—y'all have been dating the same man?!"

Lacy gave a hollow laugh, full of disbelief. "Apparently."

Ava scrambled for her phone. "Hold on, hold on—this can't be—" She pulled up a recent selfie Patrick had sent her: him in a sharp navy suit, grinning, flashing that familiar watch Lacy had given him for his birthday. Bree leaned over, saw it, and cursed under her breath. "That's him."

Lacy closed her eyes briefly, a sharp pain slicing through her.

Ava looked shattered. "I didn't know, Lacy. I swear to God, I had no idea."

"I know," Lacy said tightly. "You didn't. He did this."

Bree's eyes darkened. "Call him. Right now."

Janelle and Kayla were already halfway across the room, phones in hand like backup singers ready for war.

Lacy hit Facetime first.

No answer.

Declined.

Ava, shaking, tried next.

And this time?

He picked up.

The second the screen lit up, Patrick's voice came through, smooth as butter.

"Hey, beautiful," he said, smiling wide—until he saw who else was on the screen.

His face paled instantly.

Six women.

One truth.

And no place left to hide.

"Patrick Ellis," Bree said, deadly calm, "meet your welcoming committee."

Patrick fumbled. "Lacy, baby, I can explain—"

"Save it," Lacy said, her voice slicing clean. "Explain to her."

Ava's hand shook but her voice was steel. "You lied to me."

Patrick swallowed visibly, scrambling. "I didn't mean for it to get this far—"

"But it did," Bree snapped.

"You had two relationships at once," Lacy said, her chest tight, her fingers curling around the couch cushion for balance. "Two lives."

Patrick's words tripped over themselves, excuses pouring out in a hot mess of nothing.

Ava ended the call with a sharp jab of her thumb.

The room exploded in noise—curses, shouted disbelief, angry laughter.

Lacy just sat there, shaking.

Bree crossed the room and crouched in front of her. "You listen to me," she said, voice fierce. "None of this is your fault."

Ava slid down onto the couch beside her, still looking gutted. "I'm so sorry, Lacy. I swear I didn't know."

Lacy turned, offering a broken, watery smile. "I know. He played us both."

Silence wrapped around them—heavy, but healing too.

Then—

Ding-dong.

Everyone froze.

Bree blinked, straightening. "Oh my God."

Kayla whispered, "It's the strippers."

The tension cracked.

A wild, relieved laugh tore out of Lacy's chest.

"Perfect timing," she said hoarsely, wiping her eyes.

And when the door opened—and a line of shirtless men strutted into the room, music blasting behind them— the room erupted in laughter and cheers.

Lacy couldn't help it—she laughed too. The kind that came from deep in her chest. Sudden and uncontrollable. It felt so ridiculous, so surreal, so perfectly timed, like the universe itself had decided she was done being sad for the night.

The strippers did their job—excellently, if the screaming and dollar bills were any indication. Champagne flowed. The music thumped. Lacy danced with her girls until her cheeks hurt. Bree grabbed her hand at one point and twirled her around like they were teenagers again, carefree and fearless.

The night became a blur of glitter, spilled drinks, off-key singing, and wild laughter.

Forget Patrick? They did.

Completely.

And when Lacy finally collapsed into bed, makeup smudged, hair tangled, body aching from dancing, she felt lighter. Not healed, not fixed—but cracked open in a way that let some light back in.

Tomorrow was the wedding.

But tonight?

Tonight had been for her.

Chapter 11

The morning after the unforgettable night was a little slower, but no less bright. The sun streamed through the windows of the house, its warmth a sharp contrast to the coolness of the night. Lacy sat in the bathroom, her hair still slightly damp from her shower, staring at herself in the mirror. The night before felt like a distant memory, even though every step, every wild moment was burned into her mind.

She'd thrown herself into the fun, danced, laughed, screamed until her voice was hoarse. But the ache in her chest was still there, lurking just beneath the surface.

A knock on the door interrupted her thoughts. "It's Andrew," came the familiar voice, a little too cheerful, a little too bright for her mood.

"Come in," she called, doing her best to pull herself together.

The door creaked open, and Andrew stepped inside, dressed casually in a button-up shirt and dark jeans, his hair freshly shaved, his eyes still carrying the remnants of sleep. He was early, like always.

"Okay, let's do this," he said with a grin, walking over to where Lacy sat, his eyes immediately scanning her as though he was already assessing what she needed. "You're going to look amazing, Lacy. You know that, right?"

She gave him a tired smile. "Thanks, Andrew. I'm kind of glad you're here early. I'm not... totally ready to face today, to be honest."

He pulled the chair out from the vanity and sat next to her, his posture relaxed but attentive. "I get that. Weddings are... a lot. But hey, you've got this. And I'm here to help however I can."

Lacy laughed softly, meeting his eyes. "Thanks. I'm not sure what I would've done without you and Bree."

Andrew tilted his head slightly, then hesitated before speaking. "What happened last night? Did you talk to Patrick?"

Her stomach sank at the mention of his name. For a second, she felt like the air around her had thickened. She took a breath, her gaze falling to her hands as she fiddled with the edge of the towel around her shoulders. "You could say last night was... eye-opening," she said, voice tight.
Andrew reached over, touching her hand lightly, his fingers warm against her skin. "Do you want to talk about it?"
She sighed, leaning back in the chair. "I'm not sure where to start. Patrick... he just wasn't the man I thought he was. It's like everything's been a lie. I found out he's been lying to me... about so many things. It hit me like a ton of bricks."
His thumb brushed over her hand, and he spoke softly. "I'm sorry, Lacy. You don't deserve this."
Lacy nodded, the weight of her emotions starting to crack through the calm exterior she'd tried to maintain. She blinked quickly, but one tear slipped down her cheek. "I love him, Andrew. I thought, he would wait... I thought I was ready for more. But now I'm just... I don't know. Lost."
Andrew's hand tightened gently around hers. "You don't have to figure it out right now, okay? I'm here for you. Take all the time you need. You deserve better than that, Lacy. You deserve someone who can meet you where you are and who isn't going to play games with your heart."
The tenderness in his voice, the way he was looking at her—like she was the only thing in the room—struck her in a way she wasn't prepared for. Before she could even process what was happening, Andrew leaned forward. His lips brushed against hers, soft and tentative at first, as if unsure whether he should, and then deeper, more urgent. His hand cupped her cheek, tilting her face upward, and all at once, the world seemed to quiet. The lingering ache from Patrick, the guilt, the confusion—all of it melted into the heat of the kiss.
Lacy's heart raced, her pulse thrumming in her ears as her mind struggled to catch up with what was happening. This was Andrew. Her friend. Her colleague.

When they pulled apart, both breathless, Lacy stared at him, wide-eyed, her chest rising and falling quickly. "Andrew..." she whispered, her voice shaky.

He pulled back slightly, his expression unreadable, but his hand still rested lightly on her arm. "I'm sorry," he said, voice low, as though unsure of himself. "I didn't mean to—"

"No," Lacy interrupted, her voice a little firmer, a little clearer. "It's not... it's not that. I just... I wasn't expecting that."

Andrew gave her a sheepish smile, his thumb running over her skin again. "I've been thinking about it for a while, actually. About you. But I didn't want to push you. Not when everything with Patrick was so... complicated."

Lacy blinked, her mind still reeling from the unexpected turn of events. "I need a moment," she whispered, trying to regain her composure. "I don't know what I'm doing."

Andrew gave a small nod, sitting back a little, giving her the space she needed. "Take your time. We'll talk later. But just know, I'm here, Lacy. Always."

The room was quiet for a moment, the soft hum of the music outside reminding her of the day ahead—the wedding, the dress, the people, the joy, the pain. She took a deep breath, then another, trying to ground herself in the reality of what was about to happen.

After a few minutes, she stood and began to prepare herself for the wedding, a swirl of emotions battling for dominance. Her heart still ached over Patrick, but there was something about the raw, unexpected tenderness of the moment with Andrew that made her feel... seen. And she hadn't realized how much she needed that until now.

The wedding venue shimmered with elegance—linen-draped tables, floating candles, a string quartet tuning up in the background. The day felt like magic, wrapped in silk and sunlight.

Lacy moved through it all with purpose, clipboard in hand and a Bluetooth headset tucked into one ear—fully in maid-of-honor mode. She'd traded her morning confusion for go-time adrenaline, and nothing was going to touch Bree's perfect day.

She found her sister in a private bridal suite upstairs, surrounded by the final touches—veil steaming on a mannequin, champagne glasses half-full, bridesmaids fluttering about. Bree stood in the center of it all in her wedding gown, radiant and a little stunned, like she couldn't quite believe the moment had come.

"There she is," Lacy said, stepping inside and closing the door behind her. Her voice was light, but her eyes shimmered. "You're a freaking dream, Bree."

Bree turned toward her, her lip trembling with emotion. "Don't make me cry again," she whispered, already blinking back tears. "We just fixed my makeup."

Lacy laughed and crossed the room, taking both of Bree's hands in hers. "Today is about you. Nothing else. Not work, not drama, not anyone who doesn't deserve to be in this space. You are marrying the love of your life, and it's going to be perfect."

Bree exhaled shakily. "You promise?"

"I do," Lacy said, and they both cracked up at the accidental wedding pun. "Now breathe, drink your champagne, and tell me what you need."

The hours flew by in a blur of silk ribbons and soft laughter. Lacy made sure everything ran like clockwork—seating charts confirmed, flower girls lined up, makeup touch-ups coordinated, DJ cued.

When it was time to walk down the aisle, Lacy stood at the front, bouquet in hand, watching Bree glide toward her future with grace and quiet joy. And yet, as the vows were exchanged and the couple said "I do," Lacy's heart tugged in opposite directions. Her smile never faltered, but inside, she was spiraling.

Images flashed through her mind—Patrick's betrayal, Ava's stunned silence, the look on Andrew's face after their kiss, the way it had made her feel everything and nothing all at once. She clutched her bouquet tighter and blinked hard.

The ceremony had ended in a swell of applause and happy tears, and Bree was now off in a whirl of guests and champagne flutes, her new husband's arm wrapped tightly around her waist. Lacy had done her job—every detail had come together like a dream—but as the crowd shifted toward the cocktail hour, she suddenly felt untethered.

The emotion she'd kept buried during the ceremony pressed in now, hot and unwelcome behind her eyes. She needed a second. Just one.

She stepped away from the reception lawn, weaving past flower arrangements and laughing guests, until she spotted him. Andrew. Leaning casually against a pillar near the bar, tie slightly loosened, hands in his pockets, his gaze scanning the crowd until it landed on her.

His smile softened the chaos inside her.

"Hey," she said, stepping into his space like it was familiar, like it was safe.

He looked her over. "You killed it out there," he said, eyes warm. "Seriously. You made today look effortless."

"Thanks," she whispered, her voice thin. "I think I've been running on caffeine, champagne, and raw determination for two days straight."

He chuckled, then studied her more closely. "You okay?"

She hesitated, and that was all it took. The walls she'd been holding up all day began to crack.

"I thought I was," she said, her voice catching. "But then the vows happened and I… I don't know, it all just hit me."

Tears slipped down her cheeks before she could stop them, and she turned her face slightly, embarrassed.

Andrew reached out, his hand gently resting on her waist as he pulled her into him. She didn't resist. Her face pressed against his shoulder, and he held her close, warm and solid.

"I'm here," he said softly. "I got you."

Something about those three words undid her. She didn't expect to cry into his chest at her sister's wedding, but there she was, and there he was—quiet and steady and real.

When she finally pulled back, her eyes were glassy, but she smiled. "Sorry. That wasn't in the maid-of-honor playbook."

Andrew's gaze dropped to her lips for just a second too long. "No apology necessary."

The second kiss wasn't careful.

It wasn't slow.

It was a collision.

Andrew cupped her jaw, his mouth claiming hers like he had finally stopped asking permission—and started taking what he wanted. It was deep, consuming, stealing the breath from her lungs and the steady ground from beneath her feet.

Lacy's heart jolted, her body responding before her brain could catch up. For a wild, weightless second, she kissed him back—heat flaring in her belly, a gasp slipping into his mouth—until reality slammed into her.

She pulled back abruptly, dazed, her fingers brushing her kiss-swollen lips. Her pulse roared in her ears.

She stumbled a half-step back, her hands trembling as she smoothed her dress, desperate for something—anything—solid to hold onto.

"That… that shouldn't have happened," she said, voice trembling.

Andrew didn't apologize.

He didn't even look away.

"No," he murmured, his voice low and sure. "But it did."

The air between them crackled, too charged, too dangerous.

Before either of them could say something that would change everything, Bree's laughter burst across the garden, jarring Lacy back into the real world.

She blinked, took a shaky breath, and stepped back—fumbling with the smooth fabric of her dress like it could anchor her. "I—I should get back."

Andrew didn't move to stop her. He just watched her go, the weight of his gaze burning into her skin as she fled.

When Lacy stepped back into the reception, the world spun too bright and too loud. Her heartbeat didn't slow. Her lips still tingled, a phantom brand of what shouldn't have happened—twice now—with Andrew.

The music pulsed around her, laughter and champagne swirling in golden waves, but everything inside her felt splintered.

She caught sight of Bree twirling joyfully with her new husband, a perfect moment frozen in time—and yet Lacy's chest ached with something she couldn't quite name.

Across the room, Andrew stood at the edge of the bar, a whiskey glass dangling loosely from his fingers, his tie loosened,.

He wasn't smiling.

He wasn't pretending.

He just watched her.

And when their eyes locked, it wasn't friendly or casual—it was charged, heavy with the weight of everything unspoken between them.

Kayla grabbed Lacy's arm, tugging her onto the dance floor before she could drown in it.

"Okay, you've been a model of grace and poise all damn day," Kayla declared. "Now it's time to get you irresponsibly drunk."

Lacy forced a laughed—too loud, too relieved. "Deal."

They threw back their first shot, then another. The tequila burned but so did everything else inside her, and she welcomed the distraction. Her heels came off. Someone turned the music up. And then the night was movement, and flashing lights, and laughter that vibrated in her chest.

Andrew joined them on the dance floor, and soon it was just the two of them again, like the world had folded inward. They danced like no one was watching, the space between them crackling with all the words they weren't saying. Every brush of his hand felt electric, every glance weighted.

They started a shot game with the bridal party—one shot for every compliment Bree received, another for every person who told Thomas he looked good his suit. By the fourth round, they were leaning on each other for balance, grinning like fools, flushed and loose and dangerously comfortable.

And when the DJ switched to something slow, Lacy didn't think twice before wrapping her arms around Andrew's neck, swaying against him. His hands settled on her waist, pulling her closer than was strictly necessary. Her head rested on his chest, and she let her eyes fall closed for just a second too long.

"I should stop this," she murmured, not moving.

Andrew didn't answer. His fingers just kept tracing slow circles against her lower back, flirting with the curve of her ass.

And that was it. That was all it took.

Later, as the party dwindled and the moon climbed higher over the quiet Palm Springs sky, they stumbled toward her room, laughing softly, their arms around each other. He kissed her like he meant it. Not cautious this time. Not surprised.

"I've been trying not to say anything," he whispered between kisses, hands sliding over the straps of her dress, "but I can't pretend anymore, Lacy. I am in love with you. I've felt it for a long time. I can't keep pretending."

The world tilted for half a heartbeat—and then she was pulling him closer, her need to believe him eclipsing everything else.

"Then stop pretending," she whispered back.

And this time, neither of them stopped.

Clothes slipped away like secrets they no longer needed to keep. Her dress whispered to the floor, his shirt undone by fingers that trembled with anticipation. It wasn't frantic, but it wasn't slow—it was a meeting in the middle, a mutual unraveling. Each kiss deepened their need, each breath more urgent than the last.

When they finally came together, it was like falling into place.

He moved over her with a tenderness that stole her breath, his body syncing with hers in a rhythm that felt both brand new and deeply familiar. Their eyes stayed locked more than she expected, searching, asking, answering. It wasn't about escape. It wasn't about proving anything.

It was a connection. Fire and comfort. Release and arrival.

Lacy's hands framed his face as he moved inside her, her nails grazing lightly down his back. He whispered her name like it was something sacred, something safe, something he'd been holding onto for too long. Her body responded instinctively, every nerve alive with sensation, her mind blissfully quiet for the first time in weeks.

And when she came, it wasn't with restraint. She let go completely—of the past, of the pain, of every question that had haunted her.

Andrew followed soon after, his body tensing, his breath catching on a groan that came from somewhere deep. He collapsed beside her, their bodies tangled, damp with sweat, pulsing with the afterglow.

For a while, neither of them spoke.

The silence between them wasn't awkward—it was full. Full of what they'd just shared, full of things neither of them quite knew how to say yet.

Lacy rolled onto her side to face him, the sheet slipping down to her waist. Her fingers traced the edge of his jaw—soft, thoughtful, a question hidden in the way she touched him.

"What happens now?" she asked, voice barely above a whisper.

Andrew's hand found her hip, grounding her. He leaned in, brushing a strand of hair away from her face with a gentleness that made her chest ache.

"I don't know," he said quietly, honestly. "But we'll figure it out."

Lacy searched his face, wanting to find certainty there—something solid to hold onto.

Instead, she found something better.

Patience.

Care.

A man who wasn't asking her for promises she wasn't ready to give. A man simply there, willing to stand in the unknown with her.

She nodded, blinking against the sudden sting behind her eyes.

"Okay," she whispered.

But when Andrew pulled her closer, tucking her into his side like she belonged there, Lacy's mind stayed restless.

Because even though every instinct told her she was exactly where she needed to be, another part of her—wounded, wary—still whispered about everything she had lost. About promises broken. About Patrick.

The ache of it lingered.

But so did the steady rhythm of Andrew's heartbeat against her ear.

The safety of his arms.

The unspoken vow that whatever came next—they would face it together.

And for now, even with all the questions swirling in her chest, that felt like enough.

Chapter 12

The office was chaos wrapped in coffee cups and clacking keyboards. The whisper of conversations and the buzz of ringing phones pulsed in the background like a live wire, while Lacy felt like she was dragging herself through molasses just to keep up.

After the whirlwind of Palm Springs—the wedding, the drama, Patrick, Andrew—stepping back into her office felt like landing in someone else's life. The walls were the same, her desk untouched, but everything inside her had shifted.

The annual book fair was weeks away, and the entire publishing house was in full throttle. High-profile clients were flying in, new talent had to be courted, and press kits were being proofed within an inch of their lives. This wasn't just another week at work—it was the Super Bowl of the industry. And Lacy, now an Executive editor, was at the center of it.

Normally, she would've thrived in this chaos. She used to live for the deadlines, the back-to-back meetings, the buzz of authors pitching their next big thing.

But today?

Her head was still in Palm Springs.

Andrew hadn't said much since they returned. Not in a bad way, not in a distant way—it was just... tender silence. Careful silence. Like neither of them wanted to break whatever fragile truth was growing between them. They hadn't defined anything, hadn't made any declarations. But the way he looked at her when their eyes met in the hallway? It said enough.

And then there was Patrick.

Her phone was a battlefield. Missed calls. Unread messages. Voicemails she couldn't bring herself to listen to.

Lacy, please call me.

I'm sorry.

Can we just talk?

He hadn't stopped. And she hadn't answered. Every buzz of her phone sent a spike of anxiety through her chest. Every time his name lit up, her stomach turned.

She sat at her desk, staring blankly at a manuscript that was due back with notes by noon. Her fingers hovered over the keyboard, unmoving. Around her, the office spun—ambitious interns darting past, seasoned editors holding last-minute meetings, eccentric authors popping in with half-finished ideas and last-minute demands.

Lacy was usually the one everyone turned to for calm. For quick answers. For leadership.

But today, she was an emotional wreck in a pencil skirt.

She inhaled deeply, rolled her shoulders back, and forced herself to type the first sentence of her notes.

One sentence. Then another. One hour. Then another.

She didn't know what the week would bring. Or what Andrew would say. Or if Patrick would ever really let go.

But for now, she had work to do.

And somehow, that had to be enough.

Lacy was on her second cup of coffee and third attempt at rewriting an author bio when the receptionist's voice crackled through her desk phone.

"Hey, Lacy? There's a delivery for you. Flowers."

She sighed. "Just sign for them. I'll come get them in a minute."

A minute later, the door to her office opened and in came a massive arrangement of roses, lilies, and something else aggressively fragrant—carried by Andrew. He poked his head out from behind the arrangement, brows raised. "These are for you."

Lacy rolled her eyes. "Thanks."

The card read:

Lacy, I'm sorry. I love you. Please talk to me. —P

She didn't even bother to read it twice. The vase landed with a dull thud on the side table, the flowers looking entirely too smug for her mood.

Andrew stepped fully into the office, closing the door behind him. "Patrick?"

"Who else sends a botanical guilt trip?" she muttered.

He crossed the room, hands in his pockets. "You okay?"

"I'm fine." She wasn't. "Just… trying to keep my head above water."

Andrew's gaze dropped to the flowers again, then to her. "Do you want to talk about it?"

Lacy shook her head. "Not yet. Not when I've got a keynote author who refuses to pick a cover, a booth design that's still not approved, and a whole damn book fair breathing down my neck."

He didn't push. Just gave a small nod, then a soft, "I'm here if you need me."

Her phone buzzed. A text from Bree.

Bree: You good? Want me to run point and get rid of flower-boy's next delivery before it reaches your door?

Lacy smirked and quickly replied:

Lacy: Too late. He just sent a garden.

She'd barely set the phone down when it buzzed again. This time, a group chat notification.

Ava:

okay so… I saw Patrick. I know, I know. But I needed answers.

He told me he was single, Lacy. Said things with you were basically done. I had no idea. I would never have gone there if I'd known.

He played us both. Lied to both of us.

He said he regrets everything. That he still loves you.

I'm so sorry.

Lacy stared at the screen, her pulse flickering in her ears.

Her expression didn't change much—but Andrew caught it anyway.

He glanced up from the file he was flipping through, brows tightening. "What is it?" he asked gently. "You look like you just got hit."

She hesitated, phone still in her hand. "Ava. She finally talked to Patrick."

That made him pause. He set the file down, giving her his full attention. "Yeah?"

"She says… he told her he was single. That we were basically over. That he didn't want to get hurt." Her voice went flat. "She's saying he lied to both of us."

Andrew's jaw tightened, but it was the question in his eyes that landed first.

"Wait… how did she not know it was your Patrick?"

Lacy finally looked at him. "The girls only ever called him HC in the chat. Hot Chocolate. I never said his name out loud. Only Bree knew it."

She let out a dry laugh. "So maybe she really didn't know."

A beat passed between them.

"At first."

Andrew didn't say anything. But the way he was watching her said enough.

"And now?" he asked, quieter this time.

Lacy shook her head. "I don't know. I just… I need to get through this week."

As if summoned by the universe itself, there was a knock at her office door—quick, polite, but confident.

Lacy glanced up, already expecting another delivery. Instead, the door eased open and in stepped Lucas, portfolio in one hand, a to-go coffee tray in the other, and that signature easy charm playing at the corners of his mouth.

"Hey," he said, closing the door behind him with a soft click. "Hope I'm not interrupting. Brought the layout concepts by for the author showcase—figured you'd want a look."

Andrew, who had still been standing just a few steps away from her desk, turned at the sound of Lucas's voice. His gaze lingered on Lacy for a moment longer than necessary before he nodded.

"I'll catch you later," Andrew said quietly, his voice even, unreadable.

Lacy met his eyes but said nothing. She didn't know what to say—not with her heart still tangled and her mind barely keeping pace.
Andrew slipped out without another word.
Lucas raised a brow as he crossed the room. "Bad timing?"
Lacy exhaled. "You could say that."
"Didn't mean to crash anything," he said, placing the portfolio gently on her desk. "I just figured you could use a distraction. And caffeine."
He held out one of the cups like a peace offering.
She took it, managing a grateful smile. "You were right on both counts."
Lucas gave a modest shrug and pulled up the extra chair. "Then let's talk shop—and if we accidentally stumble into talking about life, well… so be it."
He spread out the designs, the scent of fresh coffee filling the space between them. His easy presence, the way he never demanded more than she could give, steadied her in a way she hadn't even realized she needed.
Because the fair was coming fast.
Because Patrick's shadow still clung to her.
Because Andrew feels so right.
And now—now Lucas was here.
And nothing in her world was as straightforward as it used to be.
The days leading up to the book fair were a blur of activity: finalizing contracts, coordinating schedules, and overseeing the design of marketing materials. Lacy worked tirelessly, fueled by a potent mix of adrenaline and pressure. Lucas, as one of the featured authors became an integral part of that rhythm. Their relationship had always carried an undercurrent of charm: coffee shop run-ins, light flirtation, conversations that danced at the edge of something deeper. But this? This was different. Working with him in an official capacity peeled back a new layer. She saw the focused, passionate side of him—the artist who cared deeply about his words, his message, the impact of his story. And he, in turn, saw her in her element: confident, decisive, the kind of editor who didn't just polish a manuscript but championed the person behind it.

The professional boundary between them gave her a buffer she didn't know she needed. It made things safer. Simpler.
She'd always known he was insightful, sharp in his quiet way, but seeing him navigate the publishing chaos with clarity and calm was something else entirely. His notes were thoughtful, his questions intentional, his ability to see the bigger picture uncanny. Their conversations—while still warm and easy—now held a different weight. He didn't just get her. He got the industry, the pressure, the unspoken politics of it all.
And somehow, amid the chaos, his presence grounded her. Not in a loud or sweeping way. Just… steady. And in a week where everything else felt tangled, that steadiness mattered more than she could admit.

Mrs. Eleanor Vance had been around more than usual lately—hovering just enough to make everyone sit a little straighter. With Delia gone, having accepted a senior role at another publishing house, the shift in the office was noticeable.
No formal announcement had been made yet, but the ripple effect was already there.
Surprisingly, Mrs. Vance had become something of a steady presence. Once skeptical of Lacy's abilities, she now recognized her talent and dedication—offering sharp critiques still, but now edged with something unexpected: encouragement. Even warmth.

One afternoon, after a particularly grueling editing session, she'd paused in Lacy's doorway.
"You have a gift," she'd said, her voice lower than usual. "You see the story before the author sometimes."
That compliment—quiet, unprompted—had stayed with Lacy far longer than any performance review or pay raise ever had.
The contrast between her professional triumphs and the complexities of her personal life was striking. And yet, in a strange way, it felt balanced.

The success at work grounded her, gave her a sense of self-worth that seeped into every other part of her life.

The fears hadn't vanished—but they no longer ruled her.

She was beginning to understand that strength didn't mean having all the answers. It meant showing up anyway—with grace, with grit, and with the quiet courage to keep going.

It had been several weeks since the wedding, and though the world had moved on, the pieces of Lacy's heart were still shuffling into place.

Luckily, the book fair had been a saving grace—a whirlwind of deadlines and logistics that kept her mind occupied and her hands too full to linger on anything else.

Patrick still called sometimes, but the frequency had waned. The barrage of texts had slowed. The flowers had stopped. The silence between them stretched wider with each passing day, and somehow, that hurt more than the noise.

Now, the evening before the event, the office buzzed with an energy that felt more electric than anxious. Mrs. Vance called an all-staff meeting, her usual polished tone replaced by a sharpened edge of urgency.

"Alright, team," she said, standing at the front of the conference room in her signature wrap dress and heels that somehow never clicked when she walked. "We are less than twenty-four hours out from the biggest book fair we've hosted in the last five years. That means I expect punctuality, professionalism, and presence. This is not the week for personal chaos. This is the week we shine."

Everyone speaking their affirmatives, some with more enthusiasm than others. Lacy sipped her lukewarm tea and took notes, her mind already jumping ahead to booth layouts, author check-ins, and whether the signage from the printer had actually arrived.

After the meeting, they did a final walkthrough of the event space. Tables were in place, banners hung, name tags sorted by alphabetical order. It was a beautiful kind of controlled chaos, and it oddly soothed her.

Andrew fell into step beside her as they did a last sweep of the vendor floor.

"It's coming together," he said, hands tucked into his pockets.

"It is," Lacy replied, offering him a tired but genuine smile.

They walked a few more steps in silence before he glanced sideways at her. "So… you and Lucas. You two seem—cozy."

She turned to him with a raised brow. "Cozy?"

Andrew shrugged. "I'm not prying. Just… observing."

Lacy huffed a quiet laugh. "We're friends. We like caffeine and sarcasm in equal measure."

"That's all?"

She stopped walking, turned toward him fully. "That's all."

He held her gaze for a beat longer than necessary before nodding. "Okay. Just asking."

They both called it a night shortly after, exchanging a quiet "see you tomorrow" before heading in opposite directions.

Lacy got home, kicked off her shoes, and was immediately greeted by the soft thud of paws hitting the floor. Leo trotted out from under the coffee table, tail high in the air, giving her a single, judgmental meow as if to say you're late.

"Hey, Leo," she sighed, bending down to scoop him up. He let her, purring as he nestled into the crook of her arm. "I missed you too."

After setting him down and refilling his food dish, she changed into her favorite oversized tee and climbed into bed. Leo leapt up gracefully beside her, circling once before curling into a ball at her feet.

Phone in hand, she pulled up Bree's contact.

The line rang once. Twice. Voicemail.

Not unusual lately.

She didn't even have time to feel disappointed before her screen lit up with a message.

Bree: Can I call you tomorrow? Everything okay?

Lacy: Sure. Everything is fine. TTYT

She tossed the phone onto the bed with a soft sigh, leaning back against the headboard.

Bree had been hard to reach since the wedding—not in a distant way, just busy. Honeymoon phase busy. Their talks had been reduced to rushed check-ins during her commute or late-night voice notes with bad Wi-Fi. Lacy understood. She really did. But she missed her sister. Missed the long talks and the comfort of being understood without needing to explain anything.

Her phone buzzed again.

Lucas: You're going to kill it tomorrow. Everything looks amazing. Proud of you.

She smiled, fingers hovering over the screen before she typed back.

Lacy: Thanks. I needed that.

Leo stirred at the sound of the phone, stretched his paws, then tucked his head beneath his tail.

And for a moment, the quiet didn't feel so lonely.

Tomorrow, the chaos would begin. But tonight, there was stillness. And that would have to be enough.

The morning of the book fair arrived wrapped in a steady drizzle that blurred the city skyline into muted gray. Lacy awoke early, nerves buzzing with anticipation and a splash of anxiety. She stood by her window for a moment, watching the rain bead against the glass before pulling herself into motion.

Today wasn't a day for second-guessing. Today, she had to show up.

She pulled her hair into a sleek low bun, letting a few loose tendrils frame her face. Her makeup was soft but precise—a warm neutral eye, bold eyeliner, and a dusty rose lip that gave her just enough color. From her closet, she chose a tailored navy jumpsuit with structured shoulders and a cinched waist that gave her an effortless silhouette. The fabric was rich and smooth, almost luminous in the dim light of her bedroom. She paired it with caramel-toned heels and a delicate gold chain around her neck—the one Bree gave her for her last birthday. A gold watch, a pair of minimalist hoops, and a structured camel trench coat completed the look.

She usually walked to work, but not today. The rain demanded otherwise. She drove, windshield wipers keeping rhythm with her thoughts, her breath fogging the glass until the car heater warmed the space.

When she arrived, the building was still cloaked in the quiet of early morning. Her heels echoed faintly through the polished marble foyer as she pushed open the doors. She was the first one there.

Well, almost.

"Morning, superstar," Andrew said, emerging from the hallway with a to-go coffee tray in hand and that familiar warm smirk tugging at the corner of his mouth.

She turned, surprised but smiling. "You almost had me."

"Close," he said with a wink, offering her a cup. "But technically, you beat me here."

They shared a quiet laugh, the tension easing slightly. Moments later, the unmistakable click of designer heels echoed through the space.

Mrs. Vance entered like she owned the morning. And in some ways, she did. Her white silk blouse was tucked immaculately into a high-waisted maroon pencil skirt that hugged her curves like it was tailored for no one else. A matching structured blazer with sharp lapels framed her regal posture. Her heels were Louboutin, red-soled and commanding, and her perfume trailed behind her in delicate floral notes that whispered old money. Her dark hair was pulled into a twisted chignon, not a single strand out of place, and her ruby earrings flashed every time she turned her head.

"Lacy, Andrew" she said with a gracious nod. "Everything looks stunning."

"Thank you, Mrs. Vance," We replied in unison.

"Let's make it a day to remember, shall we?"

And with that, the room seemed to wake up.

Staff began filtering in, setting up tables, arranging books in glossy towers, and placing placards with authors' names at signing stations. The scent of fresh coffee and rain-damp coats mingled with the rich aroma of paper and ink. The buzz of activity filled the air—phones ringing, voices coordinating, footsteps moving swiftly across the floor.

Then came Lucas. He arrived with a canvas tote slung over his shoulder and a rolled-up sketch pad in one hand. He looked effortlessly cool in a charcoal button-up with the sleeves half-rolled, dark jeans, and weathered leather boots. His hair, slightly damp from the rain, curled at the edges, and when he smiled at Lacy, it was the kind that settled warmly into your chest.

"You weren't lying. This place is buzzing," he said, setting down his things.

"Welcome to the chaos," she replied, her eyes catching his for a beat too long.

Andrew stood nearby, clipboard in hand, checking off names and micromanaging the schedule with his usual cool-headed precision. He moved like he belonged in every room, his calm presence making people feel steadied just by proximity.

The fair was officially underway. Attendees trickled in despite the weather, umbrellas folded and coats draped over arms as they browsed new releases and chatted with authors. A string quartet played softly in the background, and the smell of cinnamon pastries from the corner café wafted into the event space.

And then, just when Lacy thought she could breathe—

"Lace."

She turned.

Patrick.

He stood there, behind her, soaked slightly from the rain but composed, his tailored coat darkened at the shoulders, and in his hands—a bouquet of her favorite flowers: white peonies wrapped in kraft paper.

Her breath caught. For a moment, her body forgot how to move, her fingers tightening instinctively around the stems.

He gave her a small smile, one that didn't reach his eyes. "Saw these and thought of you. Figured you could use something beautiful today."

She took the flowers slowly, heart thudding. "Thank you... I didn't expect you to come."

"I wouldn't miss it."

And for a moment, all the noise around her—the music, the chatter, the movement—faded into something muffled, like she was underwater. Holding flowers in one hand and her composure in the other.

Chapter 13

"Girl. Patrick showed up? At the book fair? What the actual hell?"
Bree's voice cracked through the phone like a lightning bolt, and Lacy—bundled in her comfiest hoodie, Leo curled in her lap like a judgmental loaf—tilted her head back and stared at the ceiling.
"Yep," she said, her tone flat with disbelief. "Walked in like it was some rain-soaked rom-com. And of course he had peonies. White ones."
"Oh no. Not the peonies. He's going full sentimental sabotage."
Lacy huffed a laugh. "Right? I was just trying to make sure Mrs. Vance didn't eat the intern alive, and then boom—there he is. Just standing there with this sad little smile and a soggy bouquet like, 'Hi, remember me?'"
"Please tell me Andrew materialized out of nowhere like a security detail."
"Like he had a sixth sense. I swear, the man must've teleported."
Bree cackled. "I knew it! He's been on Patrick Watch since that whole Ava fiasco. Did he say anything?"
"Nope. Didn't have to. He just stood there, right next to me, all quiet backup energy. Lucas saw it too—he didn't come over, just kind of clocked it from across the room. He checked on me later, though."
"Damn. The tension in that room must've been crackling like bad wiring."
"It was… a lot. But Patrick left without causing a scene. I told him I'd listen. That's all I gave him."
"Which, coming from you—and considering where you are now—is a lot."
Lacy sighed, dragging her fingers through Leo's fur. He yawned like none of it was his business.
"Leo says I should've kicked him in the shins and kept it moving."
"Leo is a wise and ruthless feline," Bree chuckled.
Lacy smiled faintly. "Honestly, I didn't even tell Andrew that I agreed to meet up with him today. I just… needed to face it on my own first. You know?"

"I get it. You've been carrying it all in that cool, polished, 'I'm-fine-really' way. But we both know your version of fine usually involves emotional repression and reorganizing your kitchen drawers."
"That's... not inaccurate."
"But listen. You don't have to do this solo. We've got you. I've got you."
Lacy felt her throat tighten a little. "I know."
There was a beat of silence, heavy and grounding.
Then Bree added, "Okay but wait—were you wearing that navy jumpsuit yesterday?"
"Oh my god, Bree—"
"I knew it! You gave him Cinematic Main Character Energy. Man shows up drenched with flowers and there you are, looking like you just walked off a power editorial shoot."
Leo let out a meow, almost on cue.
"Even Leo agrees," Bree said smugly.
Lacy chuckled. "Y'all are chaotic."
"Chaotic and correct." Bree laughed

The late afternoon sun broke through the thinning clouds, casting a muted gold across Lacy's living room. Her apartment was quiet, except for the soft sounds of jazz streaming from her Bluetooth speaker and the rhythmic swish of Leo's tail as he lounged on the windowsill, watching the world. Lacy moved slowly through her space, tidying up—folding the throw blanket on the couch, rinsing a few dishes in the sink, fluffing the pillows she never let anyone sit on. It was her kind of decompression. The kind that asked nothing of her but presence. The events of the book fair still clung to her like perfume—faint but unmistakable. It had gone better than she could have imagined. Authors were thrilled, attendees lingered well past their allotted time slots, and the post-event buzz online was already calling it a revival.

It was the best book fair the company had ever had, and considering this was only their third attempt in ten years—and the first in five—that meant something. It meant she had done something. Something big.

She caught her reflection in the hallway mirror as she passed, bare-faced now, hoodie on, hair pulled into a loose braid. Still her. But steadier somehow.

Her phone buzzed on the coffee table, vibrating next to the half-folded laundry. She glanced at the screen, already expecting a "Great job!" text from one of the junior editors—or maybe Lucas, who'd sent her a doodle of a peony in her inbox earlier.

But it wasn't Lucas.

Patrick.

She stared at the name for a long second. Then she picked up.

"Hey," she said softly.

"Hey," he replied, voice quieter than usual. "Hope I'm not interrupting anything."

She sat on the armrest of the couch. "Just me and Leo. He's not great at conversation though."

A pause.

"Can I come over?" he asked. "I'd like to talk… properly."

Lacy's breath caught. She looked toward the kitchen, at the soft halo of afternoon light washing over the counter where the bouquet of peonies now sat in a mason jar. Too beautiful. Too tender to throw away.

Too much.

"I think… I'd rather meet somewhere," she said carefully. "Neutral ground."

"Neutral ground?" His tone sharpened. "I thought we were past the games, Lacy."

There was a pause, like he was trying to reel it back in.

"You said we'd talk. I assumed that meant at your place. Like we used to."

Lacy said nothing for a beat. She could hear the shift in him—tight, then tender, like he couldn't decide which version of himself would win her back.

"It's not that I don't want to see you," she added quickly, her voice trembling at the edges. "I'm just—my heart's still trying to catch up."

Patrick's reply came softer now. "I understand. Just tell me when and where."

"I'll text you," Lacy said with a sigh, the phone already starting to feel heavy in her hand.

They exchanged goodbyes, and Lacy set the phone down, pressing a hand to her chest.

Leo hopped down from the windowsill and rubbed against her ankle, his soft meow grounding her.

"Yeah," she murmured, bending to scratch behind his ears. "I'm not sure I'm ready either."

But she would show up anyway.

The café near Lincoln Square was tucked beneath the awning of a restored brownstone, its ivy-covered exterior glistening from the lingering drizzle. Late afternoon light filtered through antique windows, casting a golden hue over worn wood floors and weathered café tables, the air warm with the scent of cinnamon and freshly ground espresso.

Lacy arrived a few minutes early, stepping from the cab with her shoulders squared against the drizzle. She had dressed in quiet armor—a deep forest green midi dress that hugged her waist and flared at the hem, black suede ankle boots, a silver chain resting against her collarbone. Her camel trench was folded neatly over her arm. Her curls were loose today, soft around her face, a stark contrast to the tight rein she was keeping on her emotions.

Through the window, she spotted Patrick immediately.

He was already there, sitting at a corner table, hunched slightly over a mug, his signature white-and-red Jordans visible beneath the cuff of his jeans.

The same pair he always wore when he was nervous.
The familiarity of it all—of him—punched something deep in her chest.
Patrick looked up as she walked in, rising from his seat with a tentative smile that didn't quite hide the exhaustion in his eyes.
"Hey," he said, pulling out her chair for her like he always used to.
"Hey," she replied softly, sliding into the seat across from him.
For a moment, the world inside the café blurred into background noise—the low hum of conversations, the clink of coffee cups, the soft hiss of steam from the espresso machine.
"You look..." Patrick started, his voice rough, then softened into something almost reverent. "Beautiful."
Lacy gave him a small smile. "Thanks."
He nodded, running a hand over his jaw like he was bracing for impact.
"I didn't mean to make a scene at the book fair," he said, voice low.
"You didn't," she said simply. "It was... surprising. But not a scene."
"I just..." He stopped, exhaling through his nose. "I needed to see you. To remind you—"
He caught himself, the words dying before they could land.
"Honestly, I don't even know. I just needed to be near you."
Lacy folded her hands around the warm mug in front of her, steadying herself against the rush of old feelings.
"I get it," she said. "And... I appreciate the flowers. I do. But Patrick—"
She met his eyes evenly. "I'm still figuring out what I want. I'm not ready to promise anything."
He leaned in, elbows on the table, voice earnest. "I'm not asking for promises. I'm asking for a chance. Just a chance."
Before she could answer, her phone buzzed sharply on the table between them, the screen lighting up.
Andrew – Calling

Patrick's gaze flicked to the name.
Just once.

But it was enough.

The air shifted—sharp, immediate. Tension curled between them like smoke, tightening in her throat.
Lacy didn't move to answer.
The phone buzzed again, then stilled.

"You two talk a lot?" Patrick asked, tone light but laced with something colder.

She kept her voice even. "He's been a friend. Someone I can lean on."

Patrick nodded, slow and stiff. His jaw flexed, and this time he didn't bother to hide it.

"Right." A beat. "Always one of those, huh? The work friend. The quiet one waiting for his shot."

Lacy blinked. "That's not what this is."

He laughed once—low, humorless. "Sure. Until it is. I've seen that movie before."

Her stomach clenched. Not from what he said—but from how he said it.
The shift.
The edge in his voice.
The way the air suddenly felt too still.

"I wasn't going to explain," she said, thumb brushing the screen to silence the call, "but I do want to be honest. I'm still working through everything. That's not about Andrew. It's not even about you."

She paused, fighting the familiar tightness in her chest.
"It's about me."

His eyes didn't soften. His smile didn't reach anything.

"And what about what I'm working through, Lacy?" he asked, voice a shade too calm. "What I gave up? What I've been trying to hold together while you figure yourself out?"

The tone. The spin. The way he made her feel unreasonable for protecting herself.
Something in her twisted—a muscle memory from long ago. Warren. The way he'd press just hard enough to make her question herself. Make her shrink to keep the peace.
She took a breath, her fingers tightening around her mug.
She wanted to tell him no. That there would be no more talks. No more spinning.

But instead—

"Let's just take it one conversation at a time," she said quietly.

Not for him.
For her safety.
To end the moment before it turned into something uglier.
Patrick didn't smile.
He just nodded, slow and cold.
And that told her everything she needed to know.

The sky had shifted from gray to indigo by the time Lacy stepped out of the café. The rain had stopped, but the sidewalks still shimmered under the streetlights, slick with quiet.

The Uber ride home was silent—blessedly so.
It gave her space to breathe.
To replay every word. Every tone.
She hadn't expected to feel so unsettled. Not just by what Patrick said, but by what it stirred in her.
The edge in his voice. The spin. The way she'd felt herself shrink without realizing it. Again.
His presence was still familiar in all the ways that made her chest ache. But something deeper had shifted. Something in her was done pretending. She could feel it—like tectonic plates shifting beneath the surface. Subtle, but unstoppable.
Her phone buzzed again just as she stepped into her apartment. Leo greeted her at the door with a stretch and a yawn, then promptly wound himself around her ankles, purring like a motor.
Lacy set down her clutch, giving him a slow scratch behind the ears before checking her phone.
Andrew:
Just checking in. Everything okay?
She stared at the screen for a beat longer than necessary, thumb hovering.
Lacy:
Yeah. Just got home. Appreciated the call.
A typing bubble appeared almost immediately, then disappeared. Then appeared again.
Andrew:
Just wanted to make sure you're good.
Also—book fair numbers are already looking insane. You crushed it, Lacy.
Her lips twitched into a tired smile.
Lacy:
Couldn't have done it without you.
She hit send, then tossed the phone onto the couch and made her way to the kitchen. The kettle was already warming on the stove when she heard the soft ping of another notification.

She walked back over and picked up the phone.
Lucas:
Congrats again on yesterday. Coffee tomorrow? My treat before your day gets hijacked again
She didn't respond right away. Instead she called Bree.
No answer.
So she opened their group chat—silent since the wedding—and typed:
Lacy: Hey ladies, it's been a minute and radio silence since the wedding. Let's get together next month and celebrate each other at brunch! Who's all in?
It took a while, but the replies came in.
Bree: Yes!! Count me all the way in. Miss y'all so much!
Ava: I'm in! I'll bring the mimosas
Kayla: I'll fly in for it. Been needing a girls weekend. Let's gooo.
Nina: Same here. I'll plan a work trip around it
Chrissy: I'm in! Just tell me when and where
Janelle: Can't make it—family thing—but I want pics!!
Lacy smiled, warmth blooming in her chest. The thought of seeing everyone again—laughing, decompressing, just being—was something she hadn't realized she needed so badly.
She typed a quick message: Love y'all. Let's make it a thing. She also text Lucas: Thank you! That sounds like a plan! I will see you at our usual spot.
Leo nuzzled under her chin, and she let herself feel at peace.

The coffee house was unusually busy that morning. The soft hum of conversation and clinking ceramic cups filled the air, mingling with the scent of espresso and fresh-baked pastries. Rain still misted lightly outside, beading on the windowpanes and casting the room in a cozy, gray glow. Lacy stood in line, shifting her weight from one foot to the other as she scanned the crowd.

Lucas was already there—tucked into a corner booth near the window, sketchpad in front of him, coffee halfway gone. He spotted her, lifted a hand in an easy wave, and that familiar, crooked smile spread across his face. It hit her, unexpectedly, how comfortable that smile had started to feel.

She made her way over, brushing a few raindrops off the sleeve of her trench coat.

"Hey," she said, slipping into the seat across from him.

"Morning, Queen," Lucas said, his tone teasing but warm. "Didn't expect to be sharing you with half the city."

"I think the whole city showed up at this place today," Lacy replied, pulling her coat off and setting it beside her. "I had to fight a woman for the last parking spot."

Lucas smirked. "Did you win?"

"Barely. She flipped me off. I waved sweetly."

"That's my editor," he said, raising his coffee cup in mock salute.

A barista set Lacy's latte down with a practiced smile, and she took a grateful sip before settling back into the seat. Her gaze flicked to the sketchpad. "What are you working on?"

Lucas turned it around without hesitation. A rough but beautiful rendering of the book fair. It wasn't detailed yet, but the mood was unmistakable—the sweeping arches of the venue, the bustling energy of the crowd, and at the center, a soft figure in a jumpsuit holding a clipboard. Her.

Lacy blinked. "You sketched me?"

Lucas shrugged, looking uncharacteristically sheepish. "It was a moment. You looked... in your element."

A beat passed. She felt her cheeks flush slightly, unsure what to say, so she took another sip of coffee instead.

He watched her carefully. "How are you really doing, though?"

She hesitated, then smiled a little. "Honestly? Kind of tired. Kind of proud. Also, kind of... overwhelmed. The fair went better than I could've dreamed. It's the biggest success the company's had in years. But also..." Her voice softened. "Patrick showed up."

Lucas didn't flinch. His face remained open, but the light in his eyes dimmed just slightly.

"I saw," he said quietly. "Didn't want to crowd you. Figured you had enough going on."

"You were right. It was... a lot."

"You okay?"

"I think so. I met with him yesterday. We talked."

Lucas nodded slowly, not pushing. Just listening.

"I didn't tell anyone I was going," she admitted. "Not even Bree. Just needed to do it on my terms."

"Good," he said. "I mean, not that you went, but that it was your call. You deserve that."

Their eyes met across the table. Something unspoken passed between them—understanding, maybe. Or a quiet promise that there was room for more when the time was right.

Lucas leaned back, running a hand through his hair. "Well, for the record, you crushed it. Book fair, that is. You made magic."

Lacy smiled, this time fully. "Thanks. I needed to hear that."

The morning after the book fair buzzed with an energy Lacy hadn't felt in a long time. As she stepped off the elevator and into the office, she was met with a burst of applause. Nearly the entire staff had gathered near the front desk, clapping and cheering as she entered, their smiles wide and genuine.

Lacy blinked, startled but smiling. "Okay, okay—y'all are doing the most right now," she said, laughing as she placed a hand over her heart.

Mrs. Vance stepped forward from the center of the crowd, resplendent in an ivory sheath dress and a single strand of pearls. "And you deserve every bit of it," she said, her voice warm and commanding. "The numbers are in. Not only was this the best-attended book fair in our company's history—it was the most profitable. We brought in new authors, press coverage, and more buzz than we've had in years."

Applause rose again, and Lacy felt her chest swell with pride.

"This," Mrs. Vance continued, "was a team effort. And in recognition of that effort, corporate has approved a four-day, company-paid cruise—leaving in two weeks. Not everyone will be attending, of course, just our top executives and a select group of high-performing staff."

Heads turned. Emails pinged.

Lacy's phone vibrated in her hand—Cruise Itinerary: RSVP Required. She opened it quickly.

Congratulations, Lacy! You've been selected as part of the celebration cruise departing in two weeks. Please confirm your attendance by Friday.

She smiled and tapped YES, her pulse still racing from the announcement. Just as she tucked the phone away, another message buzzed in—this time from the group chat.

Kayla: Hate to do this, but I'm gonna have to miss the brunch. Work's a beast right now. I'll make it up to y'all with a weekend visit. Promise!

Lacy sighed but typed a quick reply:

Lacy: We'll miss you, but we'll hold you to that visit. Brunch won't be the same without your mimosa commentary.

The rest of her morning moved quickly—back-to-back meetings with new authors, follow-ups from the fair, and a conference call with a publisher on the West Coast. Everyone was riding the high of the fair's success, and Lacy found herself offering more handshakes, warm smiles, and congratulations than she could count.

Just as she wrapped up a final Zoom call, Andrew appeared in the doorway, holding a small stack of takeout menus in one hand and a mischievous grin in the other.

"You've officially been productive enough for one morning," he said. "It's time to eat, and I'm not taking no for an answer."

Lacy raised an eyebrow. "You came with menus?"

"I came with options," he corrected, stepping in and fanning them out like a blackjack dealer. "Thai, Indian, or that vegan place you pretend not to like but secretly love."

She laughed. "I do not secretly love it."

"You do. You're a tofu traitor."

"I hate you."

"No you don't," he said, settling into the guest chair across from her.

"Come on, Mrs. Executive Editor. What are we feelin'?"

Her phone buzzed.

Patrick: I know you're busy, but I just wanted to say I'm proud of you. The fair was amazing. Truly.

She glanced at the screen, let the message linger a beat too long, then set the phone aside.

"Indian," she said finally. "But only if you're getting the garlic naan this time."

"Done and done," Andrew said, already typing in the order.

The room settled into a warm rhythm—quiet, comforting.

Until her phone buzzed again.

Ava:

I've been holding this in, but I needed to tell you… I'm four months pregnant.

Lacy stared at the screen.

The words blurred.

Her pulse stuttered.

She blinked, read it again.

Then again.

Her stomach twisted—tight and low.

Andrew glanced up, catching the shift in her expression.

"What is it?"

She didn't respond.

Another message came through.

Ava:

It's Patrick's. I haven't told him yet. We've still been… talking. I don't know what I'm doing. I just… I needed you to know.

The phone slipped in her hand before she caught it, setting it down face-down like that could contain the scream rising inside her.

Andrew leaned forward, voice low and gentle.

"Lace?"

She pressed her palms to her thighs, grounding herself.

"Ava's pregnant," she said, her voice like glass.

A swallow.

"And it's Patrick's."

Andrew went very still.

For a long, suspended second, the only sound was the faint tick of the wall clock behind them.

"They've still been... talking," she added, barely more than a whisper. "This whole time. Even after... everything."

Andrew's jaw flexed, anger sparking behind his steady eyes, but he said nothing.

He didn't push.

Didn't offer useless words.

"Are you okay?" he asked quietly.

Lacy shook her head once, a small, broken movement.

"I don't know," she whispered.

Grief, betrayal, humiliation—all of it tangled in her chest so tightly she couldn't tell one feeling from the next.

Without a word, Andrew stood and crossed the small space to her side.

He didn't touch her—he just stood there. A quiet barrier between her and the world unraveling at her feet.

Lacy inhaled shakily and pressed her fingertips to her temple, trying to force the spinning to stop.

Four months.

That meant Ava had known.

Through the group chats, through the wedding planning, through the wine nights and brunches and inside jokes.
She had smiled.
She had hugged her.
And she had known.
The betrayal tasted different than Patrick's.
Sharper. Dirtier.
Like a cut she hadn't even seen until it was too late to stop the bleeding.
Lacy drew in another breath, shaky and uneven.
This wasn't the kind of surprise you smiled through.
It wasn't the kind that left space for healing.
It drew lines.
It made enemies.

Chapter 14

The knock on the door was hard enough to rattle the hinges.
Lacy jumped, her tea nearly slipping from her hand as Leo launched from his perch on the windowsill and bolted down the hallway. She wasn't expecting anyone, and after the last few weeks, surprise visitors set her on edge.
She crossed the apartment, heart already thudding. When she pulled the door open, the sight that met her made her stomach plummet.
Patrick.
Soaked from the rain, his hoodie clinging to his shoulders, his signature sneakers muddied at the soles. His eyes were wild—not angry, but desperate.
"Lacy," he said, voice rough. "You blocked me."
"No kidding." Her voice came out flat, arms folding tightly across her chest. "What are you doing here, Patrick?"
"I just found out—Ava told me I might be the father. I didn't even know until today. I tried calling, texting—I needed to talk to you."
Her jaw tightened. "You think showing up unannounced makes this better?"
"I didn't mean for any of this to happen. She said she was on birth control. I didn't think—" He dragged a hand through his wet hair, eyes pleading. "Yeah, I was still talking to her. But I thought we were done. You and me—we had a chance again, didn't we? I felt it."
"You don't get to say that." Lacy's voice cracked, and she hated it. "You don't get to stand there and act like you were all in with me when you were still sleeping with her."
Patrick stepped forward. "I didn't mean to hurt you, Lacy."
"But you did. Repeatedly." Her voice rose. "And what kills me is I almost gave you another chance. I wanted to believe you meant it when you said you loved me. But while you were handing me flowers, you were also giving Ava a family."

"That's not fair—"

"Fair?!" Her voice echoed off the walls. "Patrick, you lied to both of us. You chose this mess. And now you're here, hoping what? That I'll comfort you?"

He opened his mouth, but she was already shaking her head.

"No. I'm done. You don't get to use my door as a confessional." She stepped back and pointed. "Get out."

"Lacy—"

"Get. Out."

He hesitated, then turned and walked slowly down the hall. No dramatics, no final words. Just his retreating figure and the slamming door that followed.

Lacy stood still for a long moment, breathing hard. Her fingers trembled as she pulled out her phone and unconsciously dialed the one person who had always shown up for her.

"Hey," Andrew answered. "Everything okay?"

"No," she whispered. "Can you come over? I just—I need to get out of here."

"I'm on my way."

Fifteen minutes later, they were walking the quiet streets toward the park. The rain had stopped, leaving the air cool and damp, the trees glistening like glass sculptures under the streetlights. Lacy kept her hands in her coat pockets, head down. Andrew stayed beside her, giving her space, saying nothing until she was ready.

When she finally spoke, her voice was hoarse. "I thought I was done crying over him."

"You are," Andrew said gently. "This isn't crying for him. This is grieving what he took from you."

They walked until her shoulders loosened, until her breaths came a little easier.

They circled the park twice before Lacy's legs began to ache. The walk had helped—cleared her head just enough to remember who she was without Patrick's shadow looming overhead.

Andrew walked her back without a word, their silence easy, comforting. At her door, he lingered.

"I'm sorry," Lacy said, voice low.

"For what?"

"For calling you into my mess."

Andrew shook his head and stepped closer. "You're not a mess, Lacy. You're someone who just got dealt too much truth all at once. And I'll always show up for you."

She opened her mouth to respond, but the words got lost somewhere behind her ribcage. Instead, she stepped forward and wrapped her arms around him. He didn't hesitate—he held her tightly, the kind of embrace that made her feel like maybe everything would be okay after all. His warmth soaked into her bones, steady and quiet, like a long exhale.

When they pulled back, Andrew's hand reached up, almost instinctively, to wipe a tear from beneath her eye.

"Thank you," she whispered.

He held her gaze for a moment. And then—like something had shifted in the air between them—he leaned in and kissed her.

It wasn't a question. It wasn't confusion. It wasn't like their tipsy, uncertain kisses at the wedding.

This was deliberate. A moment anchored in something real. His lips were soft, his hand warm against her cheek, and when he finally pulled away, her breath was completely gone.

Lacy stood frozen, eyes wide, heart beating against the cage of her chest like it was trying to escape.

"I should go," Andrew said softly, but his smile was faint, knowing.

She didn't stop him. She couldn't. Not because she didn't want to—but because something inside her was still catching up.

The office was quieter than usual—less buzzing energy, more recovery mode.

Lacy had thrown herself back into her work like it was oxygen. Meetings, edits, check-ins with the new authors they'd landed from the fair. She barely had time to process anything beyond her calendar.

But the silence between meetings was brutal. Her thoughts wandered—back to Patrick's doorstep confession, Ava's message, and that kiss from Andrew that still lingered on her lips like a secret.

Mrs. Vance had been a whirlwind of motion all week, praising the entire team and teasing the upcoming cruise like it was a royal celebration.

Every time someone mentioned "Top Performer's Getaway" or "sunset cocktails," Lacy felt the tiniest flicker of hope—like the trip could be the break she didn't know she needed.

She sat through back-to-back meetings that morning, pitched two fresh authors, and even restructured one of the department's editorial calendars.

By noon, she was massaging her temples when a knock tapped at her office door.

Andrew, with a stack of takeout menus and a hopeful expression. "I know you're busy, but I'm also not above bribery."

She smiled despite herself. "I'm not hungry."

"Cool, then I'll just sit here and eat obnoxiously until you give in."

Ten minutes later, they were sorting through Thai and tacos, cross-legged on her office floor like college students. They didn't talk about their feelings. Not yet. But the way he looked at her—so steady, so sure—made her heart ache in a way that didn't hurt.

Later that afternoon, an email dinged across her screen with the cruise itinerary. She opened it, scanned the guest list, and smiled softly when she saw her name beside Andrew's.

Then, her phone buzzed.

Nina: "Hey babe, I hate to do this, but I'm gonna have to miss brunch. Work's a madhouse. BUT I promise I'll come visit the weekend after if you're around."

Lacy sighed but smiled. Another one down. Just a handful of them left now.
She minimized the message, pushed her chair back, and stared out the window.
Seven more days.
Ocean air, sunlight, maybe peace.
She could make it.

Each day crawled by, stretching longer than it had any right to. But somehow, Lacy managed to stay busy enough to keep the emotional mess at bay.
Tuesday brought in final edits on the big fall release. Her red pen flew across the pages, mind sharp, emotions dull. Leo had started sleeping at her feet when she worked late—his way of keeping her company without prying.
Wednesday, she and Andrew sat in on two strategy meetings with Mrs. Vance. When he passed her a note during a particularly dull budget breakdown, it simply read:
"Sunsets. You and me. Top deck. I'll bring the drinks."
She smiled, folded it into her planner, and never responded out loud.
By Thursday, the office was humming with cruise chatter. Outfit plans. Sunblock debates. Who was in charge of the playlist. Who was sneaking rum into checked luggage.
Lacy nodded along when asked if she was excited, smiled politely when her assistant asked about her beachwear plans. She even gave Kayla a thumbs-up in the group chat after seeing her Amazon haul of floaty maxi dresses and oversized sunglasses.
But truthfully, she hadn't packed a single thing.
That night, alone in her apartment with Leo curled on the windowsill, Lacy finally opened her suitcase. She tossed in clothes without thinking. A swimsuit she hadn't worn in years. The linen pants Bree swore made her look ten feet tall. A notebook. A pen. A single bottle of wine.

Just in case.

She paused only once—holding up the navy wrap dress she'd worn to the last author gala. The one Patrick had liked.

After a long beat, she folded it and put it back in her closet.

Friday morning came with the usual flurry—last-minute calls, signatures, and a full inbox. Mrs. Vance walked through the building like the cruise ship was already docked outside.

At noon, Lacy finally carved out a moment to decompress at her desk when a familiar knock came at the door. Lucas leaned in, smiling easy with two to-go cups in hand.

"Didn't think I'd see you before your big ocean getaway," he said.

"I wasn't sure I'd survive the week."

Lucas laughed, handing her the coffee. "You'll love it. Salt air clears the head."

"Are you speaking from experience or artistic exaggeration?"

"Both," he grinned, tapping the rim of her cup with his. "Bon voyage, Editor Extraordinaire."

He didn't stay long—just enough time for a little warmth, a little lingering look that reminded her how nice it was to be around someone who didn't need anything from her.

By the end of the day, her out-of-office reply was set, her desk was clean, and her nerves were finally humming with something that felt close to hope.

Maybe it was time to step away from the wreckage.

Maybe the ocean really could clear her head.

The morning of the cruise has finally arrived. Lacy stretched slowly, her arms reaching for the ceiling as sunlight spilled through the slats of her blinds. The soft rustle of waves from her white noise machine had already lulled her halfway into a vacation state of mind. She blinked at the ceiling, a giddy smile creeping across her face.

Cruise day.

The thought rolled over her like a warm breeze.

Her phone buzzed on the nightstand, and without looking, she answered the FaceTime call.

"Girl!" Bree's face filled the screen, framed by her silk bonnet and oversized coffee mug. "It's cruise day! You up? You ready? Are you packed?"

"I'm up," Lacy said, still nestled in her sheets, voice groggy but smiling. "Mostly packed. Final touches after coffee."

"You better be more than mostly packed," Bree said, eyes narrowing with mock suspicion. "You know cruises wait for no one. I need you in that port on time, living your best life."

"I got this. I even printed my boarding pass like a real adult."

Bree snorted. "Okay, okay. Proud of you. But for real, listen—first-time cruiser tips. One: pack a swimsuit in your carry-on. Don't be that girl waiting on her luggage while everyone else is on the pool deck with a drink in hand."

"Duly noted."

"Two: pace yourself with the food. It's all delicious until day three when you start dreaming of vegetables."

Lacy laughed. "Why is that so specific?"

"Because I lived it. And three: flirt with somebody. Just one person. For the vibes."

Lacy raised a brow. "You're ridiculous."

"I'm right," Bree said. "And you deserve to be seen and spoiled, not stressed and dodging drama."

The mood shifted slightly, and they both knew why.

Lacy sighed, tugging the sheet up to her chest. "Ava left the group chat."

"Because I told her she was outta line," Bree said without hesitation. "She should've said something. I tried to be gentle—tried to be fair. But I'm not about to make space for someone who hurts my people and then acts like it's all love."

Lacy nodded. "I don't blame you."

She stared at the ceiling for a moment, jaw tightening.
"When I first met her… I had a feeling."
A bitter laugh slipped out. "I shrugged it off. Didn't want to be that girl who assumes things. Guess I should've listened to myself."
"You were right," Bree said firmly. "But being right doesn't always make it hurt less."
Lacy exhaled slowly. "It's not even about her anymore. It's the knowing. That she knew… and still chose what she chose."
"I know, Lace. I know," Bree said, softer now. "But this trip? It's your line in the sand. Leave that mess on the dock. Go, breathe. Be soft again."
They talked a little longer—about brunch plans still moving forward even if they were a few girls short, about Leo's temporary food handler's license (aka her assistant, Jasmine, who'd happily agreed to feed him), and about Lacy's list of outfits. Bree demanded pictures.
Once they hung up, Lacy showered and got dressed, leaning into easy chic: a flowy pale-blue maxi dress cinched at the waist, oversized sunglasses, and her hair freshly braided into neat, mid-back-length twists. She pinned a few away from her face, letting the rest fall gracefully down her back. Her favorite travel tote was packed with the essentials—lip gloss, sunscreen, a paperback, and Dramamine.

She did one final sweep of the apartment—dishes done, lights off, food and water bowls filled. Leo flicked his tail at her in protest before hopping onto the windowsill, the very picture of dramatic indifference.
"I'll be back before you can miss me," she whispered, reaching up to scratch under his chin.
Her phone buzzed just as she slid into the back of her rideshare. A text from Andrew.
Andrew:
So I just found out you blocked my number… Oh wait. Wrong dramatic moment.

Just wanted to say I could've picked you up this morning, but I'll forgive you if you let me carry your bags again.

Also—first cruise too. So we're in this together. No pressure. Just adventure.

Lacy couldn't help it—she smiled at the screen, the kind of smile that warmed her chest before it reached her face.

Lacy:

I'll let you carry one bag. Maybe.

Let the adventure begin.

Chapter 15

The port was buzzing with life—families, couples, and wide-eyed first-timers rolling suitcases behind them, all funneling toward the towering cruise ship gleaming in the morning sun. It rose like a floating palace above the docks, sleek and elegant, the painted name arched in bold lettering across the side.

Lacy stepped out of the rideshare and took a moment to drink it all in. The salty breeze caught the hem of her soft linen wrap dress, and she felt it flutter around her legs like the first note of a song she already knew she'd love.

She had traveled before—girls' trips, solo getaways, even a few work retreats—but never a cruise. Once she got married, those spontaneous adventures became rare, then nonexistent. A cruise had always lingered on her list of "someday"s. And now, standing at the edge of something so grand and unfamiliar, her heart did a quiet leap.

"Okay, Lacy," she whispered to herself, popping the trunk and eyeing her embarrassingly large suitcase. "Definitely not your usual carry-on kind of trip."

As if summoned by the thought, a voice called out from behind her. "Need a hand?"

She turned just as Andrew stepped out of a sleek blue BMW x6, effortlessly handsome in a crisp white polo, tailored navy slacks, and those aviators that made him look like a GQ cover model with too much charm. His duffel bag was slung over one shoulder like it weighed nothing.

Lacy's breath hitched for a fraction of a second—not from surprise, but from the way he looked at her. Like the ship wasn't the only thing gleaming that morning.

"I packed light," she said with a grin, gesturing to her full-sized suitcase, a carry-on, and her oversized tote.

He chuckled, already reaching for the handle. "Looks like you're moving in."

"Four days is not overnight," she said, arching a brow. "Besides, I came to enjoy myself."

Andrew's smile widened. "Good. That's the plan."

They wheeled their luggage toward the check-in line together, falling into easy conversation as passengers boarded in clusters. The terminal buzzed with that electric energy only the beginning of a vacation could bring—half anticipation, half disbelief that real life had been successfully paused. As they stepped onto the ship, a wave of cool air and fresh citrus scent swept over them, the entryway grand and golden with gleaming floors and sweeping staircases. Staff in polished uniforms greeted them like royalty. They made their way to the staff meeting point near the atrium, where the rest of their coworkers had begun to gather in little groups, laughter echoing under the vaulted ceiling. Lacy glanced around, catching the familiar faces of editors, designers, and marketing leads—everyone dressed down, but glowing, like they'd already shed the stress of deadlines.

Then came Mrs. Vance, standing off to the side with a man none of them had ever seen before. She was all elegance in a flowy silk kaftan and oversized sunglasses, her trademark poise still intact, but the sharp edge dulled by what looked suspiciously like vacation joy. Lacy smirked. Andrew leaned in and said low, "I don't know who that man is, but she hasn't stopped smiling since they got on board."

Lacy laughed. "That's not our Mrs. Vance."

He nudged her. "She's undercover."

As room assignments were handed out and the group started to disperse, Lacy looked up at the open decks stretching above her, the ocean just beyond the glass walls, the thrum of the ship's engines beneath her feet. It was like being on a floating five-star resort. Everything gleamed—from the towering glass atrium to the marble floors that caught the afternoon light just right. The grand chandelier above the central staircase sparkled like ice suspended in air. Music played faintly, jazzy and luxe, a soundtrack to the hum of excited guests mingling and exploring.

Most of the staff group veered off toward the right with a cheerful cruise coordinator. But Mrs. Vance, perfectly put together in a tailored cream linen set and oversized sunglasses, glanced over her shoulder.

"This way," she said smoothly, and Lacy and Andrew exchanged a look, their interest piqued as they followed her in the opposite direction.

"I feel like we're being recruited for something secret," Andrew murmured as they passed through a more exclusive corridor, this one noticeably quieter, more refined.

"I wouldn't be mad about it," Lacy whispered back, half-smiling.

They took a glass elevator up several floors, the blue of the ocean stretching endlessly on the horizon beside them. At the top, a staff member in a pressed white uniform greeted them by name and handed each of them personalized keycards.

"This is… definitely not window suite territory," Andrew said, just as Mrs. Vance paused at a polished hallway with a subtle velvet rope—one that the attendant quietly removed to let them through.

She turned to face them with a rare, sincere smile.

"The book fair was a turning point for this company," she said simply. "And it would not have been possible without you two. These are balcony suites—our thanks to you both for exceeding every expectation. Enjoy yourselves. You've earned it."

Then, with a nod that somehow still managed to feel regal, she disappeared into her own suite two doors down.

Lacy blinked and turned toward her door. The keycard slid in with a satisfying click.

The door swung open.

"Oh. My. God."

The suite was something out of a travel magazine—no, a dream. Spacious and glowing in soft natural light, the room had sleek, modern furnishings with gentle nautical touches. Pale driftwood floors, a king-sized bed dressed in crisp white linens with a navy throw at the end, and plush seating arranged near a glass coffee table. A vase of fresh orchids sat in the center, subtly perfuming the air.

But it was the floor-to-ceiling sliding glass doors that stole her breath. They opened out onto a private balcony, the ocean so close it felt like it was reaching for her. Two cushioned loungers waited outside, angled perfectly for sunrise or sunset views.

The bathroom was all luxury: double vanity sinks, a rainfall shower with built-in bench, and complimentary spa products lined like little gifts on the counter.

A chilled bottle of sparkling water and a personalized welcome note sat on the table:

Welcome aboard, Lacy! Here's to four unforgettable days at sea. — Your Cruise Concierge

She flopped onto the bed and let out a low, giddy laugh.

A knock came at the door, and she opened it to find Andrew leaning in the doorway of his suite across the hall.

"So," he said, arms crossed but eyes bright, "Wanna pretend we're royalty for the next four days?"

She grinned. "Only if we get to act completely spoiled about it."

"Deal."

Before the cocktails and celebrations could kick off, Lacy and Andrew were ushered with the rest of the company group into the Coral Theater—a sleek, modern space with tiered seating, polished chrome railings, and a ceiling dotted with lights that mimicked stars.

The ship's cruise director, a sharply dressed man with boundless energy, took the stage with a wide grin.

"Welcome aboard the Celestia Maris! Over the next four days, you'll explore three ports, enjoy gourmet dining, live entertainment, and more fun than you know what to do with. But first—let's talk safety."

A short but engaging video began to play on the large screen behind him, walking guests through muster stations, life jacket locations, and emergency evacuation procedures. The charming animation and subtle humor kept the mood light. It wrapped with a firm but friendly: "Now that we've got the serious stuff covered, let's get to the good part!"

The director returned to highlight the daily itinerary, pointing out special events like poolside yoga, wine tastings, trivia nights, and the captain's dinner on Day 3.

"For those of you here with a corporate group," he added, "your company has reserved a few private events—including a sunset cocktail hour and a private excursion at our second port. Details will be delivered to your stateroom daily."

Mrs. Vance barely reacted to the mention of private events, but Lacy caught the knowing glint in her eye.

With that, the lights came back on and the guests began to scatter—some to the deck, some to explore, and others to stake out loungers by the pool. Andrew leaned toward Lacy as they stood.

"So… yoga in the morning?" he teased, eyebrows raised.

"I'm on vacation," she grinned. "I'll be sleeping in and eating things with extra syrup. And with that Im hungry, lets find food"

They wandered toward one of the open-air decks, drawn by the scent of something buttery and fried drifting on the breeze.

"I'm starving, too," Andrew said, scanning the row of food stalls tucked along the outer promenade. "Think they've got anything dangerously greasy?"

Lacy chuckled. "If they don't, it's not a real cruise."

They ended up sharing a basket of truffle fries and skewers from a pop-up tapas stand, shaded by oversized striped umbrellas. The ocean breeze swept over them, warm and salty, and below, the buzz of voices rose from the lower decks where the Sail Away Party had kicked off in full swing—music pumping, staff tossing leis around guests' necks, the ship gently swaying as it began to pull away from port.

Andrew nodded toward the festivities. "Want to check it out?"

Lacy hesitated, then shook her head with a lazy smile. "Nah, I want to be fresh for dinner. I think I'll go wash the travel off, maybe try on a few dresses I packed last-minute and pretend I didn't stress over them for a week."

He laughed, tipping his water bottle in salute. "Fair. I'll go see what the hype's about and report back."

They parted at the elevator bank with a shared grin and an unspoken "see you later." The short walk to her stateroom gave Lacy a moment to breathe in the view from the top deck—sapphire waves glinting under a cotton candy sky. The ship had left the shore behind, and with it, the stress of the last few weeks. Her room greeted her like a quiet luxury, and after a cool shower,

She stepped onto her private balcony wrapped in a towel, letting the breeze dry her skin.

The sun was dipping low, melting into the horizon in a blaze of amber and rose. The ocean sparkled like it had been kissed by firelight, and the salty air danced across her skin, cool against the warmth left by her shower. Lacy closed her eyes and breathed it in—the sea, the hush of waves, the faint sound of laughter rising from lower decks. It was magic, and it was hers for the next four days.

She leaned against the railing, towel cinched just above her chest, letting the breeze run through her braids. There was a small thrill in it. Unrushed. Indulgent.

Free.

Finally, she stepped back inside.

The suite around her was hushed, cast in the dim, golden glow of the setting sun filtering through the sheer curtains. Lacy dropped the towel and reached for the emerald satin gown she had hung hours earlier.

The dress she choose felt like poetry—fluid, sleek, and lush as it draped over her. It hugged her curves in all the right places and moved with the grace of ocean water. The back dipped daringly low, while the neckline swept across her collarbone with an understated elegance. Her skin, still kissed by the sun, shimmered softly under the dim lights.

She pinned her braids into a loose crown, gold cuffs catching glints of light. A few tendrils were left out on purpose, framing her face like brushstrokes. Her makeup was dewy and effortless, all glowing bronze and soft shimmer, with a glossy nude lip that said she wasn't trying—but was absolutely winning.

Gold hoops, a dainty chain, a single cuff bracelet. Metallic heels that made her feel a little dangerous.

She gave herself one final once-over in the mirror, tilting her head as the last rays of the sun painted the room with golden warmth. Her heart fluttered. The first formal night of the cruise. A fresh chapter. A new version of herself.

Yeah. She was ready for this.

By the time she stood in front of the mirror, zipping up her dress, Lacy felt lighter. Ready.

And so the evening began.

The first formal dinner was held in the main dining room, a grand, glittering space that looked like it had been plucked straight from a dream. Chandeliers floated like constellations overhead, casting soft gold light across rich mahogany tables and crystal-clear glasses that caught the sparkle. Velvet-lined chairs and gleaming silverware completed the scene, and as the staff began to usher in guests dressed in their finest, the air buzzed with elegance, celebration, and just the right hint of flirtation.

Lacy arrived a few minutes early, her heels clicking over the polished marble floor as she stepped into the foyer just outside the dining room. She was still smoothing her dress, tugging gently at the fabric across her hips, when she heard a low whistle behind her.

"Wow."

Her fingers froze.

She turned slowly, and there he was.

Andrew stood just inside the entrance, freshly shaved and impossibly elegant in a tailored black tux that fit like it had been made for his body alone. A crisp white shirt opened just enough at the collar to keep things interesting, and a slim black bow tie was expertly knotted beneath a chiseled jawline. His skin glowed warm beneath the light, and his deep brown eyes—always so composed—drank her in with open admiration. His gaze swept over her from head to toe, lingering at the subtle shimmer of her dress, the way her braids framed her face, the confidence in her posture. A slow smile spread across his lips, equal parts charm and heat. "You look…" he stepped closer, eyes locking with hers, "like you walked off the cover of a magazine. No—scratch that. They'd be lucky to have you."

Lacy's breath caught.

Andrews eyes flicked to her lips for a fraction of a second before returning to her eyes, softer now, sincere. "Seriously, Lace… you're stunning."

She swallowed hard, heart thudding against her ribs. "I can't lie… you're really trying to test my focus tonight. I didn't realize we were dressing to destroy."

He grinned, that teasing spark back. "So you're saying I clean up well?"

"I'm saying," she stepped a little closer, "if there's a Best Dressed award, you might actually give me competition."

They stood there, a beat too long, heat simmering just beneath the surface. The kind of moment that stretched out, wrapped around them, and made the rest of the world blur.

A bell chimed softly, signaling the opening of the main dining room doors. Andrew offered his arm. "Shall we?"

Lacy nodded, slipping her hand into the crook of his elbow, and together, they walked in.

The main dining room glowed under crystal chandeliers, each table set with gleaming silverware and delicate candlelight that flickered like stars above fine china. Floor-to-ceiling windows showcased the ocean wrapped

in dusk, while soft music from a live string quartet gave everything an effortless elegance. The company had arranged seating by department, most of the staff seated in lively clusters. But Lacy and Andrew were at a two-top by the window, with a view so breathtaking it felt curated—just like the seating arrangement.
She raised an eyebrow as she took her seat. "So, we're the only ones who got the private upgrade?"
Andrew gave her a slow grin, leaning in slightly. "Might've run into Mrs. Vance while you were decompressing. Asked if we could skip the group table."
Lacy blinked, both surprised and impressed. "You just… asked?"
"She was surprisingly cool about it. Said something like 'You two earned it.' I think she winked, but that could've been the wine in her hand."
Lacy laughed, unfolding her napkin. "So you're charming even Mrs. Vance now?"
Andrew picked up his glass and clinked it lightly against hers. "I'm charming when it counts. And let's be real, I didn't want to share you with payroll and marketing tonight."
She smirked, swirling her wine. "Possessive. Bold move, Mr. Mitchell."
"I said what I said," he replied, biting into a roll like he wasn't affected—but his eyes lingered on her a beat too long.
Their conversation meandered through sharp observations and inside jokes—who would win the onboard trivia championship (Lacy, obviously), how they'd both nearly got lost trying to find their rooms, and why the onboard espresso bar should be considered a miracle of modern travel.
"Okay, but be honest," he said, slicing into his filet. "Would you rather eat dinner with the authors from your most recent submissions… or the legal team?"
Lacy snorted. "That's evil. Authors. At least they're creative when they spiral."
"Legal's more dramatic though."
"Not in a fun way," she deadpanned.

As dessert arrived—a trio of artfully plated sweets that looked like they belonged in an art gallery—Andrew eyed Lacy's untouched strawberry tart.

"You're not gonna eat that?" he asked.

"It's too pretty to ruin." she said

"Then I'll ruin it for you." He reached across with his fork.

She blocked him without missing a beat. "Touch it and you're going overboard. And I'm not jumping in after you."

He laughed, sitting back, utterly unbothered. "Noted. No dessert theft. Still worth the risk."

Lacy finally gave in, taking a small bite and groaning softly. "Okay. Maybe it's worth sharing."

Andrew leaned in again, quieter this time. "You really do look incredible tonight." She glanced at him, warmth creeping up her neck despite the breeze from the nearby doors. "Thank you. And you… you wear that suit like it was custom-written into your DNA."

"Custom-written?" he smirked. "I like that. Might have it printed on my business cards."

She laughed behind her glass. "You'd cause a suit shortage if you made that your brand."

Their eyes met across the table, the banter giving way to something slower, deeper. The room blurred for a moment, the sounds around them softening, until the music shifted and the waitstaff began clearing plates.

Andrew finally leaned back, stretching just a little. "Think they'll kick us out if we stay here until breakfast?"

"I don't know," Lacy said, gathering her clutch with a sly smile, "but I'm definitely not sharing my tart if we do."

After dinner, they explored the upper deck, stopping by a lounge where live jazz played under dim lighting. They didn't dance, but they stayed for a while, sipping nightcaps and soaking in the music. The leather armchairs were plush, the bartender's pour was generous, and Andrew found an espresso martini that made him dramatically declare he was never leaving the ship.

Lacy, toes still tingling from her heels, sipped her bourbon cocktail with a citrus twist and leaned back with a sigh. "Why does everything taste better on a cruise?"

Andrew raised his glass. "Because there's no one here to judge how many you have."

"That sounds dangerously accurate," she said, her smile slow and amused. When they finally decided to head back, they took the long way. The ship rocked gently beneath their feet, and the ocean air wrapped around them—warm, salty, and just soft enough to make the moment stretch.

Halfway to their room, Lacy paused and slipped off her heels with a dramatic sigh of relief.

"That's it. My feet have surrendered."

Andrew turned to see her barefoot, holding her heels like a proud rebel. "You okay, Cinderella?"

"I'm thriving," she said, swinging the shoes by one finger. "But I'm not responsible if I start skipping."

"That's fair," he said, taking her shoes and offering his arm. "Allow me to escort your royal barefootness."

They got turned around somewhere near a stairwell that didn't lead where they thought it would. "Weren't we supposed to turn at that big glass sculpture thing?" Lacy asked, squinting.

Andrew looked around. "There are, like, six big glass sculpture things. This ship has a theme."

"Luxury maze?"

"Exactly," he laughed. "Okay, new game. We only get three wrong turns before we have to ask for help."

"Challenge accepted. But if we find the room first, you owe me another espresso martini tomorrow."

"Deal."

They wandered past a closed art gallery, accidentally stumbled into a karaoke bar mid–Whitney Houston tribute, and discovered a quiet sundeck with lounge chairs that faced the sea, empty and peaceful under the stars.
"Okay, this is kind of perfect," Lacy murmured, resting her arms on the railing.
Andrew stood beside her, the light from the moon casting a soft glow on both of them. "You sure you still want to go back to the room?"
She tilted her head. "If we don't, I'm taking a nap right here. Barefoot and all."
He grinned. "Tempting, but I don't want you waking up to pool towel patrol."
They eventually found their suite—three wrong turns later—and Andrew triumphantly pointed to the door. "We made it. Just in time for room service and highly questionable decisions."
Lacy laughed as she punched in her keycard. "No questionable decisions yet. Just... a little buzz and an early appreciation for cruise life."
He leaned against the doorframe, not quite ready to say goodnight. "First day down. You having fun?" She glanced over her shoulder at him. "More than I expected. You?"
"I'd follow you barefoot through any luxury maze," he said with a smirk.
Lacy shook her head, biting her smile. "You're ridiculous."
"Accurate."
She slipped inside, still smiling. "Goodnight, Andrew."
"Night, Lacy."
The door clicked shut, but her grin lingered.

Chapter 16

The next morning on the ship began with sunlight slipping between the sheer curtains of Lacy's balcony door. She stretched beneath the cool sheets, eyes already open. For a second, she thought she'd caught the sunrise—but a glance at her phone told her she'd missed it by fifteen minutes.

She sighed, not quite disappointed, and lingered a moment longer before finally sliding out of bed. The balcony breeze teased her braids as she stepped outside, arms outstretched, wrapped in one of the plush, hotel-quality robes the cruise line so kindly provided. Below, the sea sparkled like scattered diamonds, and the hum of distant waves reminded her she wasn't in the office, or at brunch, or anywhere but exactly where she needed to be.

She made her way to the ship's café, sunglasses on, lips glossed, slides clicking against the polished deck. She ordered a cappuccino, a fresh fruit cup, and a buttery croissant that flaked apart the moment she picked it up. Every table had a view, and Lacy picked one overlooking the ocean, letting herself simply breathe.

Not ten minutes into breakfast, her phone buzzed.

Andrew: You missed the sunrise. Amateur move.
Lacy: I was fifteen minutes late. That's fashionably late.
Andrew: I'm fashionably located at the pool deck. Come find me.
Lacy: Is this the beginning of a treasure hunt?
Andrew: Yes. X marks the lounge chair with the hot guy holding two smoothies.
Lacy: Be right there.

She swapped her robe for a sleek, high-cut two-piece in soft ivory that made her sun-kissed, carmel skin glow and highlighted every sculpted curve—thank you, Pilates. A light linen cover-up drifted around her as she walked, more for style than modesty, doing nothing to hide how incredible she looked. Lacy felt good—better than good. This was her moment, and she owned every step of it.

When she stepped onto the pool deck, sunlight danced over her skin like it had been waiting all morning just to show her off. A few heads turned, but only one reaction mattered.

Andrew.

He was stretched out in a lounge chair like he had no worries in the world, mirrored sunglasses on, two smoothies—one green, one orange—resting on the table beside him. But the second he caught sight of her sauntering his way, he sat up fast, sliding off his shades like he wasn't sure his eyes were working right.

"Amazing," he said, voice low and full of quiet admiration.

His gaze moved slowly, deliberately, taking her in like she was some kind of vision—and maybe, in that moment, she was.

"You look absolutely stunning. Thank you Pilates!" he grinned

Lacy smirked as she took the green smoothie from his hand and settled into the chair beside him. "I thought the same thing when I looked in the mirror. Pilates is the ish"Lacy laughed

Andrew laughed with her, dragging his gaze away long enough to recover. "Mission accomplished."

Lacy sipped her smoothie, lips curving into a smug little smile. If this was how day two started, she couldn't wait to see what came next.

The pool deck was already buzzing. Music played from hidden speakers. A few families splashed in one section, while most of their fellow coworkers lounged or hovered near the swim-up bar, clearly embracing vacation mode. Mrs. Vance was nowhere to be seen—possibly still in her chic mystery disguise.

"Want to hit the excursion fair later?" Andrew asked. "They're doing sign-ups for tomorrow's port stop. Beach day or hiking or something with ATVs."

"Yes," Lacy said, "to whatever includes sunscreen, snacks, and minimal chance of injury."

He laughed. "You're the dream travel companion."

By mid-morning, they joined a few colleagues for a round of mini-golf—surprisingly competitive and complete with pirate-themed obstacles. Lacy nailed a hole-in-one and didn't let Andrew forget it for the rest of the game. They lost track of time wandering through the art gallery, laughing at a few abstract pieces and pretending to critique like seasoned collectors. After lunch at the open-air bistro (ahi tuna sliders for Lacy, gourmet flatbread for Andrew), they hit the top deck where a pop-up dance class was drawing a small crowd. Lacy couldn't resist. Andrew claimed two left feet—until he realized she was going to join with or without him.

They spent the next thirty minutes learning a salsa-inspired routine from a cruise staffer with far too much rhythm and an encouraging smile. Lacy laughed so hard she almost missed a step. Andrew surprised them both by keeping up.

By the time late afternoon rolled around, they were both sun-kissed, slightly salty from sea air, and completely relaxed.

"I'm officially convinced cruise life is my real life," Lacy said as they strolled back toward their rooms, already talking about naps and the evening's dinner theme.

Andrew nodded, grinning. "You were made for this. Barefoot mazes, sunrise misses, and dance battles."

She arched a brow. "Careful, you're starting to sound like someone who's having a good time."

"I plead the fifth." he laughed.

Evening settled slowly over the ocean, the horizon dipped in watercolor shades of apricot and rose. Lacy stood barefoot in her suite, hair in a loose wrap, scrolling through her phone when a message buzzed in from Andrew.

Andrew: Come to my room. Comfy clothes. Sunset surprise.

Her brows lifted in amusement, curiosity blooming behind her eyes. She slipped into soft lounge pants and a fitted tank top, tossed a cozy cardigan over her shoulders, and padded barefoot across the hall to Andrew's suite. When she knocked lightly, the door swung open almost immediately.
"Perfect timing," Andrew said, stepping aside.
Lacy took one step in and stopped, breath catching just behind her lips.
His balcony had been transformed.
All the furniture was cleared except for a wide cushioned nest of pillows and blankets spread across the entire space—layered throws, oversized cushions, her favorite plush textures. The lounge chairs had been moved inside, and the sliding glass doors were open wide, letting in the breeze and the distant hum of the sea. Soft flickers of artificial flame danced in safe corners of the room, casting a warm, golden glow.
On a small table nearby, her favorite snacks were laid out—dried mangoes, dark chocolate-covered almonds, popcorn dusted in truffle salt. And two glasses of chilled white wine waiting, catching the last blush of the sunset.
"You did all this?" she asked softly.
She turned to face him. Her throat tightened unexpectedly — no one had done something like this for her in a long time.
Andrew shrugged. "I've been told I'm an overachiever."
"You remembered all my favorites."
"I pay attention."
Lacy smiled—soft and full—and let herself sink into the cozy setup, folding her legs under her. Andrew sat beside her, kicking off his shoes and settling in just close enough to brush her shoulder with his.

For a few minutes, they simply watched the sun dip behind the sea, casting a soft golden veil over the horizon.

Then, Andrew turned to her, voice quieter. "Can I ask you something personal?"

Lacy hesitated, then nodded. "Yeah."

"You once said there was a reason you didn't want to live with Patrick... and you don't talk much about your past. What really happened?"

She didn't answer right away. Instead, she took a sip of wine and stared out at the ocean, the waves soft and patient.

"I was married once," she said eventually, her voice steady. "Ten years. Most people don't know because... I don't bring it up. Not because I'm ashamed. I just... I've done the work. Bree helped. Therapy helped. But I don't carry it with me anymore."

Andrew watched her, giving her the space to continue.

"He was very controlling. At first, it was small stuff—how I dressed, how I wore my hair, how much I spent on coffee. Then it turned into who I could talk to, when I could leave the house, and where I could work. I stopped recognizing myself. I wasn't Lacy anymore. I was his idea of me. It was very toxic and eventually abusive."

Her voice wavered, but she kept going.

"I left with nothing. Literally. Bree picked me up in the middle of the night, while he was out yet again doing God knows what. I was scared, broke, and I lived in her guest room for a while. I climbed my way back piece by piece. That's why I love my independence. I finally got it back, after loosing it for so long."

Andrew reached over, gently taking her hand in his. For a moment, neither of them spoke. The hush between them was full but unpressured.

Then he said quietly, "I loved someone like that once. Not in the same way—but deep. She was my high school sweetheart. We dated for years, and I was ready to do long distance when I left for college. But she thought it would be easier to break up and stay friends."

Lacy glanced over, listening closely.

"We tried. The friendship didn't hold. And even though I said I understood, the truth is—I was heartbroken. I wanted to marry her one day. Have kids. I thought she was it."

He paused, running a hand along the railing.

"Eight years later, I ran into her at a publishing conference. We picked things up like no time had passed. It felt easy again. Comfortable." He gave a small, wistful smile. "But we weren't the same people anymore. I was deep into building my career, and she wanted the marriage, a family, the whole nine. And I couldn't give her that. Not then."

Lacy tilted her head. "Do you want kids now?"

Andrew looked at her for a long moment, then back out at the sea. His voice was low, full of quiet admiration. "As of right now? No. I can't say I do. But who knows what the future holds?" He looked at her then, his smile quiet, meaningful.
Lacy's lips curved slightly. "So... a soft maybe."

"A soft maybe," he echoed, gently.

She nodded, more at peace than she expected. It wasn't a firm answer—but it was honest. And it was his truth.

"I'm so sorry you went through that," he said after a pause. "But damn, Lacy... you're incredible."

She let out a breath, her smile soft but certain. "Thanks for not looking at me like I'm broken."

"I wouldn't dare," he said, smiling gently. "You've already done the hardest part. The rest of us are just lucky to be here now."

He leaned in then, brushing a tender kiss against her lips—no hesitation, no questions. Just a moment of quiet affirmation, full of care.
And when she kissed him back, the air shifted.
It deepened, their hands finding each other, mouths meeting again—this time slower, bolder. Andrew's hand cradled the back of her head as he pulled her closer, their bodies melting into the nest of blankets. There was no rush, no pressure—just the weight of the moment building between them, soft gasps and deeper breaths shared like secrets.
Then Andrew pulled back, pressing his forehead to hers, voice husky.
"If we don't stop now... I'm not sure I'll be able to."
Lacy's lips were parted, eyes slightly dazed, wanting more but understanding.
"I hate how responsible you are," she whispered, teasing but breathless.
He grinned, brushing a thumb over her cheek. "You'll thank me when we're two cocktails deep winning trivia in the piano lounge."
She groaned playfully. "Fine. But only if there's dancing after."
"Deal." He helped her up, fingers lingering just a second longer as he pulled her to her feet. Their hands stayed loosely entwined as they stepped back into the suite, the warmth of the night wrapping around them like a second skin. Laughter bubbled between them, light and easy. Lacy stopped in her suite to put on her sneakers and then they were off to tackle the night.

The hallway buzzed with activity as Lacy and Andrew made their way toward the lounge hosting "Cruise Ship Showdown: Team Trivia Edition." A small sign outside the door welcomed them in big, glittery letters, and the faint sounds of 80s music and competitive shouting bled through the walls.

They slipped inside, greeted by the warm hum of conversation, the clink of glasses, and a scatter of teams already forming. The host—a woman in a sequined captain's hat and far too much charisma for the hour—waved them in like celebrities.

"You two look like trouble," she grinned.

"Only the good kind," Andrew replied, nudging Lacy's elbow as they found a table near the middle.

"We're definitely winning this," Lacy said as she slid into her seat.

"Oh, so it's a competition now?" Andrew asked, grinning.

"Always."

The game began with ridiculous team names ("Quizteama Aguilera" and "Les Quizerables" drawing the most laughs) and a fast-paced round of questions that had them shouting over each other, laughing through wrong answers, and high-fiving every time they nailed a hard one.

Lacy leaned in close during a particularly tricky question about Oscar winners. "Don't overthink it. I know it was Lupita," she whispered, her voice brushing his ear.

He glanced sideways, amused and a little distracted. "I'll don't doubt you."

"Smart man."

By the time their team—"Bookends"—won second place (narrowly edged out by a group of competitive retired teachers), they were breathless with laughter and clinking glasses of celebratory champagne handed out by the host.

"I'm still calling it a win," Andrew said as they exited into the hall.

"Oh, absolutely. I got free champagne and the sweet, sweet taste of superiority. Let's go dance it off."

He offered his arm, which she looped hers through with a playful twirl.

The nightclub on the upper deck had transformed into a glowing escape of low lights and pulsing beats, a blend of old-school and modern hits setting the rhythm. Couples and solo dancers moved like silhouettes beneath the soft glow of ceiling lights, and the scent of sea salt clung faintly to the air. Andrew led her to the dance floor like he'd done it a thousand times before—confident, smooth, and so handsome she almost forgot how to step.

Lacy's braids swayed as she laughed, letting him spin her once, twice, then pull her close with a smirk.

"You're showing off," she accused, breathless.

"I'm winning second place again," he teased, his voice low near her ear. "And I'll take the prize in kisses this time."

She raised a brow. "Oh? Pretty confident for someone who fumbled the Shakespeare question."

He feigned a dramatic gasp. "You swore we'd never speak of that."

Their dancing turned more playful—shoulders bumping, fingers laced, bodies naturally syncing. At one point, he dipped her just slightly, her hand gripping the lapel of his open collar, her laughter husky in his ear.

They didn't rush to leave. Why would they? Time felt soft and slow, the kind of night you never wanted to end.

Around midnight, with aching cheeks from smiling and too many "just one more song" moments behind them, they wandered off in search of snacks.

Lacy walked next to Andrew along the quiet corridor lined with moonlit windows. They stumbled into a cute little café still serving croissants and cookies, dimly lit and nearly empty.

They sat on the same side of a booth, thighs brushing beneath the table as they split a chocolate croissant and passed a cup of tea between them.

"Best day ever," she sighed, letting her head rest lightly on his shoulder.

"I'm gonna need a new benchmark," he said. "Because if this isn't the top, I don't know what is."

He turned to her, and without a word, kissed her again—slow, sweet, unhurried. Like he was learning her, not claiming her.

She smiled against his lips. "You're kind of good at this."

"Years of trivia shame prepared me for this moment."

They eventually made it back to her room, fingers loosely linked, their conversation trailing off in quiet laughter and half-whispered words.

The night had been electric, all teasing glances and too-long touches, but now it slowed to something softer as they stepped onto the balcony outside her room.

The stars were out in full, scattered like glitter across the velvet sky. The soft sound of the ocean below provided the perfect soundtrack to their quiet laughter as they collapsed onto the cushioned bench beneath them.

"I don't think my feet will ever forgive me," Lacy said, wiggling her bare toes and stretching with a sigh.

Andrew tilted his head back, arms draped along the top of the bench. "They'll get over it. You danced like you were trying to win a medal."

She laughed, curling her legs up under her. "You weren't so bad yourself, loverboy."

"Loverboy?" he echoed with a smirk, leaning a little closer. "That what you're calling me now?"

"I don't know," she shrugged, eyes twinkling. "Kinda has a ring to it."

A silence fell between them—not awkward, but charged. The kind that hummed with possibility.

Andrew's gaze drifted from the stars to her. "You ever think about how weird it is that we ended up here?" he asked quietly. "I mean, not just here on this cruise, but… here. You and me."

Lacy didn't answer right away. Instead, she reached for one of the mini bottles they'd snuck from the dance lounge, cracked it open, and handed it to him before grabbing her own.

"To weird," she said, raising hers.

Andrew smiled and clinked his bottle to hers. "To weird."

They drank, then settled back against the cushions, the sound of waves filling the spaces between their breaths. At some point, Lacy leaned into his side, and he instinctively wrapped an arm around her. Her head fit perfectly against his shoulder.

"I don't want this night to end," she murmured.

"It doesn't have to," he said, just as softly.

They stayed there for what felt like hours—just the two of them and the sky and the sea, no office, no drama, no past to haunt the moment. Just now.

Eventually, Lacy yawned, and Andrew chuckled.

"Okay," he said, helping her up. "Time to get horizontal before you pass out on me."

Back inside, the room glowed faintly from a bedside lamp. Lacy climbed onto the bed, Andrew following close behind. They didn't even bother changing—just slid under the covers, still tangled in conversation, snacks, and the last shreds of laughter.

They fell asleep like that—barefoot and smiling, curled into each other like they'd always belonged there.

Chapter 17

At first, she didn't open her eyes. She simply inhaled and let the moment settle—his steady breathing, the weight of his arm across her waist, the way her bare feet were tangled with his under the sheet. It was the kind of morning she thought only existed in movies. Or daydreams. When she finally did open her eyes, Andrew was already watching her. His voice was low and husky from sleep. "Morning, beautiful." Her lips curved. "Morning, handsome." He grinned, his hand brushing a braid away from her cheek. "I think we passed out halfway through a bag of trail mix." "And halfway through a story about how you nearly got banned from karaoke night in college," she teased, stretching beneath the sheets. Andrew laughed. "It was a false accusation, by the way. Totally innocent." "Mmm hmm." She turned onto her side to face him fully. "You always wake up this charming?" "Only when I get to wake up next to someone like you." That earned him a soft kiss—a gentle press of her lips to his before she rolled away and sat up. "We should probably start the day." He groaned dramatically. "Or... we could pretend it's still night and go back to cuddling."

Lacy turned, arching a brow over her shoulder. "Tempting."

Andrew propped himself up on one elbow, eyes roaming the curve of her back as sunlight filtered through the sheer curtains. "Is that a yes?"

She didn't answer right away. Instead, she shifted onto her knees, crawling back across the bed with a playful smirk. His breath caught. The sheet slipped slightly, and he saw more than she revealed the night before. Her skin was glowing, braided hair cascading down her back, and all he could think was damn.

When she leaned in and kissed him again, it wasn't soft like before. It was deeper—intentional. A question and an answer all at once.

He broke the kiss only long enough to whisper, "I want you"

Lacy's response came in the way her fingers slid into his hair, her mouth moving against his, and the way she whispered, "I want you too" like she meant it from the marrow of her bones.

He flipped her gently onto her back, taking his time, intentional in the way he explored her like she was something sacred. He kissed a path down her collarbone, her ribs, lower—her breath hitched as he disappeared beneath the sheet. Her fingers gripped the fabric. Her legs tensed around his shoulders.

When she came undone, it was quiet and gasping and messy in the most beautiful way.

He came back to her slowly, kissing her hip, her stomach, until he met her mouth again. "You still want me?"

She answered by pulling him to her, wrapping herself around him like gravity.

Their bodies moved together like waves—slow and urgent, hungry and tender. No pretenses. No hesitation. Just two people finding each other in every breath, every kiss, every inch of skin. It was a claiming without pressure, a surrender without fear.

And when they finally collapsed against the pillows, tangled again but in a brand-new way, neither of them said a word for a while.

Eventually, Andrew whispered against her shoulder, "Okay... now that is definitely the best way to start a day."

Lacy chuckled, breathless and glowing. "I can agree with that."

He kissed her shoulder. "Let's shower before we're late for our date with Mrs. Vance and her mystery excursions."

She rolled her eyes but smiled. "Fine. But I'm picking the water temperature."

Andrew was already out of bed, offering his hand. "Only fair. You already raised it in here."

She took it, letting him lead her into the bathroom, both of them stealing one more look—one more smile—before the water washed the night (and morning) from their skin.

The shower was quick but intimate, the space small enough that every movement brought them closer, the warm water streaming down their bodies.

After the shower, the bathroom filled with soft steam and the scent of citrus shampoo, Lacy wrapped a towel around herself and padded into the room to grab her athletic wear for the excursion—breathable leggings, a cropped tank, and her trail sneakers. She dressed quickly, tying her hair into a high, efficient bun as she moved through the room with a lightness in her step.

Andrew, still half-damp and grinning, reached for the clothes he'd worn the night before, now a little more wrinkled than he'd prefer.

"I'll change in my suite," he said, slipping the shirt over his head. "Can't exactly show up to a company excursion smelling like you."

Lacy gave him a smug, teasing look. "That sounds like a you problem."

He laughed as he buttoned the shirt halfway, shoes in hand. "Five minutes. Try not to miss me too much."

"You're across the hall, your not going to war."

"Still," he said, backing toward the door with a sexy smile, "the separation anxiety could hit fast."

Lacy tossed a rolled-up pair of socks at him as he ducked out. She lingered at the door for a second longer than necessary, then shook her head, grabbed her small daypack, and finished getting ready. Sunscreen, sunglasses, water bottle, lip balm—all the essentials tucked neatly inside. She slung the bag over her shoulder. By the time Lacy stepped into the corridor, Andrew was already waiting outside his suite, now dressed in fitted athletic shorts, a moisture-wicking tee, and trail shoes. He looked good. Too good for a company excursion. She arched a brow.

"You changed fast."

He glanced down at himself. "I was motivated."

She let out a soft laugh as they walked toward the elevators, the low hum of other guests and early morning movement filling the hallway. A sense of anticipation was building in the air. Whatever Mrs. Vance had cooked up, it was going to be anything but ordinary.

"Ready to bond with coworkers over questionable outdoor activities?" Lacy asked as the elevator doors opened.

Andrew smirked. "As long as there are snacks."

Together, they stepped in and descended toward the meeting point, sun creeping higher in the sky, adventure just around the corner.

The moment Lacy and Andrew stepped off the tender boat and onto the dock, the warm, honeyed air of the island wrapped around them like a welcome hug. Lush palm fronds rustled above, and the scent of hibiscus and saltwater danced on the breeze. The scene ahead was straight from a travel magazine—vibrant market stalls, smiling guides holding signs, and the backdrop of thick jungle and turquoise shoreline. It was tropical paradise with a polished, curated edge.

"Wow," Lacy breathed, tightening the strap on her pack. "Okay, this is definitely not your average 'team-building' getaway."

"No icebreakers or trust falls in sight," Andrew replied, scanning the bright signage ahead. "Just pure vibes."

A sleek white tent marked the welcome point for the Seaglass group. A large banner read: "El's Island Excursions: Choose Your Own Adventure" in bold, elegant script.

An enthusiastic staffer greeted them with cold towels and fresh coconut water before pointing to a tall display board that listed the available excursions, color-coded by theme:

Couples & Connection (sunset hike, tandem kayaking, wine tasting cave)
Solo Thrills (ATV jungle ride, aerial zipline maze)
Family Fun (eco tour, animal encounter)
Mystery Route (???)
Relax & Rejuvenate (beachside sound bath, spa tents)

Lacy tilted her head. "El's? Who's El?"

Before Andrew could respond, a familiar voice chimed in behind them. "That would be me," said Mrs. Vance, stepping out from the side of the tent with a sunhat, oversized sunglasses, and a confident grin that made her look ten years younger.

Lacy blinked. "You're El? Well I guess it makes sense, El-anor."

"In the flesh," Mrs. Vance said, offering them a wink. "El is what my friends call me—and apparently, now my brand too. This island and these excursions? My little side project."

Andrew let out a low whistle. "You own this place?"

"I built it. Curated every trail, meal, and hammock you're about to see," El said, spreading her arms with theatrical flair. "I figured if I was going to get people to bond and unwind, I might as well do it somewhere beautiful."

Lacy looked around again, this time with a new sense of awe. "Of course you did."

Within minutes, the group was loaded into an open-air jeep, winding through the island's lush interior. The ride was bumpy, filled with laughter and curiosity as palm trees gave way to dense jungle and the sounds of tropical birds echoed through the canopy.

As they bounced along the dirt road, Lacy found herself seated next to El, who leaned in conspiratorially.

"So," El said, not looking directly at her, "how's the cruise treating you so far?"

"It's been...unexpected," Lacy replied, glancing at Andrew, who was deep in conversation with one of the other guests. "In a good way."

El nodded, smiling to herself. "I figured. Something about the sea air brings clarity, doesn't it?"

Lacy gave a small laugh. "And maybe courage."

El turned to her then, her expression softening. "That's exactly what I hoped this week would be for you all. Not just a break from work—but a push toward whatever you've been holding back."

The jeep slowed as they approached a hidden clearing—hammocks strung between trees, guides setting up what looked like a low ropes course and a station for making herbal oils. There were no crowds, no noise. Just connection. Curated chaos and calm.

As Lacy stepped down from the jeep, Andrew offered his hand—steady, simple, warm.

The air was thick with tropical bloom, and the sound of birdsong threaded through the trees around them. Before anyone could ask where exactly they were, El clapped her hands once and turned to face the group.

"Welcome to the mystery excursion," she said, eyes glinting behind her sunglasses. "Hope you wore real shoes."

It turned out the day's surprise was a guided hike through the island's interior—lush, winding, and full of stories. Two local guides led the way, and El—somehow more alive and magnetic here than she ever seemed behind her desk—walked beside them, narrating as they moved.

The trail was shaded and fragrant, the earth soft beneath their feet, with bursts of tropical color at every turn. Lacy and Andrew fell into an easy rhythm, trading quiet jokes and glances as the group climbed steadily uphill.

"You see that tree?" El called out, gesturing to a crooked fig with thick roots that fanned across the ground like fingers. "I planted one just like it the day I bought this land. That was my way of saying I was staying for the long haul."

Andrew, just behind Lacy, let out a low chuckle. "That actually sounds like something you'd do."

She turned halfway, one brow raised in amusement. "Oh? What's that supposed to mean?"

He grinned. "You act like you're just passing through life's moments, but then you leave roots behind without even realizing it."

Lacy laughed, the sound light and bright in the humid air. "I'll take that."

Lacy rolled her eyes, but her smile gave her away. "Don't psychoanalyze me while we're surrounded by paradise."
"Can't help it," he said, gazing warmly. "You're fascinating in any setting."
She gave a soft laugh, then bumped his hip with hers as they walked. "Keep talking like that, and I might start thinking you're trying to charm me."
He leaned in a little closer. "Wouldn't be the worst idea I've had."
About thirty minutes in, the trail opened into a hidden cove—crystal-clear water lapping against smooth black rocks, and a wooden platform extending into the sea with ropes and anchors for jumping, floating, or simply lying under the sun.
El turned to the group. "This is your playground for the next few hours. We've got snorkeling gear, cliff jumping, hammocks, paddleboards. Lunch will be served here later. You're free to do as much—or as little—as you'd like."
Most of the group broke away excitedly, gravitating toward the water.
Lacy and Andrew lingered near the edge of the platform, watching the sun glint on the surface.
"This place is insane," she said, awe and gratitude in her voice.
Andrew nodded but didn't answer right away. He was watching her—closely.
Lacy kicked off her shoes and stood at the edge of the platform, letting the breeze play with her hair "This doesn't feel real."

Andrew came up beside her, barefoot and grinning. "If this is Mrs. Vance's side hustle, I'm rethinking my entire career path."

El was in her element. She moved through the group with a relaxed confidence, sharing stories, laughing easily, clearly watching everyone enjoy what she'd created. When she passed by Lacy and Andrew again, she tossed them both a pair of snorkel masks. "There's a reef just past those rocks. Go explore."

Underwater, the world turned silent and surreal. Schools of fish darted past them in flickers of silver and neon, and Andrew reached for Lacy's hand beneath the surface. They swam like that—connected and floating, weightless and easy.

Later, they lay side by side in a shaded hammock, the gentle sway and the lull of ocean waves making it hard to tell if they were napping or just suspended in the kind of peace neither of them got nearly enough of.

"You know," Lacy said softly, head turned toward him, "I don't think I've ever seen you look this relaxed."

Andrew smirked. "That's because I'm currently suspended between two palm trees and not answering emails."

She reached over to brush a bit of sea salt from his temple. "You're kind of perfect like this."

His eyes flicked open at that. "Yeah?"

"Yeah."

They kissed again—lazy, warm, unhurried. Everything about the day felt like permission to breathe.

As the sun began to dip lower in the sky, casting long golden shadows over the island, the group gathered around a rustic table for a shared meal. The air was thick with the scent of grilled seafood, roasted vegetables, and fresh tropical cocktails that made Lacy's senses come alive. El stood to make a short toast, her words heartfelt and genuine.

"To new beginnings," El said, raising her glass with a smile. "To unexpected paths. And to the kind of people who make this journey unforgettable."

Laughter rippled through the group, glasses clinking in a chorus of joy. Everyone was so relaxed, so carefree. The island was alive with possibility, and for a few hours, everything felt untouched by the weight of reality. Lacy caught Andrew's eye, a playful twinkle passing between them as they traded quiet jokes about the food and the island's strange quirks. For once, there were no questions about their pasts, no thoughts of what might come next. It was just the two of them—free, happy, and living in the moment. The tightness that often pressed against Lacy's chest felt lighter, almost nonexistent, as the evening stretched on.

But all good things must end, and as the sun began its descent, the night crept in, carrying with it a shift. The warmth of the day gave way to a cooler breeze, and the group began to gather their things to return to the boat. The ride back to the ship was quiet, but not in a heavy way—instead, it felt like the world had slowed down just enough to let them both breathe and share a few unspoken thoughts.

The boat docked back at the cruise ship, and the evening ahead beckoned. They parted ways briefly, each heading to their suites to change for the captain's dinner.

Lacy slipped into her room, the space now feeling like a sanctuary, quiet and familiar. She had decided on an all-black ensemble for the black-tie event—sleek and simple, with a deep plunge at the back that made her feel both bold and elegant. She ran her fingers over the fabric, letting the silk slip through her hands as she admired the way it made her feel—like someone who was ready for a night that wasn't just about the event, but about her and Andrew. About what they were building, however slowly it was happening.

As she applied a quick swipe of red lipstick, her mind wandered to him—Andrew. How effortlessly they had fallen into step with each other over the past few days. He wasn't just the man she worked with anymore. He was someone she could laugh with, someone she could tease without worrying about what it meant. But there was also something deeper, something that buzzed under her skin when their hands brushed or when they shared a quiet glance.

As she finished getting ready, she caught her reflection in the mirror. The silk dress hugged her curves in all the right ways, the slit at the side just enough to be flirtatious without overdoing it. She smiled, feeling a flutter in her chest. Tonight, it was more than just a dinner. It was their night, a night that was somehow all about them, even among all the guests.

Lacy gave herself one final look and grabbed her clutch, heading out the door. She didn't know what was going to happen next, but she was pretty sure she was about to have one of the best nights of the trip.

Chapter 18

Andrew, was waiting just outside his suite. He'd chosen a navy and black tuxedo—classic, fitted perfectly, and just the right amount of charm. His tie was a deep, rich burgundy, a subtle nod to the tropical vibes of the island that had begun to feel like home. He stood by the door, adjusting his cufflinks, when Lacy's arrival stopped him in his tracks.
She was every bit the vision he had imagined—elegant, breathtaking, and just the right kind of confident. The hazel eyes that had laughed with him on the island now seemed to hold something more—an invitation, maybe, or a shared secret they weren't ready to fully speak.

"Wow," he said, his voice just low enough to send a shiver down her spine. "You look... incredible."
Lacy laughed, a light and playful sound that made his heart pick up a beat. "I could say the same for you," she teased, stepping closer. "I see you've gone for the classic look. A little James Bond?"
Andrew grinned, his eyes warming as he stepped in to close the distance. "If only I had the license to kill," he said, voice smooth with a hint of flirtation.
Lacy raised an eyebrow, stepping back as if appraising him. "You might be dangerous, Mr. Mitchell," she said with a wink. "But we'll see if you can keep up tonight."
Andrew chuckled, offering his arm as he led her out of the suite. "I think I'll be able to handle whatever comes my way," he said confidently, but his grin deepened when he saw the playful gleam in her eyes. "Shall we?"
Together, they stepped into the bustling hallway, their hands brushing lightly as they walked toward the grand dining room. There was no rush, no pressure—just a feeling that tonight, they were something more than two colleagues dressed to impress. They were them, and whatever the night held, they would share it.

As they entered the grand dining room, Lacy couldn't help but feel the weight of the evening's magic. The room was bathed in soft, golden light from crystal chandeliers overhead, with tables draped in white linen and set with fine china. The air smelled faintly of fresh roses and the delicate scent of ocean salt that still clung to the air from the island. A string quartet played softly in the corner, setting a romantic, almost whimsical tone.

Lacy and Andrew's arrival didn't go unnoticed. A few eyes drifted toward them, but most of the attention seemed to linger on the two of them as they walked in side by side. This wasn't the same as arriving together as friends—it was different. There was an ease between them now, the kind that made them look like a perfect match.

"Shall we?" Andrew asked, his hand lightly brushing her back as they made their way to the table. His touch was light, but the warmth in his palm lingered long after he'd moved his hand away.

Lacy nodded, her smile just a little wider than usual. "Lead the way, Mr. Mitchell."

They were seated at a table for two, close to the edge of the room with a perfect view of the sea through the large windows. The evening was warm, but the breeze was cool enough to be refreshing as it drifted in from the open air beyond.

Dinner began with a champagne toast, and as the bubbles rose in her glass, Lacy clinked it lightly against Andrew's. She caught his eye, a playful glint still in hers. "To unexpected paths," she said, echoing El's toast from earlier, "and to finding exactly what you didn't know you were looking for."

Andrew smiled, his gaze warm and appreciative. "I'll drink to that."

They both took a sip, and the conversation flowed easily from there. They talked about their favorite moments from the excursion, exchanged jokes about some of the guests they'd met, and mused over the oddities of island life. But the more they talked, the more they noticed just how much they already knew about each other—the way they could read between the lines, catch the smallest cues, finish a thought without needing the rest of the sentence.

At some point, the conversation shifted from playful to something quieter. Andrew leaned in slightly, a soft smile tugging at the corner of his lips. "It's funny," he said, voice low and warm. "We've only known each other a few months, but sometimes it feels like longer."

She tilted her head slightly, fingers brushing the rim of her glass. "That's rare, you know," she said. "Feeling that kind of ease with someone."

Andrew's gaze held hers. "It is."

She smiled. "Maybe you're just unusually charming."

Andrew chuckled. "Unusually?"

She raised an eyebrow, teasing. "Let's not start inflating your ego too soon. There's still dessert coming."

Their meals arrived—an elegant three-course offering, starting with a delicate lobster bisque, followed by a perfectly cooked steak, and finishing with a rich chocolate mousse that almost melted on the tongue. They ate slowly, savoring the flavors and the easy flow of conversation, and though there was laughter, there were moments of quiet too—moments where the connection between them was almost palpable.

As the night wore on, the space around them seemed to disappear. It was just Lacy and Andrew, and the quiet sounds of the string quartet that felt like the perfect backdrop to the chemistry between them. The tension from earlier—subtle and unspoken—had shifted into something more tangible now. They were comfortable, but the undercurrent of attraction was undeniable.

When dessert was served, Lacy took a bite of the mousse, her eyes lighting up at the rich flavor. "This might just be the best thing I've had all day," she murmured, savoring the sweetness.

Andrew's gaze never wavered, his smile warm. "I thought I was the best thing you'd had today," he teased.

Lacy raised an eyebrow, leaning forward slightly. "Mmm, maybe you are," she said, her voice soft and teasing. "But I think you're going to have to work a little harder to top this."

Andrew's laugh was low and rich, but there was a glint in his eyes that hinted at something more. "Challenge accepted," he said, his voice a little more intimate now, the playful tension between them thickening.

The rest of the evening passed in a blur of conversation, laughter, and flirtation. As the dinner came to a close, Lacy found herself reluctant to leave the intimate setting they'd created together. Andrew stood and held out his hand. She slid hers into his without a second thought.

"Shall we?" he asked, his voice warm, but with that familiar teasing edge.

Lacy smiled, standing to join him. "We shall."

They left the grand dining hall laughing, the echo of live jazz trailing behind them like a secret. Lacy's heels clicked in rhythm with Andrew's polished dress shoes, their hands brushing until he finally laced his fingers through hers.

"You wear that tux like you've got stock in GQ," she said, bumping her hip against his.

He leaned in, voice low at her ear. "And you in that dress? It's a miracle I didn't completely lose it during dessert."

Lacy's smirk was slow and knowing. "I noticed. You stabbed your crème brûlée like it owed you money."

They reached their suites, and she turned to him in the doorway. "Go change. Meet me back here in ten. I'm not ending this cruise without ice cream and bad karaoke."

He gave a mock salute. "Copy that."

Inside, Lacy shimmied out of the black gown, hanging it carefully on a hanger before slipping into her favorite soft matching set—shorts and an oversized sweatshirt that hung off one shoulder. She tugged her braids into a loose topknot, touched up her gloss, and padded barefoot to the door just as the knock came.

Andrew stood in the doorway in black joggers, sneakers, and a simple tee —clean, effortless, and somehow still devastatingly handsome. He leaned against the frame like he owned it.
"Ready for one last night of bad decisions?"
Lacy slipped on her shoes, already grinning. "Lead the way, trouble."

The ship had a different kind of magic at night—less sparkle, more mystery. The hallways were quieter, lit in a warm golden glow as passengers lingered in lounges or drifted back to their cabins.

Lacy and Andrew wandered the upper decks, gelato in hand, the ocean breeze warm and salted with the night air. Everything felt slower, softer, like the ship itself was exhaling.
"I can't believe you picked pistachio," she said, licking her spoon with exaggerated judgment. "That's the most dad-at-a-barbeque flavor."
Andrew raised an eyebrow, letting his spoon hover near her mouth. "Try it and say that again."
She leaned in, lips grazing the spoon before taking a bite. Her eyes closed, a little hmmm of surprise slipping out. "Okay, fine. That's stupid good."
His grin widened. "I know."
They hit the arcade next, where Lacy dominated at skee-ball and air hockey, crowing with delight every time Andrew groaned in defeat. But every laugh, every playful bump of shoulders, felt different now— charged, intentional. His hand lingered at her waist a second longer than usual. Her glance held his just a beat past teasing.
They stumbled out onto the top deck sometime after midnight, breathless and buzzing. A few other couples wandered nearby, voices low and scattered like sea foam. The pool was closed, but the water glowed faintly under soft lights. Most of the lounge chairs sat empty, shadows stretched long beneath them. Above, the stars stretched wide and endless.
Andrew stepped behind her, arms sliding around her as she leaned against the railing.

"I don't want this night to end," she whispered.

His lips brushed just beneath her ear. "Then it won't. Not yet."

She turned in his arms, their bodies aligning perfectly. They stood like that for a long moment—no words, just the quiet pull of want thick in the space between them.

Finally, he spoke, voice low and warm. "Come with me. I've been planning this all week."

Her brow arched with a teasing smile. "Of course you have."

Andrew grinned, brushing his thumb across her knuckles. "You didn't think I'd let our last night on board end without a little magic… did you?"

He kept her hand in his as they walked the quiet corridor back to the suite, the low hum of the ship's engines beneath their feet, the hush of the ocean all around. At the door, Andrew paused, his fingers tightening slightly around hers.

"Close your eyes."

Lacy gave him a side-eye. "Seriously?"

"Come on," he said, that teasing smile tugging at the corner of his mouth. "No peeking."

She huffed dramatically but obeyed, and he gently guided her inside. A few more steps, the soft click of the door behind them, and—

"Okay," he whispered, brushing his lips against her ear. "Open."

Her lashes lifted, and the breath caught in her throat.

The suite had been transformed. The curtains were drawn open to reveal the private patio drenched in moonlight, now layered in plush throws and oversized pillows—more abundant, more intentional than before. It looked like a private escape, built just for them. Strings of fairy lights flickered like fireflies around the space, casting everything in a soft, golden glow.

Just inside, on the low table by the sliding door, stood a tall glass vase filled with perfect white peonies—her favorite. Fresh, full, impossibly fragrant.

She turned to him, stunned. "Andrew…"

He looked at her like she was the only thing worth seeing. "You said the sunset was your favorite part of yesterday. I thought… maybe we'd end our last night under the stars."

Her eyes found the flowers again. "You remembered the peonies."

"I remember everything when it comes to you."

A breathy laugh escaped her—one of those soft, overwhelmed ones that slipped past words—and she threw her arms around him. "This is… it's unreal. You planned all this?"

"I may have called in a few favors."

"Of course you did."

They stood there for a moment, wrapped around each other, the glow from the patio brushing their skin. Outside, the sky stretched wide and open, stars blinking into place like they were showing up just for them.

Andrew pressed a kiss to her temple. "Come on," he murmured. "Let's get comfortable."

Lacy slipped off her shoes and stepped onto the patio, her foot sinking into layers of plush throws and pillows. The sensation was soft, almost indulgent—like walking into a cloud spun just for her. She let out a quiet breath, overwhelmed in the best way, and lowered herself onto the nest of fabric, surrounded by fairy light and moonlight.

Andrew followed, kicking off his sneakers before settling beside her with a look that said he'd been waiting for this.

A small tray of chocolate-covered fruit and a chilled bottle of wine waited nearby—another perfect detail she hadn't even noticed until now.
"Seriously," she teased under her breath, "are you trying to ruin all future nights for me?"
He chuckled, arm draping lazily around her shoulders. "No. Just setting the bar. I intend to keep outdoing myself."
"You already are," she whispered, curling in closer.
They sipped wine under the stars, wrapped in warmth and the kind of silence that only came with comfort. The moonlight carved silver lines across the ocean. Somewhere below, music drifted faintly from another deck, mellow and slow. Lacy's head rested against Andrew's chest, his thumb tracing lazy circles on her arm.
"Tell me something you've never told anyone," she said softly.
He was quiet for a beat. "I once turned down a promotion because I didn't want to leave the team I built. Everyone thought I wasn't ambitious enough, but… it felt like leaving something good just to chase something louder."
She tilted her head, looking up at him. "That's not unambitious. That's loyalty."
"Yeah? You don't think it makes me boring?"
She shook her head slowly. "Not even a little. It makes you…" Her voice dipped, eyes locking with his. "Steady. Intentional. Sexy."
He kissed her then, soft and lingering. But something shifted when she kissed him back—no longer teasing, no longer gentle. She reached up, grabbing the back of his head, pulling him in with a low desire in her throat. His hand slid to her waist, then her hips, drawing her against him. She whispered against his mouth, "Is this where you outdo yourself again?"
His response was a growl of a laugh, muffled as he kissed her deeper. "Oh, you have no idea."
They tumbled down into the nest of pillows, a tangle of limbs and whispered gasps. His hands found the hem of her sweatshirt, lifting it

slowly, tenderly. Her fingers roamed beneath his shirt, tracing the warm planes of his back, the steady beat of his heart.

"I love the way you look at me," she breathed.

He hovered above her, gaze locked on hers, voice rough. "That's because I love you."

Time froze. The stars held their breath. And in that moment, something in her cracked open—wide and safe and full of light.

"I love you, too," she whispered, like she'd known it for a while but only just now dared to say it.

He kissed her then with everything he had—like the words had pulled something primal and tender from his chest. Every touch after that was purposeful, skin to skin, heavy with heat and heart.

Their bodies moved like they'd done this in dreams too many times to count—and now, finally, they didn't have to imagine anymore. There was urgency, yes, but also care. The kind that said this isn't new, but it still means everything.

They undressed each other in quiet, hungry stages, lips brushing skin, hands mapping familiar territory like it was sacred. When they finally came together, it was more than just motion—it was connection. Rhythm. Release.

They made love like it mattered. Like it always had. Like it always would. And afterward, they stayed that way—wrapped around each other, tangled in sheets and moonlight and unspoken things that finally had names.

By the time they drifted off to sleep—bodies bare, hearts full—it wasn't just about making love.

It was about making something real.

Chapter 19

The sun was barely cresting the horizon when Lacy stirred, the soft pink light spilling across the patio and warming her skin. For a moment, she didn't move—just listened to the quiet rhythm of Andrew's breathing and the distant hush of waves against the ship. His arm was still draped over her waist, and his legs were tangled with hers in the most natural way.
She turned her head slightly to find him already awake, watching her.
"Mornin'," he whispered, voice low and sleep-rough.
Lacy smiled, stretching lazily. "Morning."
"Sleep okay?" he asked, brushing a stray braid from her face.
"Better than okay," she said softly. "You?"
He nodded, a smile tugging at the corner of his mouth. "Didn't think I'd fall asleep out here. But with you? Yeah… I could've stayed like that forever."
A beat passed between them, tender and unspoken.
But reality always comes eventually.
A soft chime over the speaker system broke the spell—the ship's final morning announcements filtering in, reminding guests to begin packing and preparing for departure.
Lacy groaned. "Back to the real world, huh?"
"Afraid so," Andrew said, pressing a quick kiss to her shoulder. "We've got, what, an hour before we're supposed to be out of the room?"
She sighed dramatically. "I guess that means I can't lay here and be spoiled any longer."
"I mean," he said with a slow grin, "we could be a little late. Blame it on the stars."
Lacy laughed, already rising to her feet, clutching the sheet around her. "Nice try, Mr. Planner."
He watched her for a moment longer, eyes full of something softer than longing. "You make even leaving feel good."

She paused in the doorway, glancing back at him with a warm, sleepy smile. "Come shower with me?"
Andrew was already moving. "Say less."
The shower steamed quickly, heat rising around them as water poured over tired limbs and sensitive skin. They hadn't planned to fall into each other again—not with time ticking—but once Andrew pressed her back against the cool tile, his mouth finding the hollow of her throat, all bets were off. It was quick, but never careless. Urgent, but tender. Like two people trying to make a moment last forever—even if it only had one more heartbeat to give.
Afterward, towels wrapped and skin flushed, Andrew leaned in and kissed her one last time beneath the spray. A little slower. A little deeper.
Then he pulled back, breath catching as he rested his forehead against hers. "I should head to my suite. Pack up, get my act together."
Lacy nodded, trailing her fingers down his damp arm. "Okay."
He gave her a look—one she was starting to recognize. Full of unspoken things and quiet promises. Then he was gone, the door clicking softly behind him.
For a few moments, Lacy stood in the quiet. Letting the silence settle like fog.
She padded into the bedroom, water still beading along her shoulders, and pulled her suitcase from the closet. One by one, she folded her clothes, each movement slow, thoughtful. Her black dress from the captain's dinner still hung by the window, catching the morning light like a memory that didn't want to fade.
She sat on the edge of the bed, fingers brushing the corner of the comforter. The same bed they'd shared their first night. The one she almost hadn't let herself get into.
And now?
Now she could barely remember what it felt like not to want him.
Her thoughts drifted—back to the excursions, the way Andrew made her laugh until her sides hurt, the softness in his eyes when he looked at her

like she was something rare. The sunset. The night under the stars. The way he said he loved her like it was the most natural thing in the world. She closed her eyes, pressing her palm to her chest, like maybe she could keep it all there a little longer.
Whatever happened next, whatever waited for them back on land… this? These days? They were hers.
And they were real.

The disembarkation process was surprisingly smooth, considering the bittersweet weight hanging in the air. The sun was still rising, casting a soft orange glow over the harbor as Lacy and Andrew wheeled their bags off the ship.
Andrew took hers without asking, his hand brushing hers with casual intimacy as they walked down the ramp.
"Let me take you home," he said, pausing as they reached the waiting car lines. "I don't like the idea of you squished in the back of someone's Prius with all your stuff."
She arched a brow. "You think I was gonna take a Prius?"
He smirked. "You were about to open that app. Don't lie."
She tried not to smile. Failed. "Fine. I was." she laughed
"Then it's settled." He opened the trunk of a black x6, BMW, tossed her suitcase in next to his, and shut it with a solid thud. "You're riding with me."
They turned to say goodbye to the Seaglass staff and a few fellow guests, who had gathered near the terminal exit. El—Mrs. Vance, or just "El" now, as everyone had affectionately started calling her—was waiting with open arms.
"You two," she said, pulling Lacy in for a hug and then Andrew, "have been the highlight of my little social experiment."
Lacy laughed. "Social experiment?"
"Oh, please," El said, waving her off. "You think I didn't see this coming from day one?"

Around them, a few staff members chimed in with grins and playful nudges.

"Y'all make a cute couple."

"It's about time." a coworker shouted she didn't recognize.

Andrew just pulled Lacy in closer, arm around her shoulder, her arm around his waist, his quiet smile growing by the second.

El touched Lacy's hand gently. "You've got something rare here, sweetheart. Don't run from it."

Lacy nodded, emotion tightening her throat. "Thank you. For everything."

El winked. "Now go. Real life's waiting—and it's even better when you've got someone to share it with."

The ride to Lacy's place was quiet, peaceful. Music played low in the background, but most of the drive was filled with the kind of silence that didn't need to be filled. The kind that spoke of contentment. And maybe a little wondering.

When they pulled up outside her building, Andrew didn't rush to get out. Instead, he turned in his seat, fingers brushing lightly over the steering wheel before finding hers.

"So… what happens now?" she asked, eyes searching his.

He met her gaze head-on. "Now we stop pretending we don't know what this is."

She swallowed. "And what is it?"

"It's real." He leaned in slightly. "And I'm all in. I want this. You. Us. I've wanted you since the moment you walked into my office and told me we were work-married."

Lacy laughed softly, heart thudding. "That was a bold day."

"And the beginning of everything." His thumb traced the top of her hand. "I hope you're all in too, Lacy. Because I want to build something with you. Something that lasts."

She nodded slowly, her eyes never leaving his. "I'm in."

He exhaled like he'd been holding that breath for days, then got out to open her door. Walked her to her building without another word, just the steady press of his presence beside her.

At her door, he cupped her face, studied her for a beat. Then kissed her deeply. Not rushed. Not goodbye. But a promise.

And when they finally pulled apart, she rested her forehead against his.

"I'll see you soon," he said.

"You better," she whispered.

Then he turned to leave and she watched him walk away, already feeling the pull of something permanent settling in her chest.

The moment Lacy stepped into her apartment, Leo trotted up like he owned the place—and missed her just enough to pretend he didn't. She crouched down, scooping him into her arms as he gave her a single annoyed meow followed by a loud purr that rumbled against her chest.

"Missed you too, fuzzy face," she whispered, burying her nose in his fur. He headbutted her chin in response, like he hadn't spent the last few days being pampered by her assistant, Claire.

Once he was sufficiently cuddled and she'd refilled his water and food bowls, Lacy finally—finally—turned her phone back on.

It vibrated like it had something to prove. She stared at the flood of notifications lighting up her screen.

Messages from Bree:

Bree: You alive?

Bree: Hello?

Bree: Should I be worried or jealous?

A string of updates from her assistant, Claire: client check-ins, a draft needing review, a note that her 2PM meeting Monday got moved to Friday. A few emails from the office that could wait. A weird number of discount codes.

One text from Lucas:

Lucas: Back from paradise yet? Hope it gave you some new perspective.

She blinked at Lucas's message, surprised by how little it stirred—like the spark that once lingered had quietly burned out.
Then—
Patrick.
Several messages.
She froze.
She thought she'd blocked him. But somehow, there he was.
Patrick: Lacy, I know you're ignoring me, but please don't shut me out like this.
Patrick: I made a mistake not telling you everything sooner. You mean more to me than you know.
Patrick: Can we just talk? One last time? Are you with that Andrew guy?
Her pulse kicked up. She immediately hit the block button again, her hands shaky as she set the phone down. Her heart still hadn't settled
And then she called Bree.
Bree's voice burst through the speaker before Lacy could even say hello.
"Girl, if you hadn't called today, I was about to organize a search party—with snacks. And glitter. You know. For morale."
Lacy let out a breath she hadn't realized she was holding. Her heart still beat unevenly, but Bree's voice wrapped around her like a hug.
She smiled, the tension loosening just enough. "I have so much to tell you…"
"Start from the top," Bree demanded. "Day one. I want the juice. I want the pulp. I want the seeds, Lacy."
Lacy flopped down on the couch, Leo hopping up to curl against her thigh. "Okay, but brace yourself. It's… a lot."
"I'm sitting. I have wine. I am spiritually prepared."
Lacy drew a breath.
Okay. So we get to the port, and El—Mrs. Vance—upgrades our rooms to balcony suites."
"Oh, that's fancy. Was this part of the reward package?"

"Apparently. But get this—our rooms were right across the hall from each other.
"Scandalous."
"Not yet," Lacy laughed. "Day one, after we got settled, I needed a moment to decompress—take in the ocean air, the quiet. When I finally came out for dinner, Andrew had already arranged for us to sit alone. Not at the big table with the Seaglass crew, not with El and her people—just the two of us at this small, candlelit table by one of the panoramic windows."
"Oh, he's a planner?"
"Apparently. He made a note on our RSVP while I was still changing. Said he wanted to start the trip with a little intention."
Bree let out a long, dramatic sigh. "That's not intention. That's romance. Continue."
"We ate, we laughed—he listened. Like undivided-attention, listened. No phone, no half-answers, just... present. Then that night…"
"Don't you dare trail off like that, Lacy."
"He asked me to come to his room to 'watch the sunset.' I thought it was gonna be some friendly wine-on-the-balcony moment. Nope. "…he had all my favorite snacks," Lacy said, tucking a pillow behind her. "The fancy popcorn I always steal from his office stash, the chocolate-covered almonds, even those weird sparkling waters I swear only I like."
Bree gasped. "Okay, wait. He didn't just plan dinner—he curated a snack situation too? Girl, that man's in love."
Lacy grinned. "Yeah… He told me he loved me"
"And you? Are you in love?"
She went quiet for a beat. "I think I've been falling for a while now. I just didn't want to admit it—not even to myself."
Bree's voice softened. "So what happened after SnackFest 2025?"
Lacy chuckled. "We talked. About everything. Life, work, what we want. And then… we kissed. Not just some light thing—it was... charged. Like the kind of kiss that shuts your whole system down."

"Lacy!" Bree squealed. "You minx. Okay, now what?"
"The next couple days were just... effortless. We explored the ship together, did all the cheesy cruise stuff. We went dancing, did a trivia night. It felt like we'd been doing this for years."
"You mean like a couple?"
"Exactly. Then the excursion day came. That's when we really got to know El—turns out she's hilarious and secretly a romantic. She put together all these little off-ship experiences—couples, singles, families. We ended up picking the one she was on, by accident."
"She totally did that on purpose."
"Oh, absolutely. We all bonded like crazy that day. The island was stunning—like, movie-stunning. And Andrew? He was so relaxed. Playful. He kept brushing my arm, whispering stuff to make me laugh."
"You two are literally a rom-com."
"That night, after the excursion… we cuddled. Talked for hours. Then, the next morning—" Lacy paused, a slow smile spreading on her face.
Bree's voice dropped to a whisper. "You did it, didn't you?"
"We did. And Bree… it wasn't just sex. This time, it was... everything." Lacy's voice softened. "We woke up wrapped around each other, laughing, still half-dressed from the night before. Then we showered together and—well. You get it."
A beat of silence.
Then—
"This time?" Bree's voice sharpened. "Wait. First of all—what do you mean this time?"
Lacy winced. "I mean... the first time kind of happened after your wedding."
Another beat.
"After my wedding?" Bree shrieked. "Wait—the reception?"
Lacy groaned. "Yaaassss. I was emotional, and tipsy, and Andrew walked me back to my room…"

"And into your sheets?" Bree gasped. "Oh my God. This man comforted you biblically while I was across the hall trying to catch my bouquet in a damn bun. Unbelievable."

Lacy started laughing, covering her face. "Well, it was well after that but It wasn't planned, Bree. It just happened."

"Clearly. But you better believe I want every detail now. Slow down. Don't skip. You're on thin ice, ma'am."

"Ok yes ma'am, so there's more. At the Captain's Dinner that night, he asked me to be his official date. Like, we walked in arm-in-arm, people from Seaglass were giving us the look."
"Oh, I know the look. That 'finally, it happened' look?"
"Exactly. Even El toasted us in her own subtle way."
Bree sighed happily. "It's about damn time."
"Then that night," Lacy continued, her voice softening, "he surprised me again. He recreated the balcony date—but bigger. He turned the patio into a whole setup under the stars. Blankets, pillows, candles. My favorite flowers—white peonies."
Bree gasped. "Shut up. How did he even get those on the boat?"
"I have no idea. I didn't ask. I was too busy being floored. We cuddled out there, talked, kissed. And then—Bree, it was the most intimate night of my life. Gentle, deep, connected. We slept under the stars, tangled up in each other."
Bree was silent for a moment. "You love him."
"I do," Lacy whispered.
"So what now?"
"We got back this morning. He insisted on driving me home, walked me to the door, kissed me like we weren't done—like this was just beginning."
"And then?"

"I went inside, gave Leo some love—he was dramatically starved for affection—and finally checked my phone."

"Say it's not so."

"Yep. Messages from the office, some junk… one from Lucas… and several from Patrick."

Bree let out a groan. "Seriously? I thought you blocked him."

"I did too. Apparently he found a workaround."

"That man had his chance and blew it. And you, my love, are clearly living in the main plotline now."

Lacy smiled, running her fingers through Leo's fur. "I think I am."

"And hey—if you ever doubt it again, just remember: a man who gets you peonies at sea is not playing games."

Lacy sank deeper into the couch, letting out a long breath. "Bree, there's one more thing I have to tell you."

Bree was quiet, waiting.

"After that night under the stars... we were lying there, and we just... talked. About everything. And then, when I told him I loved the way he looked at me, and he said it's because I love you—Bree, I felt it. In my chest, my whole body. It wasn't just words. It was real."

Bree sighed, her tone thick with emotion. "You said it back?"

Lacy smiled, her heart swelling. "Yes. I told him I loved him too."

"Finally! It's about time you two got on the same page." Bree's voice bloomed with that familiar, fiercely supportive energy. "That's everything, Lacy. It's exactly what you deserve. And look at you—this trip? It's been life-changing. You're living your own damn love story."

Lacy laughed softly. "It really does feel like something out of a movie. I wasn't expecting any of this. I didn't even know I was ready for this... but here we are."

"I'm so happy for you. You've been through so much, Lacy, but you're finally getting your happy ending."

Lacy leaned back, looking at Leo, who was curled up at her feet. "I think I'm just getting started. But the reality check's hitting hard. You know?

We're back to real life now. We can't just float in this perfect bubble forever."

Bree's tone shifted to a more practical one. "Yeah, real life is messy. Just ask Thomas and me."

Lacy raised an eyebrow. "Oh? How's that going?"

Bree sighed. "Let's just say living together after the wedding has been... interesting."

She let out a small laugh.

"Honestly? Sometimes I wish we'd lived together before—just so I'd know what I was signing up for. But in the end, it doesn't really matter. I love him. I'd still choose him."

Lacy smirked. "I thought you guys were always on the same page."

"We are. We are!" Bree insisted. "But it's like moving in with your best friend and realizing that best friend is somehow allergic to laundry hampers. We're still adjusting."

Lacy laughed. "Well, that's... real."

"Yeah. But it's good. It's us. We're finding our rhythm."

Lacy nodded slowly. "I get that. I just... I don't know what comes next for Andrew and me. I definitely don't want to rush it."

Bree's voice softened. "You don't have to rush it. Just take it one step at a time. If he's already told you he loves you and you've said it back, then you're already in it. Let it unfold. But also... don't let fear hold you back. If it's real, don't fight it."

Lacy went quiet for a moment. "You know what's wild?" she said softly. "With Patrick, I never felt completely safe. I don't mean physically—I mean... I could never fully relax. Something in me was always bracing."

Bree's voice dropped. "Your intuition."

Lacy nodded, even though Bree couldn't see it. "Probably. It's like... he didn't want to share my life. He wanted to take it over. Everything with him felt like it had to orbit around him. Like he wanted to consume me."

She let out a slow breath.

"But with Andrew?" A small smile curled into her voice. "It's different. I feel... grounded. Seen. Like I could move in with him and still be myself. He wouldn't let me lose that. He'd protect it."

Bree was quiet for a beat. Then: "Damn. That's it right there."

She exhaled. "That's the difference between love that drains you and love that pours into you."

Lacy blinked fast, her chest tight in the best way. "Yeah. That's exactly it."

Chapter 20

The morning came fast, and Lacy was ready to hit the ground running. She stretched, letting the quiet of her apartment settle around her—a gentle contrast to the whirlwind waiting just outside her front door.

Her mind naturally drifted to her to-do list, the meetings, the emails, the follow-ups stacked like dominoes. But for once, she didn't let the pressure take over. She exhaled, rolled her shoulders back, and let herself feel the stillness.

She'd said a lot the day before. Felt a lot, too. And somehow, it had left her lighter.

The air was cool, the kind of morning breeze that hinted at a new season. She decided to walk to work. A little fresh air. A little movement. A good place to begin again.

Standing in front of her wardrobe, she pulled out an outfit that would make a statement. She opted for a tailored, deep navy-blue pencil skirt that hugged her curves perfectly, paired with a crisp white blouse that had a subtle ruffle detail along the collar. Over it, she added a sleek, fitted blazer in a dark grey, its sharp lines giving her a powerful, professional look. She finished the ensemble with a pair of black patent leather pumps that clicked confidently as she moved.

Her hair, still braided from the cruise, cascaded down her back in a neat yet effortless way, and she added a swipe of bold red lipstick to complete the look. Lacy took one last glance in the mirror, feeling the sense of purpose that came with knowing she was about to crush this day.

After grabbing her purse, she slipped on her sunglasses and stepped outside, inhaling the cool morning air. The city was still waking up, but the energy of it all made her smile. She decided to make the most of her walk to work and stopped by her favorite coffee shop along the way.

As she entered the cozy shop, the familiar hum of morning chatter filled the space. The barista greeted her with a smile, already knowing her order. Lacy took a moment to enjoy the warmth of the cup in her hands as she glanced around, her thoughts drifting momentarily to Andrew and the events of the past week.

It felt strange being back, but as she sipped her coffee and began walking toward the office, she felt a renewed sense of purpose, ready to dive back into the hustle of her career. Today was going to be a good day.

She'd missed this rhythm, though there was a part of her that still longed for the laid-back ease of the cruise, for the simplicity of being with Andrew, away from the noise and demands of work. But today, she was back, and she was determined to make the most of it.

As she rounded the corner, she spotted a familiar face up ahead. Lucas. He was leaning against a brick wall outside a boutique, scrolling through his phone, his signature coffee cup in hand. Her heart skipped a beat at the sight of him, the way his dark curls bounced as he looked up.

"Hey!" Lacy called out, her smile wide. She jogged over and threw her arms around him in a quick, warm hug.

He grinned as he pulled back, his eyes scanning her. "Well, well. Look at you—glowing." His gaze flicked over her, noting the subtle changes in her appearance. "Did that cruise agree with you, or is it just the whole… post-vacation glow?"

Lacy laughed softly, feeling the warmth of the compliment. "You could say it was the cruise, but honestly, it's more the company," she teased, winking. "It was an unforgettable trip."

"I bet it was," Lucas replied, a slight knowing smile pulling at the corners of his mouth. He raised an eyebrow, eyes twinkling. "So, I'm guessing you've got stories. Lots of stories."

"Maybe," she said playfully. "We'll see if I can squeeze some time to share them. But right now, I'm back to the grind. First day back at work." She shifted the coffee cup in her hands, feeling a little more grounded in the present now that the conversation was shifting to something familiar.

"Well, welcome back to reality," Lucas said with a soft chuckle. "I'm looking forward to hearing about the rest of it."

Lacy smiled, her heart fluttering a bit at how easy their banter felt. "Let's set up some time soon," she said, "I'm in the office all day today, but we should grab coffee or lunch this week. I owe you that much."

"I'll hold you to it," he said, still smiling. He glanced at the time. "You'd better get going or you'll be late. I'll catch up with you later."

"Definitely," she agreed, taking one last glance at him before starting her walk to the office.

Her thoughts briefly flickered back to Andrew, but she quickly brushed them away, focusing on the day ahead. The morning had been a nice surprise—seeing Lucas was always easy, and it was a welcome reminder of the balance she had in her life. Now, time to tackle work.

Lacy walked into the office building with a steady pace, feeling the weight of the day ahead of her. The familiar smell of coffee and fresh paper hit her the moment she stepped off the elevator. She exchanged a few pleasantries with the receptionist, grabbed a coffee from the break room, and walked into her office, ready to tackle the mountain of work that had surely accumulated during her time away.

Her assistant, Claire, had already left a few messages on the desk. Lacy smiled as she scanned through the notes, knowing Claire was always on top of things. Leo, had been well taken care of, and there was a note about a few calls and emails that needed her attention.

"Good morning!" Claire called from the door as she walked in, a bright smile on her face. "Welcome back! How was your trip?"

"It was amazing," Lacy replied with a grin, her mind immediately drifting back to the cruise and the unforgettable time she'd had with Andrew. "I'm glad to be back, though. What's the scoop?"

"Well, you've got a few client meetings this morning," Claire began, pulling a file from the pile on Lacy's desk. "And there are some emails you'll need to catch up on. A few things from your regular clients... and there's an interesting one from a publishing house in Switzerland. I think you'll want to take a look at it."

Lacy raised an eyebrow. "Switzerland?"

"I know. Pretty exciting, right?" Claire smiled before walking out to grab more papers from the printer.

Lacy opened her laptop and started sifting through the emails first, responding to the more pressing ones before getting into the deeper conversations. As she worked, a text pinged on her phone.

It was from an unknown number.

Unknown Number: "Lacy, it's Patrick. I've been trying to reach you. I know you blocked me, but I need to talk. I can't let you walk away like this."

Her heart skipped a beat. Patrick. She hadn't expected to hear from him again, let alone this soon after she blocked him again. She set the phone down and took a deep breath, pushing the message aside for the moment. It wasn't the right time to deal with it.

The morning went by quickly as she settled into her routine. The first meeting was with a new client, a promising entrepreneur who needed Lacy's expertise with a new book launch. They discussed timelines, marketing strategies, and a potential partnership. She felt invigorated—this was what she did best, and her time away had only given her more drive to help others achieve their goals.

Afterward, she caught up with a few long-standing clients, making sure everything was on track and addressing any concerns they had. Each call was a reminder of how much she had built in her career, and how much more she still wanted to do.

Lunchtime rolled around, and Lacy's phone buzzed with a message from Andrew:

Andrew: Escape for lunch? I'm bringing sarcasm and snacks.

She smiled down at her phone, already feeling lighter.

Lacy: Meet you in five. Sarcasm better be extra spicy.

When she stepped outside, he was already standing by a lamppost like he had nothing better to do than wait for her—hands in his pockets, head tilted in that easy way that always made her want to smile wider than she should.

"Wow," he said as she approached, giving her a slow once-over. "You survived the morning meetings. I owe you a cookie."

"You owe me an entire bakery," she shot back, bumping her shoulder lightly into his as they fell into step together.

They ended up at a small café ducked off on a quiet side street—one of those cozy spots with fresh baked muffins and a chalkboard menu that changed every day.

They grabbed sandwiches and claimed a booth by the window, sliding into the kind of conversation that felt less like catching up and more like picking up an old, familiar thread.

"So," Andrew said around a mouthful of turkey club, "how's Lacy vs. The Inbox looking today?"

She groaned dramatically. "It's winning. Send reinforcements."

He smirked, nudging her foot under the table. "You need a plan. Fake an important call, slip out early, meet me for pizza and bad life choices later."

Lacy laughed, easing back into her seat. God, it felt good to laugh. To let the world blur for a minute.

"I might take you up on that."

"Standing offer," he said, raising his drink like a toast.

When they returned to the office, Lacy's phone buzzed again—this time, the group chat. Bree, Nina, and Chrissy were full-throttle planning brunch, firing off emojis and outfit ideas like it was a competitive sport.

She smiled, fingers flying as she fired off a few heart reactions—but a flicker of hesitation tugged at her.

The brunch she'd planned weeks ago was still on... but it felt different now.

Not because of the girls.

Because she wasn't the same girl who'd sent those invites.

Her phone buzzed again.
Another text—this one from Andrew.
Andrew: In case no one's told you today: you're killing it. And when you're ready to stop saving the world, I'm still down for pizza and terrible decisions.
Lacy's heart twisted in that soft, dangerous way it only did with him now.
Lacy: You're trouble, Andrew. But I might need a little trouble later. I'll let you know.
She tucked her phone away, letting the normalcy of work swirl around her —emails, meetings, deadlines—all while a new, fragile truth hummed underneath:
She wasn't just falling.
She was starting to trust the landing.

Later in the afternoon, she met with Mrs. Vance in person. El, as she'd come to know, was as insightful and wise as ever. They chatted about future projects and ideas for upcoming book launches, but there was a comfort between them now, a familiarity that came from the shared experiences of the cruise and the growing friendship they had developed. Before the day ended, Lacy returned to her office and opened the email from the Swiss publishing house. Her pulse quickened as she read the first few lines.
Subject: Exciting Opportunity: Managing Editorial Position
She skimmed through the details—an offer for a managing position in one of Switzerland's leading publishing houses, with a focus on international book deals. The pay was generous, the benefits exceptional, and the opportunity—life-changing. The kind of move she'd always dreamed of but never thought would happen.
Her fingers hovered over the reply button, the weight of the decision hanging over her.
She set the phone down for a moment and took a deep breath, feeling the intensity of the crossroads she was at. The cruise had been a whirlwind, a

moment of clarity. But now, with work in full swing again and unexpected opportunities on the horizon, Lacy had to ask herself: What did she want? What was her next step?

Later that evening, after a day full of back-to-back meetings and inbox chaos, Lacy and Andrew found themselves snuggled into a booth at their favorite Italian spot. The lighting was soft, the jazz mellow, and the tension of the day slowly melting away with every sip of wine. Andrew stretched one arm along the back of the booth and gave her that easy, familiar smile—the one that made her stomach flip for no good reason anymore.

"So, did your inbox survive the assault?" he asked, sipping his wine.
Lacy gave him a dramatic look. "Barely. Claire's a saint, but I'm pretty sure she deserves hazard pay for whatever was waiting in my drafts folder." She nudged his knee with hers. "You? Still charming everyone in the building?"
"Naturally." He grinned. "It's exhausting being this beloved."
She laughed, leaning into the curve of his arm. "Poor thing. Must be hard carrying the weight of your own ego around all day."
"I manage," he murmured, brushing his fingers lightly over her shoulder. "But this? Right now? Easily the best part of my day."
Lacy grinned, tipping her glass toward him. "Impressive. Saving the world and squeezing in a stolen lunch with me? Truly heroic."
Andrew smirked, his eyes dancing. "What can I say? I know where the real priorities are."
"Oh really?" she leaned in a little, her eyebrow lifting. "So you strategically plotted your whole lunch schedule just to sneak away with me?"
His smirk softened into something quieter, something truer. "If that's what it takes to get time with you... yeah. I'll plan around you every time."

Lacy felt her heart flutter slightly, a smile tugging at the corner of her lips. "Well, I guess I can't complain about that."

"But, don't think I didn't notice," he added, his eyes lingering on her. "You're glowing, Lacy. It's not just the wine."

She rolled her eyes playfully, though the warmth in her chest was undeniable. "I'm glowing because I finally had a chance to get away and actually relax for once. You've been pretty good at showing me how to do that."

Andrew smirked, leaning forward. "Guess I've got a few more lessons to teach, huh?"

Lacy laughed. "I think I'm up for the challenge."

Chapter 21

The week passed in a blur of meetings, emails, and the usual whirlwind of work. Lacy barely had time to think about anything other than getting back into the swing of things, but there were moments that kept her grounded—moments with Andrew, of course, but also the unexpected joys of reconnecting with old friends, like Lucas.

One afternoon, they grabbed lunch at a new Mediterranean café that had just opened. She'd been looking forward to catching up with him, the easy banter and the way they could talk about anything, no matter how big or small.

As she walked into the café, she spotted Lucas right away. His familiar, easy grin was waiting for her, and she couldn't help but smile in return.

"Hey, you," she greeted, sliding into the seat across from him.

Lucas raised an eyebrow, giving her a once-over. "Damn, Lacy, you're glowing. Seriously, what's going on with you?"

She laughed, taking a sip of her water. "I've been asked that a lot lately. Maybe it's just the sunshine."

"I think it's more than that," Lucas said, his tone playful but sincere. "You look... different. In a good way. How was the rest of your cruise?"

Lacy leaned back in her chair, feeling a twinge of warmth in her chest. "It was... life-changing. In a way I didn't expect. Andrew and I—" she hesitated, then smiled softly, "—we're more than just coworkers now. We made it official."

Lucas's eyes lit up. "Well, damn, about time! I was wondering how long that was going to take."

Lacy chuckled, feeling a little giddy. "Yeah, it was like the universe finally decided it was time to throw us a bone." She paused, her smile turning more thoughtful. "It's still all a bit surreal, to be honest."

Lucas leaned forward, his tone teasing but also warm. "I mean, if anyone could pull off a sudden romance, it's you two. You've got that... power couple vibe."

Lacy rolled her eyes, though there was a flush on her cheeks. "Stop it, I'm still getting used to it."

"Well, you look like you're glowing in all the right ways," Lucas said with a wink. "So, what's next? You and Andrew planning a big announcement or something?"

Lacy laughed, shaking her head. "Let's not get ahead of ourselves. We're just taking it one step at a time."

Lucas nodded, then tilted his head, his tone softening. "Can I tell you something kinda dumb?"

Lacy raised an eyebrow, amused. "Always."

He smiled, but it didn't quite reach his eyes. "Back when you told me you were seeing someone... I thought you meant Andrew."

Her eyes widened slightly. "Wait—really?"

He gave a half-shrug. "Yeah. I mean, you two just had this... thing. The way you talked about him, the way he looked at you anytime I stopped by the office? It didn't seem like just coworkers. So yeah, I figured it was him."

Lacy opened her mouth, then closed it again.

Lucas went on, more gently now. "But then the book fair happened, and dude showed up. That guy—Patrick, right?" He gave a small shake of his head. "That's when I realized I was way off."

There was no bitterness in his voice, just quiet honesty.

"And then I saw Andrew's face when he noticed him. Saw yours, too. It was like... watching a storm roll in that only he knew how to stand in. You didn't even flinch when Andrew came over. You just kind of... melted. Like your body remembered safety."

Lacy blinked fast, her throat tightening.

Lucas leaned back with a soft, crooked grin. "Anyway, I was wrong. But seeing you now? With Andrew? It just makes sense. And for what it's worth, I think the universe finally got one right."

She managed a small smile, deeply touched. For a moment, neither of them said anything.

Then Lacy nudged his leg gently under the table, her tone lifting. "So, what's the deal with you and relationships, huh?" she asked, dipping her pita in the hummus. "Still avoiding commitment?"

Lucas shot her a playful glare. "Is it that obvious? I'm just not in a rush. I've got other things to focus on, like... finding the best coffee in town."

Lacy laughed. "Your priorities are something else, you know that?"

"I've got my own rhythm," he said with a shrug. "But I'm genuinely happy for you, Lacy. Whatever's going on with you and Andrew, it seems like it's real."

She smiled, her eyes softening. "Thanks, Lucas. It feels different this time. I've never been so sure about anything, and I'm not looking back."

The weekend arrived quicker than expected, and Lacy found herself standing in front of her closet, trying to decide what to wear for brunch with Bree, Nina, and Crissy. It had been far too long since they'd all gathered, and despite everything else going on, Lacy was excited to catch up with them.

She settled on a casual, yet stylish, outfit: a flowy beige blouse with delicate floral patterns, paired with dark-wash jeans and brown ankle boots. After a final glance in the mirror, she grabbed her purse and headed out the door.

The hostess led Lacy to a sunny corner booth tucked beneath a canopy of hanging plants and soft golden lighting. As she rounded the corner, a wave of joy swept over her—there they were. Bree, Nina, and Crissy. The gang, minus a few.

"Oh my God, look at you!" Bree was the first to rise, arms already stretched out for a hug.

Lacy squealed, practically diving into Bree's arms. "You're married now and somehow even hotter. That's unfair."

"Stop it," Bree laughed, pulling her in tighter before Nina and Crissy stood to join the group hug.

Nina stepped back with a grin. "Okay, but seriously—you look amazing, Lacy. Like, radiant. Cruise must've been more than cocktails and sea views."

"Right?" Crissy added, sliding her sunglasses into her hair. "What kind of glow-up happens in a week? Who do we need to thank—sunshine or someone tall, dark, and emotionally available?"

Lacy laughed, sliding into the booth with a dramatic sigh. "Let's just say it was a very full itinerary."

"Start from the top," Bree said, eyes sparkling. "Even though I already know... pretend I don't."

Lacy shook her head with a mock sigh, but her cheeks flushed with the kind of joy that couldn't be faked. "Alright. So... day one, work boy and I get upgraded to balcony suites, across the hall from each other, totally unexpected."

"Girl, you manifested that," Nina cut in, smirking.

"Maybe," Lacy said with a wink. "Anyway, that night, he sets up this private little sunset date on his balcony. All my favorite snacks, music I love, even one of those tiny little candles I keep on my desk at work."

"Awwwww!" Crissy and Nina harmonized like a practiced choir.

"And then?" Bree leaned in like she hadn't heard it all over FaceTime at least twice.

Lacy bit her bottom lip. "And then... we made out. Like full-on teenage-level, messy-hair, knock-your-soul-loose kissing. It was wild."

"Okay, okay," Nina fanned herself. "We've skipped all the way to the best part. What else happened?"

Lacy told them everything—the excursions, the long walks, the nights of laughter and whispered confessions. About Mrs. Vance's surprise group outing and how Andrew always found small ways to make her feel seen. She softened when she got to the part about them sleeping under the stars, and her voice dipped as she mentioned the intimacy they shared—the way he looked at her and told her he loved her. How she'd said it back, and meant it.

She breezed past the details, just like she had with Bree before.
Bree arched an eyebrow and said, "And that wasn't even their first time."
Lacy whipped her head toward her. "Bree."
Nina blinked. "Wait, what?"
Chrissy's fork paused mid-air. "Hold up. First time when?"
Bree smirked, casually tearing her croissant. "After my wedding reception. While the rest of us were eating late-night tacos or passed out with our lashes on, someone was having a secret tryst."
"You're kidding," Nina said, eyes wide. "You didn't tell us that!"
"You've been holding out on us," Chrissy added, pointing her fork at Lacy.
Lacy sighed, cheeks flaming. "Because it wasn't supposed to mean anything. We were... drunk, emotional. It was late. We ended up on the balcony talking for hours, and then... he walked me to my room."
Bree grinned. "And she let him in. Literally."
"Oh my god, Bree!" Lacy hissed, but couldn't fight the laugh bubbling up.
"So what, was it awkward?" Chrissy asked, eyes alight with curiosity.
"It was... soft. Sweet. Kinda blurry around the edges," Lacy admitted.
"And also the scariest thing I've felt in a long time. Because deep down, I think I knew it wasn't just a one-time thing."
Nina let out a dreamy sigh. "So y'all have been sitting on a love story this whole time like it's a casual Thursday?"
Bree raised her mimosa. "To secrets, slow burns, and finally getting it right."
"I am so happy for you, Lace," Crissy said, touching her hand. "Like, for real. You deserve all of this."
"And work boy? Never would've guessed, but... wow. What a man," Nina added. "We've got to stop calling him 'buttoned-up work boy' now
Lacy laughed. "Y'all don't even know. He's still buttoned-up, but there's... layers. It's a thing."
They all burst into giggles as their food arrived—French toast for Bree, shrimp and grits for Lacy, and matching smoked salmon bagels for Nina and Crissy.

They clinked their mimosas, and conversation turned to the usual girl talk—Crissy's recent promotion, Nina's new dating experiment involving a life coach-slash-saxophone player, and Bree's honest take on married life.
"Marriage is wild," Bree said, shaking her head. "One minute you're dancing barefoot in the kitchen, the next you're arguing about the correct way to load a dishwasher. I love that man, but if he leaves one more cereal box open, we might not make it to our next anniversary."
"That adjustment is real," Nina said knowingly. "You still love them, but also maybe want to strangle them—gently."
Everyone laughed again.
Then Chrissy leaned in. "Okay but... what about Patrick?"
Lacy didn't even flinch. Her voice was steady. "Giiiirrrll—he's still trying to reach out. I thought I blocked him, but apparently not all the way. He texted me again the other day. I didn't respond. And I'm not going to."
Bree's jaw tightened. "Good. Let him stay exactly where he is—with Ava and all that chaos."
Lacy nodded, calm and sure. "Yeah. I'm not holding any of that anymore. I'm good. Really good."
The moment passed—quiet, but solid. Like something had finally settled. Lacy looked down at her plate, then back up. "Okay... I wasn't going to say anything but... I had an interview yesterday."
All eyes turned to her, wide and blinking.
"For what?" Bree asked slowly.
"A publishing house. In Switzerland."
"Switzerland?" Crissy choked on her mimosa.
Lacy held up her hands. "Just an exploratory interview. I don't even know if I'll get a second round. I didn't want to have any regrets, you know? Life is good here, great even—but the opportunity came out of nowhere and I just... wanted to know."
"Did you tell work boy?" Nina asked gently.

Lacy shook her head. "Not yet. I will if it becomes something real. But I needed to do this for me first. To make the choice without anyone else's voice in my head."

The girls sat back, contemplative, proud.

Bree reached over and squeezed her hand. "If you get it—and I have a feeling you will—you better promise me one thing."

"What's that?" Lacy asked.

"Follow your heart. Whether it keeps you here or takes you across the world. You've earned the right to choose you."

Lacy felt her eyes sting, but she nodded. "I will. I promise."

Later that Night, Lacy lit a couple of candles in the living room, the warm scent of vanilla and sandalwood curling into the air. She was in her favorite oversized tee and a pair of silky lounge shorts, barefoot, hair loose, a glass of cabernet in one hand. The evening buzzed with the The laughter from brunch still echoed in her chest, but now she wanted quiet. Not silence—just him. The one person who didn't need her to perform or pretend. The one who felt like calm.

A knock pulled her out of her thoughts.

Andrew stood in the doorway in a dark green henley and jeans, a bottle of wine in one hand and that familiar spark in his eyes.

She opened the door with a smile. "Wow. You bring wine to all your midweek visits?"

He stepped inside with a grin. "Only for women I'm trying to impress."

"And how's that going for you?"

He kissed her—light, near the corner of her mouth. Familiar. Natural. "I'll let you be the judge."

She closed the door behind him, her cheeks warm. "You hungry?"

"Only if we're counting wine and whatever snacks you call dinner."

"Popcorn is a perfectly valid meal," she said, leading him toward the couch.
Leo sat on the armchair like a silent judge. Andrew gave him a respectful nod.
"Still not buying it," she said under her breath.
"He'll come around," Andrew whispered, settling in beside her. "So... how was brunch?"
Lacy exhaled, a soft smile playing on her lips. "Good. Needed. There's something about being with them—it just pulls me back into place. Like... everything makes sense again."
He nodded, his arm brushing hers. "I love that for you."
She glanced at him, wineglass in hand. "And what about your day, Mr. Important?"
"Forgettable. Except for this part."
Her smile deepened. She tucked her legs beneath her, leaning into his shoulder.
He looked at her for a long moment. "I've got an early meeting," he said quietly, "but... I brought wine anyway."
She met his gaze, warmth blooming in her chest. "So, then, your staying?"
He nodded once, soft and sure. "Wouldn't want to be anywhere else."

The TV played low in the background as they sungled into the couch, curled under a throw blanket. Lacy rested her head on his chest, his arm wrapped around her back. The rhythm of his heartbeat steadied her.

They talked about small things—favorite childhood memories, the books that changed them, the places they still wanted to visit. There was laughter, there was quiet, and there were long moments where they didn't need to speak at all.

Eventually, Andrew brushed his lips across her temple, then her cheek, then paused just before her lips.

"Hey," he whispered.

"Hey," she murmured back, her fingers curling into his shirt.

The kiss started slow—tender, careful. But there was history now, tension carried through every touch. What began as closeness deepened into something heavier, headier.

He scooped her up without saying a word, carrying her toward the bedroom like it was a promise. There was no urgency—just reverence. They undressed each other with deliberate care, hands mapping familiar skin like rediscovery.

Lacy pulled him down beside her, tangled in sheets and candlelight, her body molded against his. It wasn't rushed. It wasn't new. It was two souls unfolding—layers peeled back, love stretched across skin and breath and movement.

They didn't need to say anything. Not in that moment.

Afterward, she lay with her head on his chest, his fingers drifting lazily up and down her arm. Leo padded into the room, took one look at the bed, and left again.

Lacy chuckled softly. "Still not a fan."

Andrew kissed her forehead. "He'll come around. I'm playing the long game."

She smiled, eyes fluttering closed, the sound of his heartbeat lulling her toward sleep.

He stayed just like that, holding her.

Chapter 22

The days blurred together, the constant stream of meetings, emails, and catch-ups consuming Lacy's time. She had managed to stay on top of everything—work, the whirlwind romance with Andrew, and of course, still finding time to nurture her relationships with the girls, especially after that long-awaited brunch.

But on one particular morning, as the sun streamed through her office window, Lacy felt a shift. She had just finished an email draft to a client when her inbox pinged. It wasn't just another client update or routine request—it was from an email address she didn't recognize, but the subject line caught her immediately:

"Editor-in-Chief, Publishing House, Switzerland - Offer for Managing Position"

Her heart skipped a beat as she clicked it open.

From: Editor-in-Chief of Edelweiss House Publishing
Subject: Managing Position Offer – Switzerland
Dear Ms. Lacy Blake,

I hope this message finds you well. I am writing to personally extend an offer for the Managing Editorial position within our company, based in Zurich, Switzerland. After reviewing your credentials and recent accomplishments, I am thoroughly impressed with the caliber of work you've accomplished at Seaglass Press.

The role would place you at the helm of a newly established department, where you would have full control over editorial strategy, team building, and operational management. We are offering a competitive salary, company car, travel benefits, and corporate housing.

The job would commence in one month, and we understand that such a transition requires careful thought. We would love for you to join our team and are confident that your experience and vision would be invaluable to our growing organization.

Please note that you have three business days to make your decision. We would be happy to discuss any questions or concerns you may have. I look forward to hearing from you soon.
Kind regards,
Seycheles Voss
Editor-in-Chief
Edelweiss House Publishing

Lacy sat there, staring at the screen, her mind racing. This wasn't just a job offer—it was a seismic shift. Full control of her own department. The chance to build something from the ground up. A top-tier salary. Housing. Travel perks. And the location?
Switzerland.
Mountains that looked like watercolor paintings. Lakes so clear they reflected entire skies. Cities where old-world charm met modern design. The kind of place that made you breathe deeper just by existing in it.
She had only dreamed of opportunities like this. And now, one was sitting in her lap—real, undeniable, and asking her to leap.

Her first instinct was to call Andrew, but then she hesitated. She had to process this on her own first. She had three days to decide, but her mind was already spinning. The job itself was a dream—a dream she had worked for—but was it the right moment? Was she ready to leave her life here in the States?

Later that day, Lacy walked out of her office, the weight of the email still heavy on her mind. She needed a break, a moment to clear her head. She grabbed her purse and stepped out of the building, heading for the nearby park. The hustle and bustle of the city seemed louder than usual, and as she walked, her thoughts kept drifting back to the email from Switzerland. She couldn't focus. She needed to talk to someone. More importantly, she needed to talk to Andrew.

Her phone buzzed in her bag—it was him.

"Hey," she answered with a smile in her voice, trying to keep things casual despite the storm brewing in her chest.

"Hey, you," Andrew's voice was warm and comforting. "How's the day treating you?"

Lacy leaned against a tree, her eyes scanning the path in front of her. "Busy, but manageable. You?"

"Same here. A ton of meetings. But I'm looking forward to seeing you later. I was thinking maybe we could grab dinner tonight? Catch up on the past few days."

Her smile deepened. "I'd love that. It's been too long since we've had time to just… talk."

"I know, right? It's been a crazy week for both of us. I'll text you when I'm finished up, but how does 7:30 sound?"

"That works," Lacy said, a little more relaxed now. "Looking forward to it."

"Me too. I'll see you tonight."

As they hung up, Lacy let out a long, slow breath. Dinner tonight would give her a chance to talk to Andrew, to reconnect, without any of the pressure hanging over her head. She still hadn't made her decision about the Switzerland job, but for tonight, she just wanted to enjoy being with him, without the weight of anything else.

The evening air carried a soft breeze as Lacy stepped into the restaurant's candlelit ambiance. It was one of their favorite spots—not overly fancy, but intimate, with low lighting, soft jazz humming in the background, and tucked-away booths that made it easy to forget the rest of the world. She spotted Andrew at their usual table, already seated with a glass of wine in front of him. His eyes found hers instantly, that familiar spark lighting up his face.

"There she is," he said, standing to greet her with a soft kiss. "You always manage to look like a dream, even after a full workday."

Lacy smiled, sliding into the booth across from him. "It's the post-cruise glow. Still hanging on."

Andrew chuckled. "Or maybe it's the glow that comes from being amazing at your job and balancing a million things without breaking a sweat."

"Well, I try." She sipped the wine he ordered for her—her favorite. "Thanks for this. I needed a little reset."

"Same here." He leaned back, watching her with that easy gaze of his. "Today was nonstop. I'm still thinking about that meeting Mrs. Vance pulled us into last minute. But the look on your face when you countered her proposal? Chef's kiss. You've got some power moves, Lacy."

Lacy laughed, setting her glass down. "You're biased. You always think I'm brilliant."

"Because you are."

They placed their orders, falling into easy conversation. Work moments, oddball client stories, the new intern who kept mixing up the printer codes—it all flowed naturally, layered with teasing and warmth. It felt like them.

"So," Andrew said, playing with the stem of his glass, "you still good for that art show next weekend? I snagged tickets, but if you're swamped…"

"I'm in. I'll need a reason to wear the dress that's been staring at me from my closet," she teased. "Besides, I miss seeing you outside the office."

He gave her a look, one of those soft, affectionate ones that said more than words. "We could fix that. More dinners, more walks, more 'you and me' time."

"I like the sound of that," she said, nudging his foot under the table.

Their entrées arrived, and for a while, they enjoyed the food, the rhythm of being together without needing to fill every silence. Lacy watched him between bites, wondering how she was supposed to bring up Switzerland—how you tell someone who's becoming a part of your daily everything that something big might shift that.

Tonight wasn't the night. Not yet.

"I'm glad we did this," she said softly as he reached across the table and laced their fingers together. "It's easy to get lost in the chaos, but nights like this... they matter."

"They do," he said, giving her hand a gentle squeeze. "You matter."

And in that moment, with the world tucked away behind restaurant walls and his eyes fixed on hers, Lacy let herself lean into it—all of it. The closeness, the comfort, the quiet burn of something solid growing between them.

Dinner ended with full bellies and hearts, a shared dessert, and one lingering kiss before they walked out hand in hand into the night.

The next day, it was impossible to get anything done.

Lacy sat at her desk, fingers frozen above her keyboard, her brain ricocheting between deadlines, layouts, and the one blinking email in her inbox titled: Offer – Zurich HQ.

She hadn't even opened it again today. She didn't need to. Every detail was already burned into her memory. Full creative control. Her own department. A team that would report to her. And Switzerland—beautiful, serene, almost unreal.

Her stomach flipped again, queasy in a way she chalked up to stress. Maybe the eggs she'd barely touched at breakfast. Or the nerves. Big decisions always hit her like this, coiling in her gut and making her second-guess everything.

But this wasn't passing. It had been lingering—on and off—for a few days now.

She pressed a hand lightly to her abdomen and exhaled. Breathe. Focus. It's just the pressure. The magnitude of it all.

Still, the nausea curled quietly beneath her ribs like it had something else to say.

A sleek office in the heart of Switzerland. A corporate apartment with a view of the lake. A salary that made her eyes water.

It was everything she'd worked for. Everything she dreamed of.

And it would take her away from everything that had slowly begun to feel like home.

Her office. Her team. Bree. Lucas. Andrew.

Her phone buzzed.

Mrs. Vance: Can you step into my office for a moment?

Lacy exhaled slowly and stood, smoothing the front of her dress. She walked the familiar hallway, heels tapping lightly, forcing herself not to think about what she might hear.

Mrs. Vance looked up as she entered, gesturing toward the seat across from her desk.

"I got a call," she said simply, hands folded. "Switzerland. The editor in chief reached out to me directly."

Lacy's heart stuttered.

"He said you blew him away—your credentials, your editorial instincts, your vision. You're at the top of his list."

Lacy stayed quiet, unsure whether to smile or swallow.

Mrs. Vance leaned back in her chair, her voice softer now. "I won't lie to you. I'd hate to lose you. You're an asset, and you've become one of the brightest parts of this team. But... if you don't take chances like this, you'll always wonder what could've happened."

Lacy nodded, throat tight.

"Do what's best for you," Mrs. Vance said. "You have three business days, but something tells me... you already know."

When Lacy stepped out of the office, the hallway felt louder, brighter, like everything was sharper than it had been that morning.

And then, there he was.

Andrew, mid-conversation with someone from accounting, glanced up and spotted her. His face lit up the way it always did when he saw her.

He excused himself and strolled over, coffee in one hand. "You disappeared on me. Everything okay?"

"Just a meeting," she said, casual, offering him a smile. "How's your day going?"

"Busy," he said with a tired smirk. "Lunch is already calling my name. You?"

"Same. Thinking of taking a walk later—clear my head."

He tilted his head. "Need company?"

She considered it, then smiled. "Actually... yeah. I'd like that."

They exchanged a few more words—nothing heavy, nothing that gave away the storm brewing inside her. Then he touched her elbow lightly before heading back to his office.

She watched him go. The man who had quietly become her calm in the chaos.

Lacy turned and walked back into her office. She closed the door behind her, sat down slowly, and stared at the email again. Then she clicked "Reply."

Chapter 23

Lacy and Andrew strolled quietly through the park, shoes crunching gently over the gravel path. The sun filtered through budding branches overhead, casting soft golden dapples across the trail. Lacy walked a little slower than usual, both from the persistent queasy feeling in her stomach and the growing tension twisting inside her chest.

Andrew was talking about a new manuscript, his voice easy and animated. She smiled faintly, nodding along, but her thoughts were miles away. She had to tell him. Now.

She stopped walking. "Andrew?"

He turned to her instantly. "Yeah?"

Her expression must've given something away, because his eyes widened just slightly. "Wait—are you pregnant?"

"What?" she choked. "No! No, heck no. Calm down."

He exhaled like he'd been holding his breath underwater. "Whew. Sorry. Just—you looked so serious. Also, not gonna lie—you've been glowing lately. And looking a little thicker in the hips... not that I'm complaining. I'm just... not ready. Yet."

Lacy raised an eyebrow, half-laughing. "Yet?"

Andrew rubbed the back of his neck, smiling sheepishly. "I mean, yeah. Eventually. I can definitely see myself marrying you. Having a kid with you. But not right now. I still want to travel with you. Get lost in little cities. Steal you away for weekend getaways. Enjoy you."

Her heart softened at that. The way he said enjoy you made her feel seen. Held. Loved.

"But anyway," he said, sobering again. "You were going to tell me something?"

She nodded, pulse suddenly loud in her ears. "Yeah. I should've told you sooner."

He looked at her, the smile already fading. "Okay…"

"I got a job offer," she said quietly. "In Switzerland. A huge one. Full creative control. My own department. It's… everything I've been working for."

Andrew didn't move, but the shift in his energy was immediate.

"I didn't tell you when I got the email. Or when I interviewed. I told the girls at brunch, and Mrs. Vance, but not you. And that's on me."

"When did you find out?" he asked, voice clipped.

"The week we got back from the cruise."

He exhaled slowly, jaw tightening. "And you waited until now?"

"I needed to make the decision on my own. I wanted to be sure it was what I wanted—not what I thought I should do for us or anyone else."

"So... what did you decide?"

Lacy met his eyes. "I said yes."

A long silence stretched between them. His expression didn't crack, but something in his posture shifted—like the ground had tilted beneath him.

"I leave in a month," she added, softer now. "I thought maybe we could still make it work. You could visit. Or maybe there's a publishing house there you could connect with... I don't know, I just—"

"You already said yes?" he asked, cutting her off. "And you're just now telling me?"

She opened her mouth, but nothing came out.

He let out a humorless breath, eyes flicking away. "If we were still just friends, you would've told me immediately. You used to tell me everything."

"I didn't mean to shut you out," she whispered. "I was scared of how much you mattered. I didn't want it to cloud my thinking."

"But I do matter," he said, his voice low. "I thought I did."

"You do. Andrew, you do."

He looked at her like he wasn't sure he believed that. Then his eyes dropped to the gravel path, quiet for a moment.

"I need to process this," he said finally.

He stepped forward, kissed her gently on the forehead, and walked back toward the office without looking back.

Lacy stood there, frozen. Her stomach flipped again, harder this time. But it wasn't nerves. Not just nerves.

Her eyes stung, tears rising fast.

She had everything she thought she wanted.

So why did it feel like something had just slipped through her fingers?

After lunch, Lacy stepped back into the office with her stomach fluttering and her head full of static. Her heart wasn't exactly lighter—more like stretched—but she'd made her decision. The hardest part—telling Andrew—was done. Sort of. And whether or not he was okay with it... she wasn't sure.

As she made her way down the hallway, Mrs. Vance was just stepping out of the conference room.

"There she is," Mrs. Vance said, a rare smile creasing her face. "I heard back from our friends in Switzerland. They said you gave your answer."

Lacy nodded, slowing her steps.

Mrs. Vance studied her for a long moment, then said, "I hope you're at peace with the decision."

"I am," Lacy replied, steady. "It's what I've worked for. And I'm ready."

Mrs. Vance's expression softened with something like admiration. "Good. Then I'm proud. Edelweiss House is lucky to have you. But Seaglass will miss you more than you know."

They exchanged a look—mutual respect, mutual understanding—and then parted ways.

Back in her office, Lacy dropped her bag in the corner and sank into her chair. Her hand hovered over her phone, then moved with purpose.

Lacy: Emergency Zoom call in 10 minutes. I have news. Bring wine. And tissues. Maybe both.
Crissy: What did you do?! Are you getting married??
Bree: If she got married without me I swear to God.
Nina: This better not be a false alarm.
Kayla: I can hop on. I need the drama to keep me awake.
Janelle: Family nap time is over. I'm in.

By the time Lacy had her laptop propped open, the entire girl gang was logging in one by one, each from their corner of the world—messy buns, cozy sweats, full curiosity.

"Okay," Lacy began once they'd settled. "So... I had a decision to make. A huge one."

Crissy leaned in, eyes wide. "We knew it. Spill."

"Switzerland," Lacy said. "The job. The one I mentioned a while back... I got it. All the bells and whistles. My own department. Lake views. Edelweiss House."

Gasps erupted across the screen. Bree, who clearly already knew, still covered her mouth in fake shock like she was on a telenovela. "She got the offer! Oh my God."

"And," Lacy said, smiling nervously, "I accepted. This morning."

"You what?!" Kayla practically shrieked.

"I leave in a month."

Jaws dropped. Nina clutched her chest. Chrissy froze with her wine halfway to her mouth.

"I know," Lacy said quickly. "It's a lot. But it's everything I've worked for. I've been playing it safe for a long time. And I just knew... this was my moment to leap."

Bree tilted her head. "And what about Andrew?"

Lacy's smile faded a touch. "I told him earlier today."

"And?" Nina asked, cautious.

Lacy exhaled. "He didn't take it well. Not because I said yes, but because I didn't tell him sooner. He was hurt."

"Understandable," Janelle said softly. "But still... ouch."

"I get it," Lacy said. "I hate that I handled it that way. I just... needed the decision to be mine. It's complicated."

The group went quiet for a moment, letting it settle.

"But you're happy?" Bree asked, gently this time.

Lacy hesitated, then nodded. "I'm scared. But I'm also... proud. I'm finally choosing the life I imagined for myself. And if it costs me something—I'll deal with that."

Bree raised her glass. "To choosing yourself. Even when it's hard."

The others followed suit.

"To Lacy."

Lacy smiled, eyes stinging. "Y'all are my heart. I mean it."

As they toasted through their screens, she felt it again—that push and pull of grief and excitement. The end of something. The beginning of something else.

Lacy was nearly out the door when the receptionist's voice crackled through her office phone.
"Mrs. Vance would like to see you before you leave."
She paused, her bag halfway onto her shoulder. She hadn't expected another check-in today, but she adjusted her blouse and made her way upstairs.
Mrs. Vance greeted her with that calm, clipped professionalism she was known for—but today, there was a softness around her eyes. Eleanor Vance stood beside her, leaning casually on the corner of the desk with a rare smile.
"So, Lacy," Mrs. Vance began, gesturing for her to sit. "Switzerland."
Lacy gave a small nod, fingers tightening around the strap of her bag. "It was a hard decision."

Mrs. Vance studied her for a beat. "We'd like to make it harder."
She slid a slim folder across the desk.
Lacy blinked, then opened it.
Her heart stopped.
Managing Editor.
 Her own team.
 Creative autonomy.
 International author scouting trips.
 Corner office.
 And a salary that surpassed Switzerland.
Lacy's breath hitched. Her vision blurred. Her fingers trembled around the folder.
"I—I need a moment," she said quickly, standing. "I'm sorry."
But before she could turn to leave, Eleanor spoke.
"Take all the time you need," she said gently. "You've earned it. Lacy, in less than a year, you've transformed this department. You've shown leadership, grace under pressure, and an eye for talent we haven't seen in years. You stepped into this place and made it better. We don't want to lose that. We don't want to lose you."
Lacy swallowed hard.
"And with Andrew going to Canada for the next six months…" Eleanor added casually, "…we figured this might feel like the right place to land."
Silence.
Mrs. Vance's eyes flicked down briefly, as if realizing she'd said too much.

Lacy blinked. "I'm sorry… what?"

Mrs. Vance looked up, her tone more measured now. "Andrew didn't mention it? I offered him the position two days ago—editorial residency in Toronto. He accepted yesterday. It's only six months, but a great opportunity for someone at his level."

Lacy's stomach dropped, but she forced a tight smile. "Oh. Yeah—he told me. I just... didn't realize it was finalized yet."

Mrs. Vance nodded, seemingly reassured by the lie. "Well, he didn't hesitate. Said the timing worked out. Especially with you heading to Switzerland. I got the sense you two had already discussed it."

"Right," Lacy said, her voice thinner now. "Of course."

But the room felt warped. Her heart thundered in her chest, her fingers white-knuckling the folder in her lap.

Two days.
Two whole days.
And he hadn't said a word.

She pushed up from the chair, smiling as best she could. "Thanks again, Mrs. Vance. I'll review everything."

Mrs. Vance gave a nod, her expression softening again. "You're going to be brilliant, Lacy. No matter where you land."

Lacy nodded, muttered something she hoped passed for gratitude, and left before her legs gave out.

The hallway blurred as she moved—heels clipping faster now, one hand still clutched around the folder, the other pressed to her churning stomach.

She turned the corner—just feet from the restroom—and nearly collided with Andrew.

He caught her instinctively, eyes narrowing in concern. "Hey—whoa. Are you okay?"

She stepped back quickly, jaw clenched, face pale.

"I know," she said flatly.

He blinked. "Know what?"

"That you're going to Canada."

His expression shifted—just slightly. Less surprise, more... caught.

She didn't give him time to dodge. "Two days ago? You accepted two days ago, Andrew. You didn't think to tell me?"

He opened his mouth, then shut it again.

"I was going to," he said finally. "I just... I wanted to make the decision for myself. I didn't want it to be about us. I needed to know I was saying yes for me."

She stared at him, stunned. Nausea surging, throat thick.

"The same Lacy speech," she whispered. "Wow."

Andrew took a small step toward her. "It's not like that. I just—"

But she was already backing away, one hand to her stomach, her face crumpling.

"I can't—" she said, voice cracking. "I have to—"

She turned and rushed into the restroom, door swinging shut behind her.

Lacy woke before her alarm, staring up at the ceiling with a heavy stillness in her chest. Her stomach churned with that same unsettling nausea from the day before—like her body hadn't caught up with the emotional whiplash of the week. She sat up slowly, hoping it would pass. It didn't.

She moved through her morning on autopilot—brushing her teeth slowly, splashing cold water on her face. For a long minute, she just stood there at the sink, willing her body to reset. But the dull, twisting ache wouldn't let go. It stayed lodged beneath her ribs, whispering that something was off—and not just physically.

By the time she got dressed, she felt drained and a little dizzy. She tugged on a navy sweater and black pants, then sat on the edge of her bed to pull on her boots.

A soft nudge brushed her ankle.

Leo.

He nudged her again, then rested his chin on her foot and stared up at her with those wide, perceptive eyes. Like he knew. Like he could see all the unraveling.

"Hey, baby," she whispered, scratching beneath his chin. "You trying to take care of me?"

He purred, curling closer. It helped. Barely.

She picked up her phone and typed a quick text to Andrew:

Lacy: Still not feeling great but heading in anyway. Might call the doctor later if it doesn't ease up.

His response came fast.

Andrew: Wish you'd stay home. But I get it. Let me know if you need anything. And please see a doctor, okay? I can go with you if you like.
Andrew: Also, still proud of you.

She stared at the screen for a long moment, then smiled faintly. It didn't reach her eyes.

He didn't know she already knew. About Canada. About the promotion. About the fact that he said nothing.

She had told him about Switzerland—even if it had been late, she told him.

And he'd repaid that by leaving her to find out from her boss.

When she got home last night, she'd curled up in her blanket and sent the girls a group message:

Lacy (Group Chat): Emergency Zoom tomorrow night? Need to talk. Big news. I mean... really big.

Five minutes later, Bree had called.

"Are you pregnant?"

"Bree!"

"I'm just saying! That's how dramatic you sounded."

Lacy had laughed then, even though her chest ached. "No. It's work stuff. I'll tell you tomorrow. Promise."

Now, standing in her kitchen, staring into a mug of tea she couldn't bring herself to sip, Lacy made herself a deal: if the nausea didn't ease up by noon, she'd call her doctor.

The office buzzed with its usual energy—meetings, emails, the background hum of publishing chaos. Lacy navigated it with muscle memory, but her mind was elsewhere. She hadn't finished her breakfast. The mint tea she'd brought in sat untouched. And her stomach... still wasn't right.

Still, there was one meeting she'd been looking forward to: Lucas.

They hadn't caught up in weeks, and today's meeting—though technically business—felt overdue. Lucas's manuscript was nearing final edits, and despite everything going on, Lacy didn't want to let it fall through the cracks.

When he arrived at the small conference room near her office, he smiled like no time had passed.

"Hey stranger," he said, sliding into a chair. "Didn't know if I'd have to start submitting updates via missing persons posters."

She let out a low laugh. "I've been... off the grid. Life things."

"You okay?"

"I will be. Just... a lot."

They dove into the manuscript, bantering through revisions, tossing ideas back and forth like old times. But halfway through, her stomach twisted hard. She pressed a hand to her abdomen, trying to breathe through it.

Lucas noticed immediately. "You good?"

"Yeah," she said, standing carefully. "Actually, no. I'm gonna have to cut this short. I'm really not feeling great."

Lucas stood too, concern replacing his usual charm. "Want me to walk you out?"

She shook her head with a smile that cost her more than he'd ever know. "I'm good. Promise. Let's finish later in the week?"

"Absolutely. But please—get some rest. You don't look like your usual world-conquering self."

She tried to grin. "Thanks for that."

Back at her desk, she picked up her phone and called the doctor. By some miracle, there was an afternoon cancellation.

"Come in at three," the receptionist said. "We'll get you checked out."

She had just dropped her phone into her bag when Andrew knocked lightly on her open door.

Her spine stiffened. She glanced up

"Hey," he said softly, lingering just inside the door. "You okay to talk?"

Lacy straightened slowly from her chair, her expression unreadable. "Yeah. Sure."

He stepped closer, but not too close. His whole presence was quieter now, stripped of earlier excitement. "I wanted to explain."

She nodded once, warily.

Andrew rubbed the back of his neck, gaze flicking around the office like he was trying to find the right place to land. "Look... I should've told you. About Canada. When I accepted. Hell, the moment I was offered the position. But I didn't. And that's on me."

She didn't respond—just waited.

"I was still... hurt," he admitted, voice lower now. "You made your decision about Switzerland. You told Bree, Chrissy, the whole group before you told me. You told Mrs. Vance. But not me."

Lacy's eyes glistened, her arms folding tight across her stomach. "I told you when I was ready."

"I know," he said. "And I'm not saying you didn't have a right. But I would've liked to be part of it, Lacy. Even just a little. I thought we were building something that included each other."

Her throat closed up.

"So I figured... if it didn't seem important to include me, then maybe it wasn't important to include you either."

She blinked slowly, trying to keep her voice steady. "And that made it okay?"

"No," he said instantly. "It didn't. I was being extra. Petty. I didn't like the way I felt, so I tried to give you the same feeling. And I hate that I did that. I hate that you found out from someone else."

Lacy swallowed hard. "When were you going to tell me?"

His gaze dropped to the floor. "Tomorrow. I was going to tell you Saturday."

Her heart splintered. She pressed a hand to her middle—not just from the nausea that still hadn't eased, but from the quiet devastation curling in her ribs.

"You were really going to wait until the last minute," she said, more to herself than to him.

"I didn't want it to come out like this," he said, his voice cracking just slightly. "I wanted to talk to you about it. Make it make sense."

She looked at him for a long, painful moment. "But you didn't."

Silence.

Andrew took a slow breath. "Maybe… maybe this is a sign that we're both supposed to focus on our careers. You've got Switzerland. I've got this residency. It doesn't mean it wasn't real. Maybe it just means it's time to keep it simple."

The words landed like a blade to her chest.

Simple.

She gave the smallest nod, but her lips were trembling. "Right. Simple."

Andrew's hand twitched at his side, like he wanted to reach for her but didn't know if he still had the right. He stepped forward, pressed a kiss to her forehead—soft, reverent, and hollow—and turned to go.

She didn't move. Not until the door clicked shut behind him.

Then, with her hand pressed to her mouth, Lacy bolted from her desk.

The doctor's office was across town, tucked in a quiet medical plaza that Lacy rarely had reason to visit. Traffic was heavier than she expected for mid-afternoon, and every red light felt like a test of her patience—or maybe her nerves. She kept one hand on the wheel and the other on her stomach, a subconscious gesture she wasn't even aware of until the third time her palm rested there like it was trying to tell her something.

The air inside her car was too quiet, too still. She flipped off the radio after realizing she hadn't heard a single lyric in the past three songs.

Her mind wouldn't stop looping the conversation from earlier. Maybe we should focus on our careers. Keep things simple.

Simple?

What did that even mean?

He was leaving tomorrow. And he was going to wait until the very last minute to tell her. Her heart twisted at the thought. If Mrs. Vance hadn't said anything, would he have ever told her at all?

He said it wasn't personal. That he was hurt. That he wanted to make the decision for himself. Just like she had.

Was that what they were now? Two people making decisions around each other, instead of with each other?

She knew he was upset about Switzerland. She understood that. But two days after the fact? That wasn't just disappointment. That was distance. That was deliberate.

He wants to break up.
He just didn't say the words.

Her stomach clenched again, tighter this time. She shifted in her seat, tried to breathe deeper, but it didn't help.

Whatever this was—it wasn't just heartbreak.

And it definitely wasn't simple.
By the time she pulled into the small lot in front of the clinic, her stomach was in knots again—not just nausea now, but nerves. The kind that whisper something life-altering is on the other side of this appointment. The front desk nurse was kind, efficient. The waiting room smelled faintly of eucalyptus and hand sanitizer. Lacy filled out the forms, barely able to focus, then sat quietly, pretending to scroll through her phone while her heart did somersaults.
Eventually, she was called back. The routine questions followed. The vitals. The sample. The familiar beige of the exam room walls.

Then came the wait.

She sat perched on the exam table, staring at a framed photo of a mountain lake on the wall. It looked like Switzerland.

That was irony, right?

The door finally opened, and her doctor stepped in with that familiar, calm smile.

"Lacy," she greeted, flipping open the chart. "We ran your labs right away."

Lacy offered a tight smile. "I appreciate it."

The doctor sat across from her, folding her hands in her lap. "So, I have your results… and it turns out the nausea, the fatigue—you're not sick."

Lacy's brows pulled together. "I'm not?"

"No. You're pregnant! Congratulations!"

The room tilted slightly. Or maybe that was just her.

"I—sorry, what?"

"You're pregnant," the doctor said again, her voice warm, but direct. "Probably around seven or eight weeks, based on your history. We'll confirm more precisely with your first ultrasound."

Lacy's breath caught. She didn't speak. Couldn't.

Pregnant.

She sat there in stunned silence, blinking at the words that had just reshaped the entire framework of her life. Andrew. Canada. Switzerland. Everything. Everything was suddenly on a new axis.

"Are you okay?" the doctor asked gently.

Lacy nodded, eyes wide, voice small. "Yeah. Just… processing."

"I'll give you a minute," she said kindly. "There's no rush."

As the door closed behind her, Lacy reached for her phone but didn't open it. She just held it, fingers trembling.

Pregnant.

She closed her eyes and exhaled.

What now?

Thank You!

Thank You! For reading my first novel.
First and foremost, my deepest gratitude goes to my family and friends, whose unwavering support and belief in me fueled this project from its inception to its completion. Their patience, encouragement, and understanding were invaluable during the long hours of writing and revision. A special thank you to my partner, who provided unwavering love and support, creating a haven where creativity could flourish. To my Chathy, thank you for the insightful critiques, the endless brainstorming sessions, and the much-needed laughter that kept me going. To my editor, thank you for your guidance, your keen eye for detail, and your unwavering belief in this story. Your expertise and support were instrumental in shaping this novel into its final form. And finally, to every reader who picks up this book—thank you for taking this journey with me.